Randolph took his place behind the King's chair. The King had already proposed one toast, which Ted had missed. He drank some wine anyway, and grimaced. It made his tongue fur up. Well, they had decided that it must be strong enough to disguise the taste of the poison.

People were beginning to relax a little. Matthew stood up and flourished his goblet at them. The red wine and the blue glass caught the candlelight and sent it reeling around the room in sparks of purple.

"My lords," said Matthew, "to the King. Both glory and length of days."

Everybody echoed him, and drank. Ted looked over the smiling King's shoulder at Randolph, and froze. Randolph looked as if he were going to throw up.

King William shook his head and put down his goblet with a thud.

"My lord?" said Matthew into the hush.

Ted got up, words from the warning labels on all the bottles of poisonous things he had ever seen going around in his head.

King William put both hands to his throat, and in the hideous light of the candles his staring and contorted face looked like a gargoyle's. . . .

✷ ✷ ✷

FIREBIRD
WHERE FANTASY TAKES FLIGHT™

THE
HIDDEN LAND

PAMELA DEAN

FIREBIRD
AN IMPRINT OF PENGUIN GROUP (USA) INC.

FIREBIRD
Published by Penguin Group
Penguin Group (USA) Inc., 345 Hudson Street, New York, New York 10014, U.S.A.
Penguin Books Ltd, 80 Strand, London WC2R ORL, England
Penguin Books Australia Ltd, 250 Camberwell Road,
Camberwell, Victoria 3124, Australia
Penguin Books Canada Ltd, 10 Alcorn Avenue,
Toronto, Ontario, Canada M4V 3B2
Penguin Books (N.Z.) Ltd, 182-190 Wairau Road, Auckland 10, New Zealand

First published in the United States of America by Ace Fantasy Books,
The Berkley Publishing Group, 1986
Published by Firebird, an imprint of Penguin Group (USA) Inc., 2003

1 3 5 7 9 10 8 6 4 2

ISBN 0-14-250143-3

Printed in the United States of America

To David Dyer-Bennet,
kindest of project managers

THE
HIDDEN LAND

CHAPTER 1

SUMMER swept on, faster, as it always did, than you expected. Ted, climbing the stairs of the West Tower on a blazing day in mid-August, wished that he had only the beginning of school to dread. It irked him how well the others had settled in. You would think they had lived in a castle all their lives, instead of in Pennsylvania. You would never think that their own elegant, symmetrical game, played over and over again every summer for nine years, had suddenly taken on a life of its own, flinging them into a country they had invented but that stubbornly refused to conform to their expectations and that, just as they were finding their feet, presented them with people they had never invented—like that weasel, Lady Claudia—and scenes they had never played—like that unexpected and awful moment in which Patrick broke the Crystal of Earth. You would certainly think that all of them might very soon be made to do in earnest the kinds of deeds that sound appealing only to the mind's ear.

Ruth was almost impossible to find; she was devouring the magic of the Green Caves as she had once devoured mystery novels, that summer three years ago when she declared that she was sick of fantasies. You would never guess that she had been obliged to change her outward behavior from that of a gentle, poetic person who had not only never hit anybody in her life but actually believed one ought not to hit people, into that of an irritable and haughty sorcerer from whose uncertain temper all the servants fled. You would never guess she'd never seen a servant until three months ago, either. And she had hit Patrick when he broke that Crystal.

Patrick himself had acquired a sort of smug silence which displayed itself during any discussion of what they were going to do, but especially in talk of how they were to get hold of the swords of Shan and Melanie. Never mind that he was a materialist and didn't believe in magic swords. Somebody whose authority he did not recognize—somebody, that is, who was neither a parent nor a scientist—had taken the swords away from him, and therefore he meant to have them back. That the swords were the only way any of them knew to return to their prosaic lives seemed to trouble him less than the assault on his dignity.

Ellen appeared to be having the time of her life. This was perhaps the most irritating thing of all, it was so normal: Ellen *always* had the time of her life. In their game she had played princesses and pages and messengers and talking animals; now she must play a princess all the time, and although she occasionally said this was boring, nobody who had been allowed to tame a unicorn not two months ago should expect to be believed when she said things like that. She probably only said them because she thought princesses ought to be bored.

So much for Ted's cousins. His little sister was both more and less annoying than they were. Laura was not studying magic, like Ruth; nor plotting against High Castle's resident wizard and its chief counselor, like Patrick; nor being lavishly rewarded for her native spunk even if it didn't accord with that of the character she should have been playing, like Ellen. She was keeping out of the way and trying not to break things. Breaking things was her special talent: since the Princess Laura, her character in the game and the person she was now obliged to imitate, had had a great deal of grace and charm, Laura was probably unhappier than anybody except Ted. His misery liked the company; but Laura's being unhappy was normal enough to be irritating, too.

Ted wondered if she had seen any visions in torches or candles or people's bracelets recently. That wasn't normal for Laura, certainly; but when it happened to her, she reacted to it in about the same way she had when the first-grade teacher told their mother Laura had a very high I.Q.: she was dismayed, and she refused to do anything about it. He should probably ask her. Not that anything she had seen so far had been much help. And that *was* like Laura; if she must have mystical visions, they would be of no use whatsoever.

Ted panted up the last steps and yanked at the door of the Garment Room. It was locked.

"Will you kindly open?" he said.

His tone was not polite, but the doors in High Castle seemed to hear only words. The door swung wide, and he went into the scent of cloves and dust. From seven of the West Tower's nine narrow windows came a thin blue light; from one only the shadow of the East Tower; and from the last a line of pinkish sunlight that had found its way between the East Tower of this inner castle and the nameless towers of one of the outer walls. The sunlight was pinkish because every other wall of High Castle's concentric five was made of violent pink marble. Ted had found this harder to get used to than the presence of Claudia, the appearance of Andrew, or even the harsh temper of Benjamin.

He picked his way among the piles of clothing. He had come to find his costume for the feast at which, in accordance with their game, Lord Randolph would poison the King, unless somebody did something. Rummaging and sneezing, he wished they had chosen some other occasion for the murder. The feasts had been the beginning of the Secret, before Laura and Ellen were old enough to play. He and Ruth and Patrick, whenever parents were going to be absent from a meal, used to dress themselves up as kings and courtiers and have their food in the barn. He had for his memories of such times a kindly feeling that he was quite sure would not survive an attempt, even an unsuccessful one, to poison the King.

He was as bad as his sister and cousins, caught between his own somewhat rash character and the meek and bookish one of Prince Edward, who everyone thought him to be. Ted, if he had been free to be Ted, would not have come obediently up here to choose his gown knowing that Randolph might kill the King and that, if he did, Ted would have to kill Randolph. Edward, not knowing these things, would not have worried and fretted as he obediently chose.

An orange velvet cloak ripped as Ted pulled apart its folds without noticing the brooch holding them together.

"Shan can turn you into a toad!" he said to the brooch. He had heard Agatha, the royal children's nurse, say this to a cat that had gotten into her sewing, and it had a better sound, in this gray castle room, than "God damn it!"

Agatha being no sorcerer, the cat in question had not turned into a toad. Ted being even less a magician than she, the brooch remained a brooch also. It had caught in the bandage on his left hand. Ted worked it free thoughtfully. The cut from Melanie's sword was not swollen or inflamed, and it never bothered him unless he knocked the palm of his hand against something, but it was remarkably slow in healing. If he had really been left-handed, it would have given him trouble. But it was Prince Edward who was left-handed.

The cut was extremely convenient for Ted, since it gave him an excuse to use his right hand.

It was true that Agatha had looked grave over the cut, and called Benjamin, the Royal Groom who was more than he seemed, to examine it. But Benjamin said that it was no more than Edward deserved for playing with enchanted weapons, whereupon Agatha looked at him sharply and shut her mouth, and Ted wished he had noticed how long it took Laura's knee to heal. Laura's knee had started this whole business: if she had not tripped and fallen on Shan's sword where it lay peacefully concealed under a hedge, they would not be here now.

Ted went on burrowing. It was a pity that they could not just play in the Secret Country. One of their old feasts would have been greatly enhanced by the costumes and food they could have wangled. He shook out a stiffly embroidered dress, thinking how much Ruth would have liked it if they had found it in her father's attic. He might have liked it himself. But he was getting tired of gorgeous colors and decoration and jewels and feathers. He flung aside piles of green, gold, blue, scarlet; and came to a gray bundle. He unfolded it carefully. It, too, was fastened with a brooch, a twisted silver one with blue stones.

"Not again," said Ted, unfastening it. The magicians of Fence's party, who probably could turn cats into toads if they could stop laughing at the suggestion long enough to say the spell, wore silver ornaments with blue stones. This one made Ted's hand prickle, very faintly: it was enchanted. He put it into his pocket so that it would not be lost in the confusion. He unfolded the gray bundle, and stood up, and shook it out.

It was a plain robe with no trimming, not even a hood, and it was less voluminous than anything else in the room.

It would not have done for the old make-believe feasts, but it suited Ted perfectly for the real one. He fingered the material, which was thin, dull, and soft. It was too soft for cotton, too sturdy for silk.

Ted gathered it up. He was not entitled to wear its brooch, not being a sorcerer. He would have to find another.

"Maybe a nice iron pin," he said, and dragged the garment with him over to the trunks that sat against the wall. It seemed reasonable that they would be full of jewelry.

The first one was full of flutes. The second one was full of what he took to be drumsticks; the third held some very tarnished horns; and the fourth a hideous mass of strings. He had just flung up the lid of the fifth when he heard footsteps on the stone stairs. As they came closer, he also heard whistling. The words to the song came up from the bottom of his mind as the names of the fencing moves, when he had his lessons with Randolph, and flowers, when he went on the Unicorn Hunt, had done.

> *The minstrel boy to the wars has gone;*
> *In the ranks of death you will find him.*
> *His father's sword he has girded on,*
> *And the great harp slung behind him.*
> *"Land of old," cried the warrior boy,*
> *'Though none beside attend thee,*
> *Still one great harp shall sing thy praise*
> *And one strong sword defend thee.*

Ted shivered, and Lord Randolph came into the room. He stopped just inside the doorway, looking at Ted. He had a smile that could stop quarreling counselors in the midst of their most cherished imprecations, but he was not using it now.

"Give you good morning," he said, on an inquiring note.

"And you," said Ted. He barely had breath to say it. Here, dropped into his lap like a late birthday present, was a last chance to talk Randolph out of his plot.

Randolph strode across the room and sat down on the trunk that held the flutes. "What are you at, then?" he asked.

"I'm choosing my costume for the feast," said Ted. A colder sweat than that generated by the August day and the close tower room was forming on his hands and creeping down his back.

"I've come to do the same," said Randolph.

Ted swallowed. "I had thought that done already," he said.

Randolph looked at him, not sharply, but as if asking him to go on. There was a stillness, a calmness, an immovable quality about him which was not usual, and which made Ted doubt that anything could make him change his mind.

Ted swallowed again. "Or is it only the mood you've chosen?"

Randolph's eyebrows went up. "That the feast chooseth," he said, slowly. "I need only choose a color."

Ted wished, not for the first time, that he had paid more attention to the trappings of the Secret Country. Colors had definite meaning here. He pushed his hair off his forehead; it needed cutting in another world, but was becoming about right here. Black was death, blue was one sort of sorcery, green another, red another; yellow was sickness, white was health, gold was faithfulness, purple was kingliness, but violet was purity. Ted saw the robe he still held. Silver was treachery. He looked up at Randolph, and held out the robe to him.

Randolph had been a little flushed from his climb. But now he turned dark red, and stood up. Ted expected him to put a hand to his dagger. But he thrust out his hand, the fingers stiffly spread, the back toward Ted, so that the blue stone in his ring caught the stray beam of sunlight and turned malevolent. The dim air of the room lightened, and here and there among the scattered clothes other gleams and glimmers answered Randolph's ring.

Ted blinked. He was too frightened to do anything except what he already meant to do. He shook the robe out as if he were an obnoxious salesman in a clothing store. It really was a fine color; why had they chosen it for treachery?

"Is this not becoming to thee, my lord?" he said.

Randolph closed his eyes and dropped his hand.

"My complexion likes it not," he said. He sounded deadly tired, but there was a glint of mischief in his tone as well.

"But does your mind like it?" cried Ted, shaking it at him. The sudden relief had left him furious.

Randolph looked straight at him, with a gaze so fierce that Ted wanted to turn away and so compelling that he could not.

"Nay," said Randolph, slowly, "nay. It likes not my mind neither."

Ted felt outmaneuvered. There was certainly a word that meant precisely the part of Randolph the robe did suit, the part of him that intended to poison the King no matter how little the rest of him liked it.

"Has Fence spoken to you?" Ted said suddenly.

"Often," said Randolph.

"Has he spoken of this?" demanded Ted, waving the gray robe again.

"Of a certainty he has not," said Randolph, sharply.

"Well, I've spoken to him about it!" cried Ted.

"Thy speaking perhaps lacked an edge?"

"I guess so," said Ted, closing the trunk full of strings and sitting down on it. He knew so. Fence had asked him if he were mad. But Fence had promised to watch Randolph. He must not have watched closely enough.

"Were I what you ween I am," said Randolph, "more than thy tongue should have an edge were thou to hinder me."

"Is that why you never practice fencing with us any-more?" said Ted. This blessing had been too welcome to be seriously questioned. Prince Edward had been learning fencing for three years, but Ted had never held a sword until he came to this country. Sooner or later, the lessons with Randolph would have betrayed him.

"I have many cares," said Randolph, "and Fence needs me also."

He sounded perfectly sincere. He must think that not practicing with Ted and Patrick was a serious lapse. Well, and it was, thought Ted, if they were going to fight a battle in the fall. Something struck him for the first time.

"If we fight the right way, we won't need fencing, will we?" he asked.

Randolph's eyebrows rose. "What flummery is this?"

"Now look," said Ted. "Everybody is always arguing whether we need soldiers or sorcerers, and nobody lets *me* read King John's Book."

Randolph looked as if this were almost too much for him. Ted watched him discard several expostulations and settle for simplicity. "The Dragon King," he said between his teeth, "hath both an arcane and a mundane army and either is deadly to us. All else aside, no sorcerer may do's work be-set with even the most mundane of soldiers. Dost under-stand, or art as willful as thy brother?"

"I hope not," said Ted, almost to himself. His brother was in fact his cousin Patrick, the most willful of a willful family. Randolph actually smiled.

"We're getting off—we stray from the point," said Ted. "What will you wear for the feast?"

"Never," said Randolph, "Shan's robe of state." And he whipped around, snatched at a mound of green on his way by, and strode from the chamber.

Ted leaped after him. "Wait! Please."

Randolph, almost around the first curve below the room, looked over his shoulder. "What's the matter?"

"Can you spare me just a couple more minutes?"

"I can spare thee all the time thou'lt take," said Randolph, and came back up the stairs. "It hath seemed to me these two months that thou wouldst take as little as thou couldst."

"You were the one who left just now," said Ted.

"Well," said Randolph, still gently, "I have not said I will sit meek under all manner of insult."

Ted stood aside to let him back through the door. Randolph dropped the mass of green to the floor and sat upon it. Ted hunched down beside him. "Is the truth an insult?"

Randolph turned red again, and in his voice the gentleness was replaced by nothing in particular. "On occasion," he said. "It is also, perhaps, ill-mannered to speak of things that speaking can but worsen."

"How if I think it can better them?"

Randolph made a wry face. "Speak, then. I am bound to hear."

Ted, wondering uneasily what ritual he had invoked, said, "What is the King's mind now, regarding the Dragon King?"

"He says he yet considereth the matter," said Randolph, "but all orders he giveth are for the mundane, not the arcane army."

"Why," said Ted, suddenly, "should I have to rely on chance encounters with you to find out these things?"

"That," said Randolph, "is between you and the King."

"Randolph," said Ted, one of his lines from the game rising unbidden to his lips, "if ever I have sons, let me not treat them thus."

Randolph winced.

"You will counsel me still when I have sons?" said Ted, still saying his lines, although they could not belong in this conversation, because in the game Edward had never dreamed of suspecting Randolph until it was too late.

"Am I thy mouse, that thou shouldst toy thus with me?" said Randolph, matter-of-factly; and he stood up.

"Stop *leaving!*" said Ted. "How can we get anything done if you keep leaving?"

"For what," said Randolph, "do I stay, my lord?"

"For your lord, maybe," said Ted, viciously. He was getting almost too good at this peculiar game of wringing too many meanings from a carelessly used word.

"Speak to the purpose, then."

"The King is set in his error?"

"He is."

"And there's no hope in his strategies?"

"None."

"And you're set in your plan?"

"Edward, Edward," said Randolph. "Thou mayst call a guard; thou mayst draw a sword; thou mayst do more than hint to Fence. But this matter is far past words. I beg thy leave to go."

"We could think of something else! Some—some—half-measure. We could say the King's sick; Fence could, and keep him out of the way. We could do something, Randolph, besides—"

"There is no 'we' in this," said Randolph, grimly. "I will have no conspiracies. I will not stain thee, I will not sully Fence, with these half-measures. That were more dishonorable yet. And I say to thee," he added, taking Ted by the shoulders in a light but merciless grip, "that I wish no harm to King William, and am sworn to defend him. Dost thou hear?"

Ted could not say a word. He stared at Randolph's face, with its ghostly kinship to his cousins': eyes greener than Ruth's, hair blacker and wilder than Ellen's; a scar on the cheek neither of them was likely to acquire; lines around the mouth and eyes neither of them, he hoped, would suffer to earn.

This was not the gay lord, the brilliant magician, the convenient hand with poison they had invented lest their plot be too easy to guess. Their Randolph would have been pleased with any way out of what had seemed to him an insoluble dilemma: the King or the Country, one must go. Their Randolph would never have said, I will have no conspiracies. Ted felt as if he had opened a door to a familiar room and found vast dark caverns. He feared Randolph as he had never feared him before: for now he was afraid, not of what he knew about Randolph, but of what he did not know.

"The gray robe, you think?" said Randolph.

Shan's robe of state, he had said. The robe of another renegade apprentice, another traitor with the highest of principles.

"As a jest, perhaps," said Ted, but his voice shook.

"Fence would take it amiss," said Randolph, "not for the gray, but for the brooch. To wear the brooch is presumption; not to wear it is denial."

"Maybe there's something else," said Ted, and began rummaging, almost frantically.

"Here," said Randolph after a few minutes. Ted turned to him. He held up a heavy and voluminous velvet robe, like those worn by the King's Counselors, but pale gray, not blue.

"I had forgot," said Randolph. "Before Shan and Melanie, the counselors wore gray; Shan and Melanie were held to have disgraced the color and the office, and so the color was changed. This will do, Edward, it will do very well."

"Think on it more," said Ted.

"This matter, as I have told you, is past words," said Randolph, "and it is far past thinking."

He put a hand on Ted's head as if Ted were Laura or Ellen, bundled up the mass of gray, and left. This time Ted let him go. He sat on in the stuffy room, staring at the vivid green of the robe Randolph had been sitting on, until the bell rang for the midday meal.

CHAPTER 2

ALL five children had exercised their imaginations on High Castle's Banquet Hall, but none of them had considered where the inhabitants of the castle would eat the humbler meals of everyday. The room in which this happened was therefore often a great comfort to visit, because it thwarted nobody's expectations. It was called the Dragon Hall, perhaps for the color of its walls and floor. It occupied the southeastern corner of the second pink section of High Castle, High Castle being constructed, most unfortunately, like a marred specimen of one of those round peppermints sometimes given away by restaurants.

The Dragon Hall was two stories high, the details of its ceiling and upper walls generally lost in smoke and shadows. A number of corridors dead-ended suddenly in balconies overlooking it, but most people coming along them did so under the impression that they were going elsewhere, and were therefore impatient of them. Only the five children and an occasional young servant seemed to have discovered the delights of unseen observation from these spots. Ted used one of them to ascertain that his sister and cousins were already eating their lunch below, and went resignedly down to join them.

The room was lit by two fires, by a few smoky torches probably left over from the night before, and by six wide bands of noon sunshine from the rose garden. In this predominantly pink light, Laura, who was normally pale, looked healthy; Ruth and Ellen, normally robust, looked a little feverish; and Patrick, normally feverish, looked bedeviled. Ted hoped it was only the light. The last thing he cared to struggle with now was Patrick in one of his moods.

All four of them greeted him with their mouths full; remarked on his lateness without giving him space to explain it, supposing he had wanted to; and returned to their discussion of whether Agatha was more than she seemed, or just extraordinarily impudent. When the woman in question sat her plump, black-haired, elegant self down at the far end of their table, there was an abrupt silence around Ted. Agatha had sharp ears and a sharper tongue.

"Why aren't you eating?" Ellen asked him quickly.

"Because I'm not hungry."

Laura and Ruth looked up.

"Why not?" said Patrick.

Ted looked around. Randolph was not there, but Fence, High Castle's resident wizard, and Matthew, the Scribe of the King's Council, were in earshot, the brown head and the red one jostled together over a piece of parchment. Ted doubted they would notice anything less than a scream, but it was just as well not to take chances.

"Come outside and I'll tell you."

"Some of us are hungry," remarked Ellen, cramming a meat pie into her mouth and stuffing two more into the pocket of her dress.

"Agatha'll kill you," said Laura, under her breath.

"I keep forgetting we can't just throw these things in the washer," said Ellen, with mild regret. "Come on, Ruthie."

"I don't want to hear any more arguments," said Ruth.

"I'm not going to argue," said Ted. "I'm just going to tell you what happened."

"Patrick'll argue," said Ruth.

"No, I won't."

"You will so, you can't help it."

"You can come back in when he starts," said Ted.

"He's doing it now," remarked Ruth, but she stood up.

Ted put his hand under her elbow as he had several times seen Randolph put his under Claudia's during the Banquet of Midsummer's Eve. "I want to ask you some things, too," he added, thinking of Claudia staring in her tower, stopped cold by Ruth's sorcery in the midst of her plots, whatever they were.

"I can't tell much to outsiders," said Ruth, standing up nonetheless.

"Well, I like that!" said Ellen.

"Good," said Ruth.

They all moved for the door.

"My lord Edward!" called Fence.

Ted started and almost tripped Ruth, who snorted and pulled her arm out of his grip.

"Sir?" said Ted.

"I would have your advice on a matter."

"Could I attend you later?" asked Ted.

"Come to my chamber," said Matthew, "and spare us all the steps."

Fence nodded, and Ted nodded, and the five children went on out.

"I'm getting tired of this," said Ellen with her mouth full, as they made for their favorite spot on the pink wall above the moat. If you sat on a pink wall, at least you got to look at a white one.

"Ruthie," continued Ellen, walking backward along the curving marble path so she could address all four of them, "has her sorcery. Ted gets to go give advice to Fence. Patrick doesn't care. But Laurie and me, we can't do anything. We can't even go to our own feast."

"Laurie and *I*," said Ruth.

"You *want* to watch the King get poisoned?" said Laura to Ellen.

Ellen wedged herself between two stones of the wall and hurled a fragment of pastry amongst the waiting ducks. The day was clear, hot, and damp, and the moat shimmered and broke and came together again in great swatches of blue and green.

"I want to go to the feast," she said, "and watch Ted save him."

"Fat chance," said Ted, bitterly. "I talked to Randolph while I was finding my costume."

"Did you find a good one?" asked Ellen.

"That's irrelevant," said Ted, sharply.

"It is *not!*"

"Let him finish, Ellie," said Ruth.

"He told me quite plainly," said Ted, "that the King is still going to try to fight the war without magic, and that he—Randolph, I mean—is going to kill the King."

"He said, 'I am going to kill the King'?" demanded Patrick, coming awake suddenly. He had been lying on a stone bench with his eyes closed, as though falling asleep were the only way he could prevent himself from arguing.

"No," said Ted. "But he told me I couldn't stop him by talking."

"That's hardly the same thing," said Patrick, closing his eyes again.

"He didn't have to spell it out," said Ted, exasperated. "We both knew what he was talking about."

"Well, that's not the point," said Patrick. "If he'd said something you could tell Fence—"

"Oh, **he** did," said Ted, realization smiting him. "He said he bore no ill will to the King and he was sworn to defend him. Isn't that just great?"

"Nobody ever said Randolph was stupid," said Patrick.

"I never did think you could make Randolph change his mind," said Ruth. "We should just stop him."

"Well, we tried to when we made Laurie wish on the magic ground in the Enchanted Forest," said Ellen. "That could still work."

"Wouldn't hurt to have a backup plan, though," said Patrick, opening his eyes again.

"Randolph told me three backup plans," said Ted, wishing he could think that was funny. "He said I could use a sword, or tell Fence, or tell the Castle guard to arrest him."

"And of course," said Patrick, "he can beat you in a sword fight, and you've already talked to Fence. And we couldn't make any sense at a trial without giving ourselves away, even if the King thought there was time to *have* a trial before the battle."

"Randolph wouldn't want to kill *you*, though, would he, Ted?" said Laura.

"That's not the point," said Patrick, overriding Ellen's customary protest that Randolph was a murderer who would probably just as soon kill Ted as anybody else. Ellen had never liked the character Randolph, and the apparent charm and goodness of the actual person had not changed her opinion in the slightest. "What Randolph meant, Laurie, was that Ted could challenge him to a duel; and if he beat Ted, that would mean he was innocent."

"Pretty sneaky," said Ellen.

"Even sneakier than we thought," said Ted, gloomily. "Patrick, I asked him to try some sort of plan with Fence and me—lock the King up and say he's sick, or something—"

Patrick sat up. "Huh," he said.

"He said he would have no conspiracies," said Ted.

"He did?"

"I think he's crazy or something."

"*Randolph?*" said Laura.

"So how are you going to stop him?" said Ruth.

"I don't suppose you know any sorcery for it," said Ted, bitterly.

"Green Caves sorcery isn't people sorcery," said Ruth. "That's Fence's kind. We do things with earth and water and plants."

"If it doesn't affect people," said Ted, "how did it work on Claudia?"

"That wasn't anything to do with the Green Caves," said Ruth, sharply. "That was Shan's Ring. I just altered a spell I'd learned from the Green Caves, to—to focus the power of the ring. But I don't know any more about Shan's Ring than you do."

Ted gave up on this line of inquiry, and picked a yellow rose from a bush that wound its way over the wall. "Well," he said, "which feast does Randolph kill the King at?"

"You mean, which feast is it supposed to be?" said Patrick, under his breath. Ellen kicked his foot, which he had propped up on the wall, but no one else took any notice of him.

"Every Man a Servant and a Master," said Ellen.

"Oh, of course," said Ruth. "Because it provides the most confusion."

"How can you do anything with everybody running around?" asked Ellen.

"If everybody's running around," said Ted, "I can run around after Randolph."

"How come Edward didn't, then?"

"Edward didn't suspect anything," said Patrick.

"But isn't *Andrew* supposed to be running around after Ted?" said Ellen.

"In the game, Randolph did the poisoning by baiting Andrew until everybody was arguing and yelling," said Ted. "And Andrew said something nasty about Edward's mother. That's why Edward didn't notice what Randolph was doing. It's essential to Randolph's whole plan that Edward not know what he's done, because Randolph has to guide him through the war or the murder's been for nothing, and the moment Edward finds out Randolph has killed the King, Edward has to kill Randolph. But I don't care about Edward's mother, so I can ignore Andrew and watch Randolph. He knows I suspect him, too, so I don't think he can do it if I'm watching. Or I'll take the cup and pour it out the window, if I have to."

"What about Edward's mother, I wonder?" said Ruth.

"I used to make up something different every year," said Ellen, with unusual diffidence.

"No," said Ruth, "I mean really. Where is she?"

Ted shrugged.

"There is a definite dearth of parents around here, when you come to think of it," said Ruth.

"Royal children are always raised by servants," explained Patrick.

"So," said Ellen to Ted, "what's your costume like?"

"Green," said Ted.

"What else?"

"Ellie, I haven't really looked at it."

"You're supposed to choose it with great care," said Ellen, darkly.

Ted, an all-too-familiar impatience overtaking him, threw the rose into the moat. "I have to go talk to Matthew and Fence," he said, and went.

Matthew had a cluttered room on the ground floor of High Castle's second white circle, overlooking the rose garden. He and Fence were sitting on the elaborate carpet when Ted came in, probably because every chair and every table was piled with documents and scrolls and books. They both looked young, bookish, and confused.

"Be welcome," said Matthew, without looking up, "and do me the honor of reading over these lines."

Ted came around behind them and peered over their bowed heads. They were looking at a very grimy, tattered, creased piece of paper, or parchment, or who knew what. Ted squinted at the swift lines of black that filled the piece, not from top to bottom, but from corner to corner, and felt a vast dismay. He did not even recognize them as an alphabet of the Secret Country that he had invented and then forgotten.

"What thinkest thou?" Fence asked.

"Not much," said Ted, still shocked.

"I thought it akin to the scribbling of the Dwarves," said Matthew, "but Fence, who saith those are not scribblings, makes it to be a riddle of Shan's. Hast seen aught of it in thy reading?"

"I don't think so," said Ted, so dizzy with relief that he had to lean on Fence's shoulder.

"Consider a little longer," said Fence, seeming not to take it amiss.

Ted took a breath to steady himself, smelled the aura of burning leaves that surrounded Fence, and sat down backward from his kneeling position. The day four years ago when he and Patrick had built the bonfire, and Ellen had found them and been furious at being left out: what ritual had they invented to placate her?

"Aren't those fire-letters?" he asked.

Matthew yelped, and Fence looked blankly over his shoulder at Ted.

"Oh, my lord, thou'rt worth a hundred of scholars and wizards such as we!" said Matthew. "Canst read 'em, then?"

"No," said Ted.

"What are fire-letters?" said Fence, mildly.

Matthew paused, as if to give Ted a chance to air his knowledge; but he was too excited to wait for long. "A device of the wandering minstrels," he said. "I know not what sorcery 'tis akin to; but they do somehow place a sheet of this," and he shook the sheet, "in the fire, and play certain notes, and speak what they would capture; and play certain notes at the ending. To make it speak, one but puts it into the fire again."

"And plays certain notes, no doubt," said Fence, dryly.

Matthew looked less exuberant. "Alas, that's true."

"So it's not much good, knowing what they are?" said Ted.

"It is great good," said Matthew, firmly. "Yet it may not come in time."

"Do you think the King's changed his mind, then, if you're still doing sorcerous research?" said Ted, hopefully.

Fence fixed him with a most unpleasant look. "It is our place to be ready an he change his mind, not to pry and speculate hath he done so."

"Have we any skilled scholars of music in the castle?" mused Matthew.

"Where did you get that, anyway?" asked Ted.

"Parts of Shan's journal are written thus," Fence answered him.

"I didn't know Shan was a musician."

"Nor did we," said Matthew. He stood up, a little stiffly. "Fence, by your leave, I will go to Celia; a most accomplished musician, she knows something of these matters and may direct us to one who knows more."

"As you will," said Fence. "I'll go on with the parts more straightly written."

Matthew bounded through the door and could be heard running down the hollow corridor.

"He's having fun," said Ted, wistfully.

"That is a scholar," said Fence, not looking up from his manuscript. "He'd welcome death itself if he learned from it what Melanie did in the Gray Lake or why the Dwarves dwindle."

"Would you?" said Ted.

"For other knowledge, perhaps," said Fence. "Not for the riddles of wizards and history."

"I guess I'd better leave you to work," said Ted.

Fence looked at him thoughtfully, with green eyes unusually sharp in his innocent round face. "Polish thy blade," he said, "with use, not with sand. I would not lose thee easily."

"If the King doesn't change his mind, you'll lose everything easily," said Ted.

"Indeed I will not," said Fence. "The Dragon King's victory will come as hard as I can make it—and that is hard, in truth." He bent his disheveled head to the scroll again. "Get thee to arms," he said.

CHAPTER 3

TED walked slowly along the dim halls. He could not walk quickly because he would trip over the green robe, and he was grateful for this. He found himself counting off the familiar landmarks of door, stair, and turn. He thought, I don't have to worry until I'm past the kitchen; I have a long way to go still; I'm safe for a few minutes.

It had been a cold and foggy day, like all the mornings before Ruth used Shan's Ring on Claudia. Outside, trees dripped, grasses drooped, the roses hung heavily, and the moat was a sheet of lead; inside, every wall and floor was cold and every torch dim. The gray garment of Shan would have suited the weather; Ted's vivid green seemed brash and useless, like flinging yourself across a banquet table at an insult.

He climbed a last stair, nodded to the man-at-arms, and turned down the corridor for the Council Chamber. It seemed to him not at all appropriate to hold the feast in the Council Chamber, but everyone except his sister and cousins appeared to think this normal.

The carved double doors were shut. He was very early, in case Randolph had planned to set something up before anyone else was around. Ted pushed, but the doors were locked.

"Open, an it please thee," he said, but the doors did not.

Ted leaned against the wall. Cold shot up his spine, but he stayed where he was. He wondered if Claudia had gotten out of Ruth's spell. He and Patrick had asked Fence, sometime in the burning middle of July, when fog would have been welcome, if Claudia could have made all those mornings in June cold and foggy. Fence's mouth quirked, and he said that he had done just that thing in his youth, so that he would not have to go hunting. "So you see, 'tis a skill mastered early," he said. "But why, think you, would Claudia work it upon us?"

Ted and Patrick had had no answer at the time, but now Ted wondered if it might not have suited Claudia's purposes very well to make waking gloomy, and getting up a trial, and being out early a misery, and seeing the sun rise almost impossible. Maybe the way cold and shadows and fog of a summer's morning made people feel was just the way she wanted them to feel. She probably liked nasty weather herself, the weasel. It would be hard to slink well without fog.

Ted jerked away from the wall. He was spooking himself. In the dim corridor shadows were beginning to crawl. He slid his hands inside the wide sleeves of his robe, rubbing his arms. There was a man with a sword not ten yards away, and there wasn't anything in the hall anyway.

Someone let a whole basinful of water down a drain all at once, just behind him. He flung himself around, tripped on the robe, and sat down next to the purple beast. It gurgled. It looked neither more appealing nor more dangerous than it had seemed on the steps of the West Tower, the night he and the others had found Shan's Ring. It had no eyes, no legs, no up or down, and no edges. It looked like spilled ink, like light blurrily reflected through a dirty window a long way off, like the water after a long afternoon of painting exclusively with red and purple. Fence and Randolph had said, more or less, that these purple beasts were the by-products of Claudia's forbidden mingling of the methods of the sorcery of the Green Caves with those of the school of Blue Sorcery.

The beast gurgled again, and sloshed itself a little, back and forth on the worn gray stones of the floor.

"Very funny," said Ted. Nobody seemed to think the things were dangerous, but they were disquieting. "Just your kind of weather, isn't it?" he said companionably. The beast was silent.

The man-at-arms poked his head around the corner at the top of the stairs. "My lord?"

"Can you come here and—" No, of course not, he couldn't leave his post. "Look at this thing on the floor; have you ever seen one of these?"

The man squinted. "'Tis too small for my eyes, seemingly, my lord."

It was the size of a beanbag chair. Ted turned to look at it again, and it was gone.

"Never mind," he said, trying not to sound as furious as he felt.

The guard grinned at him and went back around the corner.

"Give you good day," his voice said then, echoing a little in the hollow stairs.

"I would that you could," said Randolph's voice, wryly rather than gloomily.

"Hath been a bad year for fogs," said the guard.

"Well," said Randolph, "they say 'tis wondrous good for sorcery."

"No doubt," said the guard, sounding like Fence; and Randolph laughed.

When he came down the corridor and saw Ted, he stopped smiling.

"Give you good day," said Ted, and was astonished at the insolence in his voice. He wondered if he would be able to summon up the same tone for the school principal the next time the principal deserved it. He wondered if Randolph deserved it.

Randolph's eyebrows went up, but all he said was, "And you."

He did not look at Ted as Ted moved to let him by. He stopped before the carved doors, stepped back, tilted his head as if he were reading, and said, "Master and servant bid thee open."

Ted looked at the door, but if its wooden twinings were letters, they were none he had ever seen. The doors swung inward, silently, and Randolph went in.

"Will it ruin the ritual if I come in and sit down?" called Ted.

"This is not sorcery," said Randolph, rather shortly.

Ted's impulse was to ask him if he minded, but he thought in time that it was probably not wise to be too courteous to a murderer. Even on the brink of the deed it was hard to think of Randolph as a murderer. Ted went to his chair and sat down. A trickle of water had come in one corner of the easternmost window and collected on the floor in a dull pool. Ted thought for a moment that it was the beast again. The room was even darker than the hall. But Randolph, who could speak to the beasts and be obeyed, only muttered under his breath and went out, leaving Ted to feel like someone in the waiting room of an unknown dentist of dubious reputation.

Before Randolph returned, Andrew and Conrad came in. They did not look as if they had walked to the Council

Room together; they had the wary and disgruntled air of people who have been startled by someone they do not like.

They made an odd pair even in appearance: Conrad large and placid, with his bald head and vast black beard; Andrew thin and wary, with his sleek hair and yellow moustache and his level eye. Conrad wore a huge and shapeless robe of some shiny purple stuff. Andrew had stayed with what Ted realized must be the newer fashion, shirt and doublet and hose. His were gold and white. Faith and health, thought Ted. There's arrogance for you.

He and Andrew had not spoken to one another since the nasty scene at the Banquet of Midsummer's Eve. There had been no need; except on just such formal occasions, they did not move in the same circles. Now Andrew took one look at Ted and frowned even harder. Conrad only grinned at him.

"Give you good day," said Ted, to the space between them.

"Well, lad, where's the wine?" said Conrad.

"I expect Randolph's gone for it," said Ted, wondering if he should have gone, too. But it was in sealed bottles, wasn't it?

Conrad sat down in his accustomed chair. Ted looked at him, remembering Ruth's remark about the dearth of parents. Conrad was supposedly Ellen and Laura's parent, but Ted did not think he had ever seen Conrad address a word to either of them. And who was their mother?

Randolph came back into the room with a wad of cloths in one hand and a collection of bottles in the other arm. He did not look pleased to see Andrew and Conrad.

"You are early, cousins," he said. He put the wine bottles untidily at one end of the table and attacked the pool of water with his cloth.

"Not so early as thou," said Conrad.

"I must depart early," said Randolph. This was news to Ted, who looked warily at him. "I thought therefore to do my serving while I might."

"Why, no man leaves this feast before its end," said Andrew.

Randolph shrugged. Ted had never seen him approach rudeness. Perhaps when you were about to murder somebody it was harder to be polite.

Randolph opened a cupboard against the wall and took out a pile of napkins, yellow and faded. Ted knew by now that the old ones were the good ones, but he wished for fresh white napkins to brighten the room. Randolph turned back to the cupboard and took out wine-glasses; they were a cloudy blue, and much finer work than Ted had seen on any table in High Castle heretofore, even at the Banquet of Midsummer's Eve.

"These are something dusty," observed Conrad, picking one up.

"Do you polish them, then," said Randolph, shortly, and handed him a cloth.

Conrad cocked an eyebrow at him, and began to polish glasses. Ted looked at Randolph, who was staring into the empty cupboard. Ted followed his gaze, and saw only a cobweb in the corner of the bottom shelf.

"That's something dusty, too," he offered.

Randolph turned on him, and suddenly laughed. "In such a castle, why should it not be?" he said, gaily. Ted blinked at him.

Randolph pulled open a drawer and began taking out candles and candlesticks. Conrad was still polishing glasses and Andrew had begun to fold the napkins into intricate shapes—a talent Ted would never have dreamed of assigning him—so Ted was left to put the candles into the sticks and light them from the torch in the hall.

They were not, in the absence of the usual augmenting torchlight, as cheering as they ought to have been. They cast great leaping shadows into the high corners of the ceiling, put an eerie halo around every head, and distorted every visage into unfamiliarity by smoothing out some features and deepening others. Ted began to wonder how, in this bewilderment, he was to keep an eye on Randolph. Follow him like a pet dog, he supposed.

Of course, it might already be too late. Had Randolph poisoned the cloth with which Conrad was polishing glasses? No, that was silly, that would get everyone. How in the world did it go in the story: how *did* Randolph administer the poison? In the wine, yes. But in what form was it: a liquid, a pill? Had they followed *Hamlet* and made the poison a pearl?

Ted cursed himself for not having asked the others when he had the chance. Then he calmed down a little. He would probably have gotten four different answers, Randolph's exact method having been one of the less stable items of their repertoire. And you could not trust the Secret Country not to come up with a fifth answer, anyway.

Matthew and Julian came in, Matthew in a red robe that quarreled with his hair, and Julian in a black one that made him look like a bad watercolor of his usual vivid self. They were given spoons and knives and plates to polish, and fell cheerfully to these duties. If he had been feeling better, Ted would have laughed to see lords and counselors, in their best clothes, doing kitchen work. As it was, he stayed within a foot of Randolph and was stepped on several times. Randolph was so good-natured about this that Ted began to despair: he must have arranged his poison already. That meant that he could not be allowed to give anything to the King. Ted wished for the others: five of them might have been enough to achieve this.

While Randolph was talking to Matthew in a far corner that contained no glasses or napkins, Ted stole a moment to look around the room. It had filled up while he dogged Randolph. As he looked at the door, the King came in. He wore red, and a crown with rubies. The light of the candles falling back from his robe and his jewels wiped the lines from his face and dyed it a healthy color. He looked terrifyingly capable.

Andrew, with a swift movement that reminded Ted of Claudia, got to the King's chair first and held it for him. Ted, seeing Randolph taking his usual seat, slid into the chair next to him, hoping that he had gotten this detail right, that people sat where they pleased at this feast.

The King raised his hand and spoke.

"My lords, my counselors, and my friends." His voice, as always, carried well, without any suggestion of effort. Ted saw that his hands lay still upon the dully gleaming table. He might be old, but he was not weak. No wonder Randolph had felt driven to poison. Ted felt a momentary panic. They had not settled on a plan for what to do when the King did not die and still wanted to fight the battle wrong.

"It is the way of things," said the King, "that ye serve me. That we should not forget that this service is of utmost value, nor that a master would be less than he is without the least of his servants, there is a feast wherein I serve ye. But tonight is the feast wherein one of ye serves us all, that he may taste the joys of that least servant, and ye may taste the joys of the King, and the King may relish his jest. And this year is the year wherein Lord Randolph Martin's son is the least servant.

"Let the feast begin."

He looked, smiling, to Randolph on his right, and nodded.

Ted sat petrified. This was the wrong speech, the wrong feast, the wrong arrangement. This should be the feast wherein all lords served one another and the King served them, that they might not forget that in the end master and servant were equal. In the joviality and confusion of that feast any lord would have half a dozen chances to poison half a dozen of his fellows, his king, and the kitchen cat, with no one the wiser until the victims began to writhe. In that feast, Randolph could poison the King with Ted at his elbow, unless Ted were eternally alert.

But if the King died at this feast, only one lord would be pointed at: the one who had served.

Randolph could not possibly poison the King tonight. If he did they would catch him, and if someone did not stab him on the spot, they would hang him almost as speedily. He would not be able to guide Ted through the war with the Dragon King and thus save the Secret Country. And since to save the Secret Country was the only reason Randolph would kill the King, and to kill the King this way would not save the Secret Country, Randolph would not kill the King this way.

Ted almost laughed aloud, but he became aware in time of the silence he would have laughed into. Randolph looked as if he had seen the sun rise in the west. Everyone else looked acutely embarrassed. This was not just the Secret Country playing tricks, then. Everyone here had expected the Every Man a Servant and a Master Feast. Did that mean the King's mind really was weakening? Was Randolph more in the right than they had thought?

Ted stopped watching Randolph's hands and stole a look at his face. He looked neither reprieved nor thwarted; he seemed, rather, amused and somehow satisfied.

"My lords," said Randolph, gathering their gazes to him.

Matthew, screened from the King's notice by Randolph's body, slipped his napkin over Randolph's arm. A bottle of wine stood at Andrew's elbow. He slid it past Conrad and Matthew and Ted to within Randolph's reach, and Randolph took it up and began to pour the King's cup full.

Ted moved like an eel and bumped Randolph's elbow solidly. The bottle knocked into the cup, tipping it over, and a pool of vigorous red spread over the tabletop in the candlelight. As Randolph reached hastily for the toppling cup, Ted bumped him again, and he dropped the bottle, which poured impartially over the table, the floor, and Conrad's and Matthew's laps. Ted's thought caught up with his hand: nobody who looked that pleased with himself when his plans appeared to have been thwarted should be allowed to do what he liked.

The King had not seen Ted; he had seen only the jerk of Randolph's arm. As the cup thumped over, he laughed. Now he said, "Hast been coddled too long, Randolph? Shouldst be a page more often, to keep thy nimbleness?"

"No doubt," said Randolph, smiling. "Your pardon, my lord."

He turned and looked down at Ted, who was wedged between him and Matthew. The smile left his face, but Ted was astonished to see congratulation in his eyes.

"Edward, a cloth, if you would be so good," said Randolph.

Ted moved back from the table and found himself six inches from the furious and panic-stricken face of Andrew, who had been perfectly placed to see Ted jog Randolph's elbow. Ted backed away from him, pushed his way to the cupboard, and brought Randolph a pile of napkins the long way around rather than pass by Andrew again. What was wrong with him? Had he poisoned the wine, too? He had been sitting right there with the open bottle before him.

"Oh, God," said Ted involuntarily.

He looked at Matthew and Conrad, who stood dripping wine onto the stone floor. Matthew was laughing; Conrad just looked rueful. Ted handed them some of the napkins, wondering how to keep them from putting their hands in their mouths.

He looked at Andrew. That young man had not returned to his seat; he was leaning against the edge of the table, fists clenched: he looked thwarted and desperate, exactly as Randolph ought, but he was not concerned with Matthew and Conrad. He was watching Randolph as if Randolph were an escaped tiger. Did he simply not care how many other people he poisoned, or was something else the matter with him? There was no reason for *him* to poison the King. Ted shook his head. His job was with Randolph, who was now holding up the King's glass and examining it for cracks.

Ted slithered forward and took it out of his hand. If there had been poison in that glass he shouldn't let the King near it. "I'll get you another, my lord," he said.

Randolph grinned at him in the manner of one conspirator to another, and Ted went back to the cupboard feeling almost dizzy. He had never known anyone who could so wholeheartedly approve of his enemy. As a weird person, Lady Ruth of the Green Caves had nothing on Randolph.

Ted brought him another cup, and Matthew handed him another bottle. Randolph poured the King's wine: his hand on the bottle jerked once and then steadied. Andrew, who had still not sat down again, was glaring at the tabletop; the tabletop was dry; Matthew and Conrad were merely damp, not dripping. They seemed perfectly healthy. How did the lines go, from which the game's version of this event had derived its inspiration? *So mortal, that but dip a knife in it, where it draws blood, no cataplasm so rare can save the thing from death that is but scratched withal.* Well, all right; they were fine if they had no scratches or cuts. Like first-aid class, thought Ted wildly, do not suck the venom from the snakebite if you have a cut or sore in your mouth.

Shut up, he told himself, it's all right now. You stopped Randolph. Enjoy your wonderful feast. And Ted became aware that he was in the wrong place for this feast. So was everyone else, but his chair was actually empty. He edged and groped his way to the far end of the table, going sideways so as to keep an eye on Randolph, and prickling with the expectation that the King would see, and embarrass him and everyone else by chiding his unreadiness, his dullness, and his lack of manners. Not to mention that someone might take it upon himself to excuse Ted by explaining that the King had the feast wrong; and if they went ahead and had the other feast, and Randolph had not actually been so foolish as to poison the cup Ted had upset, then Randolph could do his murder after all.

But nothing happened. Matthew was asking the King if he knew of any learned and accomplished musicians in the Castle, and explaining about the fire-letters in Shan's journal. Apparently Shan's journal was not a touchy subject, and the King knew something about fire-letters. This conversation occupied the King nicely while a few other lords also found their proper seats, and Randolph poured everyone's wine.

Randolph was beginning to look a little strained, which alarmed Ted until he realized an innocent reason for it. All of the preparations for this feast were wrong now. The feast the King thought it to be was much more elaborate. It was pure luck that both feasts began with wine. Most of the feasts did not: Ted and his sister and cousins, having more taste for sweets than for wine, had created most of the feasts with three desserts, one at the beginning, one at the middle, and one at the end.

Randolph came around behind Ted and poured his wine. Ted looked at him, involuntarily. Randolph looked back with so fierce a gaze that Ted was impelled to say something.

"Are you going to be able to manage?" he asked, and did not know if he had intended the double meaning he saw as he said it.

Randolph's smile was not so radiant this time. "The preparations will serve the need," he said.

He took his place behind the King's chair. The King had already proposed one toast, which Ted had missed. He drank some wine anyway, and grimaced. It made his tongue fur up. Well, they had decided that it must be strong enough to disguise the taste of the poison.

People were beginning to relax a little. Matthew stood up and flourished his goblet at them. The red wine and the blue glass caught the candlelight and sent it reeling around the room in sparks of purple.

"My lords," said Matthew, "to the King. Both glory and length of days."

Everybody echoed him, and drank. Ted looked over the smiling King's shoulder at Randolph, and froze. Randolph looked as if he were going to throw up.

King William shook his head and put down his goblet with a thud.

"My lord?" said Matthew into the hush.

Ted got up, words from the warning labels on all the bottles of poisonous things he had ever seen going around in his head.

King William put both hands to his throat, and in the hideous light of the candles his staring and contorted face looked like a gargoyle's. Matthew knocked his chair over backward and took hold of the King.

"Fetch Fence!" he shouted.

Several people stood up, getting in Ted's way.

"Randolph," said Matthew. "Where's Fence?"

"Atop that tower of his, I'll warrant," said Conrad. "Give him wine, Matthew. My prince, fetch Fence."

"No; the wine's at fault," said Andrew. "Randolph, where is Fence?"

Andrew drew his dagger; Conrad took hold of Andrew's wrist. Randolph shook his head.

Ted knew where Fence ought to be.

"I'll go," he said, but no one heard him; they were all clustering about the King, doing this and that, and talking until he wanted to hit them. The room swam and shuddered before him. He put his hand to the heavy door, and was caught from behind by someone who closed both arms around his shoulders and held on. Ted kicked backward, and was dodged. He bit at one of the imprisoning arms and got a double mouthful of gray velvet. He shook it out and opened his mouth to yell, when there was a thud behind him.

The arms let go of him. He turned and bumped into Lord Randolph, who looked at the King, and neither moved nor blinked.

"Randolph," said Matthew, leaning on the table with the King in a heap at his feet. Well, they had said it would be a quick poison.

"So swift," said Randolph. He looked calm and a little abstracted, but he was whiter than Ted had ever seen anyone.

He shivered, turned for the door, and fell over. His head would have cracked against the stone floor, but it hit King William's knee.

"Two!" said Conrad. He and Matthew both knelt over Randolph, and nearly bumped heads. Conrad looked over his shoulder at Ted. "Thy father's dead," he said. "This one lives."

"I'll get Fence," said Ted, and went running.

"None must leave!" Andrew called after him, but he ran on. He could not stay in that room.

He was supposed to run all up and down Fence's steps before he found him in the rose garden, but it no longer mattered what anybody was supposed to do. He went straight down past the startled guard and out into the damp gray evening. He blundered past the rain-heavy roses, scattering petals on the wind as his robe slapped them, and came, in the center of the garden where the fountain was, upon Fence and Claudia.

They looked at him, Fence with sharp concern and Claudia with irritation. She was out: out of the spell of Shan's Ring, and thence easily out of the tower where Jerome had imprisoned her. Ted had no time for her. He stood catching his breath and looking at Fence.

"Edward?"

"The King," said Ted, lurched to his knees, and threw up. Fence held his head, with cold but extremely steady hands.

"Thou cream-faced loon!" exclaimed Claudia. "Where gotst thou that goose-look?"

"Hold your tongue," said Fence, absently.

Ted's stomach finished with him. Maybe they had all been poisoned by Andrew, and that was why Randolph fell over.

Fence picked him up off his knees and steered him to the fountain. "Wash thy face," he said.

Ted put his head into the water obediently. It was cold, and when he had stood up and blinked the drops from his eyes, he could see clearly for the first time since they had lit the candles in the Council Chamber.

He shook back his wet hair and turned to Fence. Claudia stood just beyond the short figure of the wizard. Her dress was brighter than all the roses, and the pallid sky behind her dark head made it regal. She looked like a queen contemplating the fate of nations.

"You did it," Ted said to her.

"What's the matter?" said Fence.

"King William is dead," said Ted.

Fence, not a fidgeter at the worst of times, became absolutely still. "How?" he said.

"Poison in the wine," said Ted. "At least, Andrew said—" he stopped.

"Who hath done this?"

"Randolph, by her will." Ted pointed at Claudia.

"In that chaos, how might you know?"

"It wasn't chaos, Fence. The King mistook the feast."

Fence remained still. "For which other?"

"Randolph's serving-feast."

"So there is no doubt?"

Ted was silent. He had remembered that it was not in his own interest to accuse Randolph now.

"Did others drink?"

"Everyone."

"Were others stricken?"

"I don't think so. Randolph fainted, or something; and I'm sick, but nobody else just—just *died* like that."

"In the cup, then, not in the bottle."

"I guess," said Ted, miserably.

"Who had a chance at the cup?"

"Search close for one that strikes," said Claudia, in her deep voice with its insinuating touch of huskiness. She sounded amused. "All may yet be very well."

"Keep the words of Shan from thy mouth," said Fence, with astonishing severity, and he put his arm through Ted's. "Go we to Randolph, then," he said.

CHAPTER 4

THEY went back to the Council Chamber in silence. Ted stole an occasional glance at Fence. For all that he was walking briskly, that same stillness hung about him, as if he had suspended all his mental processes and half his bodily ones. Ted kept wanting to make sure he was breathing. But it was comforting to have something so steady so close. Ted felt as if he had just stepped off one of the nastier carnival rides, the kind you could never let Laurie go on because she threw up.

They came up the last flight of stairs. It was colder than ever. The man-at-arms had his sword out and held it to block the stairway. He, too, looked sick. Seeing Fence seemed to make him feel sicker; he did not move the sword, nor did he speak when they came up to him.

"I have an errand to the King," said Fence, formally.

"You are too late," said the guard.

"That," said Fence, "is for the King to say."

The guard opened his mouth, looked at Ted, shut it, and moved out of their way.

"You must learn to speak for yourself," said Fence, as they went down the hall. "You are no sorcerer's puppet; give none cause to say you are."

Ted could not answer him. He had forgotten that by failing to stop Randolph he had made himself King.

Both doors of the Council Chamber stood open, but two people with swords barred their way. One of them was the yellow-haired woman with the scarred forehead who had sat next to Matthew at the Banquet of Midsummer's Eve. She looked peculiar with a mail-shirt dragged on a little askew over her red dress, but the sword suited her well enough. Her companion's mail half-covered what looked remarkably like a nightgown, insofar, among the odd fashions of High Castle, as you could tell a fancy nightgown from a plain dress; her red hair was mussed and her sharp face a little bleary. But she, too, looked quite at home with her sword. Ted wondered what in the world was going on.

"What hath been accomplished?" Fence asked the yellow-haired woman.

"All save Randolph and Matthew have been taken under guard, 'til they give account of what hath occurred. Jerome awaits you, at your leisure."

"The King?"

She looked at Ted for a moment, and then back at Fence. "Within," she said.

"Thanks," said Fence, imbuing the single word with more formality than Ted would have believed possible.

The guards lowered their swords and Fence went between them into the Council Chamber. Ted had no desire to go back into that room. He looked at the yellow-haired woman, who had been kind at the banquet. She saluted him with her sword and stood a little more aside. Ted sighed and went in.

Someone had straightened out the King's body and spread a dark-blue cloth over it. Randolph sat on the floor with his head on his knees. Matthew leaned on the table between him and the body of the King. He looked exasperated and helpless, and his whole face lit up when he saw Fence.

Fence got to his knees beside Randolph with a swiftness

most people achieve only in jumping up, and put his arms around him.

"He, too?" he asked Matthew.

"He says not," said Matthew; "he says 'tis but some gain-giving as might perhaps trouble a woman."

Ted thought that the women at the door had no gaingivings troubling *them*. Then he thought that Randolph must know that, too. Some such gaingiving, he thought, as might perhaps trouble a woman who has poisoned the King. Or anybody with any sense.

"A looketh ill to me," said Matthew.

"So do you," said Ted. "So do I, I bet."

"Matthew," said Fence, still holding Randolph, "what happened?"

Matthew said slowly, "Many came early, thinking this the feast where all must serve. We set bottles and napkins and cups in place; Andrew had the opening of the bottles; 'tis some joke a hath with Conrad."

He looked at the top of Randolph's head. "As befitted the feast, we were all helter-skelter when the King arrived. Each of us, Fence, hath polished a glass, set a napkin or a plate. The King spoke to us and we saw he had mistook the feast." He cleared his throat. "Randolph was on the King's right; Edward to his; I to his; Conrad to his; Andrew to his. Now, when we saw the King was wrong, I put a napkin along Randolph's arm; the King could not see for that Randolph was between us. Andrew had all the bottles before him, and he did push one past Conrad, and me, and Edward, to Randolph, who began to pour, the King's cup having been set already."

Matthew looked at Ted, who, not understanding the look, just shrugged at him. "Randolph was o'erhasty in his pouring," said Matthew, still looking at Ted, "and striking the cup wi' the bottle, he o'erturned it; then, striving to right the cup, he dropped the bottle. He did require Edward to bring him a cloth, and Edward did do't." He turned back to Fence. "Now the cup had been marred by the striking of the bottle, so that Edward brought him another; and, Andrew being sulky, I did take a new bottle and give it to Randolph, who poured for the King and for all."

Matthew stood away from the table and crossed his arms. "All drank the wine, and took no harm therefrom; also, in the spilling of the first bottle, Lord Conrad and I were wet, but took no harm."

"My best thanks to you," said Fence. "Edward?"

"What he said," said Ted, a little wildly. Either Matthew had not seen him bump Randolph, or he thought it best not to say so. From Matthew's looks, it was probably the latter. In any case, he would prefer not to have to explain his actions.

Randolph brought his head up and looked over Fence's arm at Ted; once again there was congratulation in his eyes. Ted stared at him, confounded; and then he knew. Now he and Randolph were in truth conspirators. It was Randolph who could save the Secret Country. If they thought Randolph was guilty they would not let him be Regent.

"Randolph?" said Fence, less sharply than he had spoken to Ted.

" 'Tis a true account," said Randolph; his eyes on Matthew were speculative. He seemed to be recovering.

"One thing other," said Matthew, still looking at Fence. "When Randolph did spill the wine, it put Andrew into a most fierce choler."

"What said he?" demanded Fence.

Matthew shrugged. "Naught," he said. "He turned color and clenched his hands."

"Yes, he did," said Ted.

"Randolph?" said Fence.

"I saw not," said Randolph.

Fence and Matthew looked at one another, but no one said anything. Randolph put a hand on Fence's arm, and Fence and he helped each other up.

"Didst thou drink?" Fence asked him.

"The servant drinks not," said Randolph.

"Shan's mercy," said Fence suddenly, "where is Benjamin?"

"He came not," said Randolph, sounding surprised.

So that's why my chair was empty, thought Ted, we were missing one. I never even noticed. Benjamin was *supposed* to be here, too. He makes a speech and says "Alas" a lot.

Fence closed his eyes and let his breath out. "One must tell him," he said.

Randolph was beginning to look sick again. Serve you right, thought Ted. Maybe nobody else cared about the King: Matthew and Conrad had seemed more worried about Randolph, but Benjamin did care. And Randolph did, of course, crazy as that seemed. That was why he was so upset. Ted wished his mind would start working normally again.

"I'll do't," said Randolph: he sounded exactly as Ted's father had when it had been necessary to put one of their dogs to sleep.

"Meanwhile," said Matthew, a little shakily, "the council lords fume and fret."

"Let Agatha examine them," said Fence. This startled Ted considerably, but nobody remarked on it. Fence regarded Matthew for a moment longer, and added, "And do you take it down, an it please you."

"It will be long ere aught pleaseth me," said Matthew, as if he were quoting something, and he went out.

"'Tis Benjamin should attend the King," said Fence to Randolph. "We will stay 'til you find him."

Randolph looked down at the King. "A will stay 'til we come," he said, and went away.

Ted and Fence stood in the darkening room. Its candles were all out. Fence was wearing his wizard's robe, and its curious twinings glowed and pulsed. Ted looked away from them to the King, and went to the window. He could not seem to stop shaking, and the air coming through the window, though damp, was warmer than the room.

"Well," said Fence. "Confusion now hath made his masterpiece. Say you still that Randolph's hand is in this?"

"I don't see how he could have done it, Fence," said Ted, truthfully enough. "I was watching him every minute."

"My mind tends to Andrew," said Fence, "but that is for a mere dislike; and he was in favor; why would a cut's own throat?"

"Could it have been a mistake?" asked Ted.

"I would I had been here," said Fence. There was a silence. "And I am remiss," he added. Ted turned around. Fence had stooped over the King and raised the blue cloth. Ted was just as pleased to be unable to see what he was doing.

"Dear heaven," said Fence.

"What?" said Ted.

"This is the very smell of sorcery."

Oh, of course. But Edward would be surprised. "*What?*" said Ted.

"This is not a natural poison. It cannot be got save by sorcery." Fence let the cloth fall from his hand and stood up. "Conrad, Matthew, Andrew, Randolph," he said. "All had a chance at cup or bottle; and all have dabbled save Andrew."

"His sister could have made it for him," said Ted, viciously.

"So she could," said Fence. He joined Ted at the window. "Or, think you, to Randolph?"

"No," said Ted. "When he spilled the wine, I gave him a different cup, and I was right next to him the whole time. Besides," added Ted, thinking that a little truth could do no harm, "he was very cheerful while we were setting the table." He had become cheerful after seeing the spiderweb in the cupboard, whatever that meant.

"And Andrew was marvelous distempered at the spilling of the wine?"

"Yes, marvelous."

"Now thou hast seen the deed, thou hast less stomach for the thought that Randolph did do't?" said Fence, belaboring the point as was his occasional regrettable habit. Ted remembered the scolding Laura, Patrick, and Ellen had gotten for disobeying Fence's orders, the night Claudia came up the stairs to Fence's tower with a sorcerous knife in her hand. Arguing had done them no good; Randolph had shut Fence up eventually. Ted was silent. Fence put an arm around his shoulders, and a little of his stillness had seeped into Ted when Randolph came back with Benjamin. They had brought two torches.

Randolph still looked sick. He stayed by the door, leaning on the wall next to the bracket he had slid the torch into. Benjamin's face, as he stared at the disordered room and the body of the King, was stunned and furious. Fence came away from the window, almost dragging Ted with him. Benjamin stooped over the King as Fence had done, and grief began to overtake the fury on his face. Then he started, and sniffed the air, and looked up at Fence.

"Aye," said Fence.

"So Melanie haunts us still," said Benjamin. He kissed the King's forehead, and looked at Fence again. Ted braced himself for the alas-speech; he had a horrible feeling that he might laugh.

"The bright day is done," said Benjamin, as if Fence were personally responsible, "and we are for the dark."

"See to thy torches, then," said Fence.

Benjamin seemed a little taken aback; then, shocking Ted, he laughed. "Aye," he said. "Fire is the test of gold." He stood up and looked at Ted. "A was better pleased wi' thee these last weeks," he said. He put his head out the door. "Bear him away," he said.

Four women Ted had never seen before came in and did so.

Benjamin looked at Ted again. "Leave all the rest to me," he said, and went after them.

"Well, my lord," said Fence to Ted. "you cannot have a council whilst your lords are penned with an inquisitor, but by your gracious will Lord Randolph and I might impart to you what we these six months have done."

"Only if you promise not to go on talking like that," said Ted.

"While we are private I will not," said Fence. He sat down in Andrew's chair and fished a map from the folds of his robe. "Randolph," he said, without looking up, "where is the Book of King John?"

"In Matthew's chamber," said Randolph. "Fence. What of the children?"

The other four children had gathered in Ellen and Laura's room. They sat, fidgeting and squabbling, on the bed with its green quilt. Around them the white horses raced unregarded across the green tapestries; the black cat slept on Ellen's discarded yellow dress. Outside above the shadowy mountains the western sky grew prickled over with stars as some wind from lands they had never seen pushed the clouds over High Castle, south and west to the domains of the Dragon King. This same wind faltered in through the unglazed window, whose shutters no one had thought to close, and tipped the flames of the lamps a little sideways. Only Laura, carefully staying out of the argument, noticed any of these things.

Ellen wanted to go listen at the door of the Council Room, but had been prevented by Ruth. Laura was not sure what she thought of Ruth these days. She had taken to wearing long white dresses, staring abstractedly into space when you were talking to her, and using her sorcerous voice for trivial things like telling Ellen that her hair ribbon did not match her dress. She was taller than ever, and wore her hair tightly braided and wound around her head, which made her look much less like Ellen and entirely too grown-up.

"I guess we'll know if anything went wrong," said Ellen, resigning herself. "They'll all shout 'Treason!'"

"Even if they did we wouldn't be able to hear it over here," said Patrick. "It's probably half a mile to the Council Room."

"Matthew has to come right by here to get Agatha," said Ellen. "So she can lay the King out."

"Why should she hit him when he's dead?" said Laura, despite her resolutions. It did not matter in the slightest, of course, because nobody paid any attention.

"Fence has to come tell *us* if the King's dead," said Ruth to Ellen, patiently. "He's Patrick's father and our uncle."

"He is not," said Ellen.

"The *King* is," said Ruth, less patiently.

"Let's *do* something," said Ellen.

"Like what?" said Patrick. "Play hopscotch?"

"I could read aloud," said Ruth.

"Can you read that stuff?" asked Laura.

"Sure," said Ruth. She picked up the book she had brought with her, a shabby affair with a much-scored leather binding, and opened it. "But King John," she read, "had been raised by an old country woman, and he knew the ways of monsters. So when the—"

"Oh, don't!" said Ellen. "I can't stand hearing any more about King John. I wish we'd never invented him. And that's *dumb*. Why should a king be raised by an old country woman?"

Ruth was exasperated, but she was interrupted before she could express herself. Fence came into the room without knocking. They all gaped at him. He was very still and remote; only the curling starry lines on his robe moved a little as the lamplight caught them.

Fence looked at them for a moment as they sat and sprawled on the bed. Then he came across the room in a flurry of stars and put his hand on Patrick's head. Patrick looked at him as if he were the worst part of a horror movie; except that horror movies never bothered Patrick.

"Thy royal father's dead," said Fence.

He appeared braced for hysteria; they simply stared at him. Laura was supposed to throw herself into his arms and howl, but she could not do it.

"I knew it," muttered Patrick.

Fence took his hand from Patrick's head and examined him much as he had examined Claudia's knife. "Did you so?" he said.

Patrick stood up and looked him straight in the face. "Ted told me what he thought."

"He does not think it now," said Fence.

Ruth was the first to recollect her part. Glaring at Patrick, she said, in strained tones. "What happened? I didn't know his Majesty was unwell."

"He was not," said Fence. He looked around at them again, and seemed to abandon whatever gentle measures he had settled on, in the face of their abnormal calm.

"The King was poisoned," he said, "with a sorcerous brew."

He went on looking at them, and they stared back. Laura thought again about howling, but she was shocked, not grieved. She wondered if Ted was killing Randolph yet. He had not wanted to; but he had not wanted Randolph to poison the King, either. So much for wishing on the Enchanted Forest, she thought. We unbroke the Crystal of Earth, but everything else is going to happen.

"Well," said Patrick, "who did it, then?"

Fence buried both hands in his robes, and his face, which had become more normal when their response perplexed him, turned remote again. "We know not," he said.

"Heh," said Patrick.

"What we may discover, you and your brother the King shall know," said Fence. Patrick's mouth fell open, which seemed to afford Fence a very dim and distant amusement, the way Laura's father would sometimes smile when you told him a joke while he was reading. Fence addressed Ellen and Laura. "Agatha hath other business than you."

"We can put ourselves to bed," said Ellen.

Fence regarded her with curiosity. "How commendable in you," he said.

Ellen, unaccustomed to sarcasm from this quarter, said, "No, not at all," like a society lady, thought Laura. Then she looked appalled.

Patrick snickered, and Ruth pulled his hair. He pushed her hand away.

"Cut it out!" he said.

"Children," said Fence.

"I'm sorry we're so unbecoming," said Patrick, sourly.

"So am I," said Fence.

They squirmed under his gaze, even Ruth, and looked at the floor.

"Whatever wildness possesseth you," said Fence at last, "tame it by tomorrow."

"You began it," said Patrick, "making Ellie look silly."

"And you shall end it," said Fence. He turned and went from the room, closing the door behind him with a thud that missed being a slam but was not a neutral noise.

"*Patrick,*" said Ruth.

"What's the use of playing any more?" demanded Patrick. "It didn't work; the King's dead!"

"You don't have to make Fence any more unhappy than he already is."

"He's not even real!"

Ruth picked up the skirts of her white dress and advanced on him. "Do you mean to tell me," she said, "that after all the things that have gone different and all the things that have gone wrong and even after *this* you can sit there and say this is all out of our own heads?"

"Yes!" shouted Patrick, standing his piece of the floor defiantly. Ruth stopped coming toward him. "And the reason it's going wrong and different is that some of us are sick in the head!"

Laura would not have spoken for anything. There was a brief but profound silence. Ellen broke it by twisting around on the bed and regarding her brother as if he were a spider that she would have liked to step on had she not been afraid it would run up her leg.

"*Who,*" she said ominously, sounding very like Ruth, "is sick?"

"Ted and Ruth," said Patrick. "And they're the oldest, so you and Laura think whatever they say, and I can't do anything by myself to keep things straight."

"Why," said Ruth, in a flat tone, "are we sick."

"You're important here and you want to stay that way. So you want it to be real."

"Why," said Ruth, more angrily, "even if that's true, is it sick?"

"Megalomania," said Patrick, scaring Laura; it sounded like some kind of cancer.

"*You're* sick!" said Ellen. "You think you're the only one who can be right, and we're all against you."

"Paranoia," said Ruth, with a sort of melancholy pleasure in knowing the word.

Laura knew that word herself, but she wasn't pleased. It was unwise to enter a family fight, but she was finding this one too much for her.

"I think you're all horrible," she said. "How can you stand there and call names when—"

"I didn't mean to call names," said Patrick. "I was trying to bring you to your senses so we can do something. You're no use if you go on thinking this stuff is real."

"What do you want to do?" asked Ruth.

"Get out of here!"

"But I need to see what *happens!*" said Ellen.

"For God's sake!" said Patrick. "This isn't a book."

"Oh, no?" said Ruth. "I thought you said it wasn't real?"

It still surprised Laura to see Patrick nonplussed. Ellen

and Ruth looked at him with a tentative sort of triumph, as if they were quite sure they were right but expected him to come up with a slippery answer.

He had an answer, but it did not seem slippery to Laura.

"It's happening *to* us," he said. "It isn't good for us. It's going to hurt *us*, and *we're* real."

"Why isn't it good for us?" demanded Ruth. "Why shouldn't it teach us things and make us better people?"

"I guess there's no reason it shouldn't," said Patrick, "but it isn't. It's making all of you—all of us—unreasonable. And emotional and grumpy. And name-calling. And callous," he added. "The King's dead and Ellie thinks he's real and she's not even sorry, she just wants to hang around and see what else happens."

"Now look," said Ellen.

"Be quiet," said Ruth. She addressed Patrick. "Lots of things that are good for the soul make people unreasonable."

Patrick sat down on the bed in a despairing movement. "It's not good for the soul," he said, "to think you're important when you're not."

"Seems to me you think *you're* pretty important," said Ellen. "You think you could make all this happen."

"I think *we* could. And that's not important, it's just normal imagination gone bad. Because it *isn't* happening, we just—"

"Who made up Lady Claudia, then?" asked Ruth.

"How should I know? What with everybody running around making up just anything and not even telling anybody, somebody could have made her up and forgotten all about her. Or just decided she wasn't a good idea."

"Why didn't that decision stick, then?" asked Ruth.

"Some of them did. Laura isn't a prince."

"Just as well," said Laura, briefly entertained. Real as everything here had always looked to her, right now she would be just as pleased if everything—even the unicorns— were imaginary. "Hey," she said, recalled, as always, to her primary problem in this country, "if it's all in our heads, why can't I ride a horse like we said I could?"

"Because you think it's real."

"So what? If the King's real, why can't me riding horses be real, too?"

"Because you know you can't!"

"I knew the King wasn't real, too, before we got here," said Laura.

Patrick seemed to be struggling with another way to make his point, and there was a pause during which Ellen fell asleep on Ruth's knee.

"I don't really care," Ruth said suddenly to Patrick, "what you think, but I would appreciate it if you would act as though this were real. It seems to me, since you're in no danger of thinking you're important, that you have less to lose by acting as if this were real, even if it isn't, than you would have by acting as if it weren't real, when it was."

Laura and Patrick looked at her in astonishment. This was a far better Lady Ruth than she had ever achieved, even at the height of her acting.

"Since you won't pay any attention to my arguments anyway," said Patrick.

"That's right."

"I guess so," said Patrick.

"Thank you."

"What do we do now?" asked Laura.

"Go to bed, I think," said Ruth, looking at Ellen.

"Shouldn't we wait for Ted?"

"I don't think," said Ruth, "that Ted is going to feel like talking to anybody."

In the clear gray morning, Fence, Ted, and Randolph straightened their backs and rubbed their eyes. The whole long council table was littered with books and maps and scribbled bits of parchment. The candles were pools in the bottoms of their holders. Ted felt like a pool in his chair. If he had not been exhausted he would have been terrified. He did not understand a third of what he had been told. He had never been fond of military history; what he liked were the tactics of single fights, like the one Prince Edward was supposed to have with Lord Randolph in the rose garden. Even if he had known about battles he would have been bewildered by the peculiar blend of normal and magical fighting that Fence and Randolph seemed to think the best way to manage things.

He had gathered something of the magnitude of their problem. Fence and Randolph, for all their youth, seemed to know a great deal about the art of war. Precepts, examples from history, episodes from their own experience, came easily to their tongues. But half their well-taught and successfully exercised theories foundered on the rock of sorcery. Neither of them had ever fought a sorcerous battle. Fence was a sorcerer, but not in the school of the Dragon King. He did not know, and apparently neither did anybody else, by what principles the Dragon King ordered his powers. He did not know his enemy; and that, said Randolph, somewhere in the cold dregs of the night, was the first rule of war.

"What about all those spies?" Ted asked.

"King John says," said Fence, "that of the information your spies gather about a sorcerous opponent, it is necessary to discount half."

"Which half, he saith not," said Randolph. He was still pale, and there were two lines of pain or weariness between his eyebrows; but he smiled at Fence with all his old charm, and Ted saw that this was an old argument between them.

"Indeed he does," said Fence.

"Ah," said Randolph, "but which half one cannot tell until one hath the whole; and we have not the whole."

"We were not permitted it," said Fence, not smiling at all; and Ted knew he spoke of the King.

As they talked on, and the west wind drove the clouds over the plain and the huge stars of the Secret Country bloomed from the clearing sky, Ted found that those precepts rescued from the rock of sorcery would drown in the whirlpool of what ought to have been the Secret Country's greatest strength: the Border Magic. To meet your enemy before he was ready, on ground of your choosing; to attack him in his weak places, so that he must abandon his strong ones to defend them; to feint back and forth over large stretches of ground until you had exhausted him—all these things would give you the victory. But because of the Border Magic, the armies of the Secret Country could do none of them.

If an army of enemies set foot in the Secret Country, the Secret Country would become a wasteland. Wherefore those wishing to defend it must fight its enemies where its enemies chose to gather. It was true that the Border Magic defeated from the start all those whose intent was to own the Secret Country, to live in it, to usefully occupy it in any way. But the Border Magic opened up vast new opportunities for the vengeful, the mischievous, the malicious. The Dragon King, by all accounts, was all three. And King John had nothing to say about the Border Magic, because the Border Magic had been contrived after his time.

"Who *by?*" asked Ted, with considerable resentment. This was not so much for the contriver as for the ruthless manner in which his own invention, of which he and Patrick had been so proud, had been logically dismantled and shown to be like a badly thrown boomerang, that not only recoils upon its wielder, but smacks him in the forehead and leaves him helpless in the hands of his enemies.

Fence shut King John's Book and pushed his damp, flattened hair out of his eyes. His round face was a little sunken; Ted could see the line of his cheekbone, and realized with a lurch of the heart that in some curious and sidelong way, Fence looked like Claudia.

"By the unicorns," said Fence, "and by the Outside Powers. The Outside Powers owed the unicorns a boon, and this was what the unicorns asked of them."

"A joke, then," said Ted.

"Perhaps. Or in part."

Ted stood up and stretched. "Fence," he said, "if King John's Book is so little use, why did you make such a fuss about using it?"

"It had been of far greater use," said Randolph out of the depths of his chair, "had we been free to gather intelligence as it bade us during these months the Dragon King hath stumbled about our borders like a cow with the staggers."

Fence chuckled. "Well, I gathered some little store. And we are free now to gather what we may," he said. "Edward. We stray from our path. Randolph, the map."

Now they were silent, and the first thoughtful murmur of awakening birds came in the windows with a stir of morning air. Ted resigned himself to a blind trust in his counselors, and looked at the two of them.

"Well," said Fence to Randolph, "when will we march?"

"Should we not have the coronation before the battle?"

"I'd rather not," said Ted, unable to be as blind as he would have liked.

"That is not the question," said Randolph.

"I, too, had rather not," said Fence.

Randolph frowned at him.

"There is no time," said Fence, "and it is not necessary."

"No?" said Randolph.

"More men believe in the Book of King John than in the speeches of Lord Andrew."

"Think you not," said Randolph, with some difficulty, "that to delay the coronation would make men to think we had doubts of the Prince in this matter of the poisoning?"

"To hasten the coronation and damage the war thereby," said Fence, "would make them to think we had doubts of the Regent."

"And is doubt of the Regent more damageful than doubt of the Prince?"

"That is not the question," said Fence.

"No?" said Randolph again. He raised an eyebrow at Ted.

"Randolph," said Ted, "everybody knows who's really fighting this war. And everybody has doubts of me anyway."

"Doubts of your skill perhaps," said Randolph. "That is nothing. It is the question of who did the murder. If you are not crowned it will be said we think you did it."

"Randolph," said Fence, "I tell you there is no time."

Randolph put the flat of one hand to his forehead and squinted at the opposite wall. "There is," he said. "We cannot leave here before seven days; we must bury the King; Edward must call a council; and we must collect those troops the King did not make ready. We must wait for Chryse; we must raise Belaparthalion. Our last reports show the Dragon King still but distant."

"Shan's mercy," said Fence. "The coronation of William was months in the making."

"I don't want a lot of fuss," said Ted hastily. What Randolph wanted did, at least, fit in with their bedraggled story. It was as King of the Secret Country that Edward had visited the land of the dead.

Fence's mouth quirked. "Very well," he said.

"Could I ask you," said Ted, "to call the council and arrange about the funeral?"

"Randolph shall call the council," said Fence; "let him have his duties for the short space left him. I'll speak to Benjamin touching the funeral."

"Thank you," said Ted.

He climbed the cold stairs to his room. Patrick was sound asleep. Ted crawled into bed and lay shivering for a while. When he fell asleep he dreamed vaguely of a herd of unicorns galloping into a purple lake while all the stars fell into it and sent it smoking into the sky. He also dreamed that he was trying to paint this scene, which seemed no more unusual to him than a good sunset, and was vexed because he could not get the right shade of purple.

CHAPTER 5

IT rained when they buried the King. It had rained all night. It was raining when Agatha woke Laura and Ellen at the hideous hour of five and made them dress in black. It was raining when Ellen discovered that they would get no breakfast until after the ceremony, said "Shan's *mercy!*" in front of Agatha, and was slapped for it.

It rained on their procession as it wound its way through the stony woods, until everyone was as black and shiny as the trunks of the trees. Ellen stopped being furious long enough to whisper to Laura, "They look like the trees walking." Laura stopped being shocked long enough to wish Ellen had not said it. The slosh and drip of foot and hoof and leaf sounded very like the noise a tree might make walking in the wet woods.

The further they went, the less Laura liked it. She finally woke up enough to wonder why, and raised her dripping head to see the gate she had left open when she walked out of her own time and met the unicorns. It was not open now. Laura realized that, unless somebody had come all the way out here, found the gate open, shut it, and not raised a fuss back at High Castle, she had not been here yet. She felt a qualm almost as strong as the one made by Agatha's slapping Ellen.

"Let's not go," she mouthed to Ellen.

Ellen's face lit up, and then she closed her mouth on a laugh and shook her head. Laura looked around and saw Agatha trudging on the other side of Ruth and watching them over Ruth's head. She would have sworn herself, if she had dared. She had almost gotten used to things, but now that the King was dead, everything else looked likely to be awful, and again she wanted to go home.

They slipped and scrambled up the hill. Laura looked for the flowers bordering the path, but there were only round gray stones.

The brilliant green of the grass inside the wall was even more startling in this rain than it had been when Laura first saw it. There were fewer flowers on the gravestones, but there seemed to be as many gravestones. Laura followed the others to the clump of people around the new grave.

"Oh, no," she said. It was the newer grave she had walked around before. She had stood over the dead King and not even known it. Not for the first time since they came to this country, she felt that she was being laughed at.

"Here, child," said Agatha's voice.

Laura blinked upward into the rain, and took the bunch of flowers Agatha handed her. They were of six or seven different kinds, but all yellow. The only ones she recognized were the dandelions. Agatha gave Ellen a bunch of purple flowers, and Ruth a bunch of red ones, and Matthew a bunch of white.

"What's this for?" said Ellen to Laura; her voice was low, because of Agatha, but held a wealth of scorn. Laura had no idea, and shrugged.

"It's part of the burial custom," said Ruth, joining them. "Everybody gets a bunch of a different color, and when the ceremony's over, we throw them over the grave and they all mix together. It's symbolic, but I can't remember what of."

"Did you make it up?" said Ellen.

"Ted and I did," said Ruth, "but it was a long time ago."

"Where is Ted?" said Laura.

"They made him help carry the coffin, him and Patrick," said Ellen. She bestowed a clinical glance upon her bouquet. "Violets," she said. "Wood gentians. Hey, what's this?"

"Shhh," said Laura; Agatha was passing their way, and gave them a quelling glance. But she did not stop. She took Matthew, who looked strange without his cheerful expression, his wild red hair flattened and darkened with rain, by the arm, and moved him toward the grave.

"Who does she think she is?" demanded Ellen.

"Whoever it is, Matthew thinks so, too," said Ruth. Matthew had smiled and bent down from his considerably greater height to say something to Agatha.

"She can't be just a nurse," said Laura.

"Nobody's just anything around here," grumbled Ellen. "Look at Benjamin."

"I think the cooks are just cooks," offered Laura.

"No, they aren't," said Ruth. "Two of them are ahead of me in sorcerous training."

"Maybe she was his nurse, too," said Ellen, looking after Matthew and Agatha.

"She's not old enough," said Ruth.

A hand came down on Laura's head, gently, but she jumped. She looked up; it was at Randolph.

"It's time, I fear," he said.

He looked, in his black clothes, as if he had been bleached, and there were lines around his eyes that had not been there the last time she saw him. Laura had once tripped over her mother's sprained ankle, and her mother had looked like that for a few seconds. But Randolph went on looking like that as he spoke again. Laura felt a desperate and foolish desire to give him some aspirin.

"Those closest to him must gather around the grave," said Randolph.

"I never even talked to him," said Laura, following him nonetheless.

Randolph turned around so suddenly that she almost fell into him, and took her by the hands. "It is too late for many things," he said, bewildering her; and he kept hold of one of the hands and took her along with him.

"He means by blood," said Ellen in Laura's ear.

Randolph made room for them between Fence and Matthew. Across the gaping grave Laura saw Ted and Patrick; Ted looked miserable, and Patrick disgusted. Both of them were wet, and very red in the face. The coffin must have been heavy.

Laura had intended not to look at the coffin, but it was so unlike what she expected that she looked at it before she knew what it was. It was a sturdy box of pale wood, spattered with rain, the running fox inlaid on the top, and a scroll of flowers, and the peculiar animals they had seen before. It was, even to someone who had been living among the beautiful things of High Castle for two months, a lovely object: Laura found herself wanting it for a moment, and then shivered.

"Will you look at that!" hissed Ellen.

"I did," said Laura.

"Look at the side, not the top."

Laura did. There, once more, in greater detail and richer color, was the story of the young man, the wizard, and the animals that they had seen on the tapestry, on Fence's dishes, and on various doors. Only the first four panels of the tapestry were on this side of the coffin. On the far right the cat and the young man with decided eyebrows were, respectively, washing and feeding the dog.

"Why couldn't we have been on the other side?" raged Ellen under her breath.

"I thought you were tired of that story."

"I want to see which last panel it is, the hole or the sun."

"Ted and Patrick can see it."

"Only if they have the sense to look."

"Stare at them," said Laura, hopefully.

She and Ellen opened their eyes as wide as they could and gazed earnestly through the misty rain at Ted and Patrick.

Randolph came around behind Ted and began talking to him. Laura forgot what she was supposed to be doing. Ted kept shaking his head, and Randolph looked as if he would have liked to shake Ted. This argument eventually attracted Patrick's attention, and at Laura's side Ellen gave a martyred sigh.

"Maybe I could find whoever made the thing," she said.

"I wonder what Randolph wants?" said Laura.

"Milady Laura," said Fence over Ellen's head, "of your courtesy, hold your tongue."

Laura looked up at him reproachfully. It was Ellen's fault they were talking, but no grown-up, even Fence, would ever bother to find out something like that before he yelled at you. Fence's mouth quirked.

"'Tis not the speech, but its substance, that I pray thee keep thy tongue from," he said.

Laura, having puzzled this out, was too astonished even to smile at him.

"Hush," said Fence, looking over her head and across the grave at Randolph. "We begin.

Randolph, standing with his hands in the sleeves of his black robe and his hair dripping into his eyes, had managed by merely looking the crowd over to make them be quiet and watch him.

"Servants, friends, and lovers," he said; and like the King's, his voice carried although he did not raise it. "We are foregathered to bid farewell to William, Celia and Conrad's son, who hath served, befriended, and loved us these fifty years."

"Fifty-two," said Ellen in Laura's ear.

Fence moved from beside her to stand with Randolph. Laura kept her eyes determinedly from his robe. Randolph asked him a question; he answered it with a short speech; Randolph asked him another; he answered it briefly.

Laura gaped at them. She could not understand a word they were saying, and yet she almost did. It was like a conversation to which she was not paying attention; if she stopped reading and listened, she would be able to understand perfectly. Their voices held a ritual intonation which made it obvious that this was the ceremony, and not some consultation about details. The rain fell down their faces.

"What're they saying?" whispered Ellen. Laura shrugged, and looked across the grave at Ted and Patrick. Patrick's face was perplexed, and Ted's resigned. Laura glanced around at Ruth, who was frowning. Everybody else was listening with a serious face; Laura could tell from an occasional nod or grimace or smile that the real inhabitants of the Secret Country had no trouble following the service.

After perhaps fifteen minutes of this, during which a number of people began blinking and sniffling, and Laura watched Ted and Patrick fidget, Randolph bowed to Fence and stepped back. Fence, in his fantastic robe, knelt on the sodden ground and picked up a handful of mud.

"In the tradition of John, by the mercy granted to Shan, in accordance with the laws of the Hidden Land," he said, and slapped the mud onto the gorgeous top of the coffin.

Laura watched him stand up, half expecting the mud to roll off his robe as if the robe were made of some new miracle fabric. But it was stained and wet, and remained so; and a fugitive gleam from a star half-muddied caught and held her eye. She saw Ted's face, covered with blood, as she had seen it before. But this time the view was wider; Ted lay on the bare and dusty ground with a great blot of blood across his chest, and Randolph knelt over him with a despairing expression. Behind them the sky was hot and empty. Laura's gaze jerked involuntarily to the real Randolph, who had come forward to hand Fence a bunch of flowers. When she looked back at the robe it was only a robe.

"What's the matter?" hissed Ellen.

"Just a minute," said Laura, staring hopefully at the stars. Nothing happened.

Randolph made a gesture with his hand, and Benjamin came out of the crowd. His eyes were red, but his face was impassive. He looked around the crowd for a moment, and finally took Ted by the arm and drew him over to Randolph. Randolph touched Fence on the arm, and Fence shook his head. Randolph jerked his head at Conrad. Fence went back to stand by Patrick, and the four others, Randolph, Ted, Benjamin, and Conrad, took hold of the ropes around the coffin and lowered it into the grave.

Laura heard a muffled sound beside her, and saw that Agatha was crying. Laura had not quite forgiven her for slapping Ellen, but she felt so guilty for not crying herself that she patted Agatha on the arm.

When the coffin came to rest it made a mushy, sucking thud that sent shivers through Laura, and she saw Ted blanch. Randolph picked up another handful of mud and dropped it into the hole. He looked almost as unhappy as Ted. Conrad and Benjamin and Ted in turn dropped a handful of earth and stepped backward.

Then the whole crowd pushed forward, and the air was full of flowers. Laura flung hers with abandon, and they landed at Randolph's feet. Laura froze, her hand still out. Randolph froze for a moment himself; but then he bowed to her, scooped up the flowers, and scattered them across the grave with a gesture that was like a salute. Laura grinned at him in her relief, but he did not smile back.

"For shame, child," said Agatha, her voice still shaky.

Laura promptly lost sympathy for her.

Benjamin and Conrad had fetched shovels from somewhere, and began filling in the grave. Laura saw Patrick eyeing the shovels, and guessed that they must be different in some way from ordinary ones. But they looked like shovels to her.

The pressure of the crowd was forcing her away from the side of the grave, and she was just as pleased to go. Ellen squelched up beside her, indignant.

"They should have put the flowers on top of the dirt," she said. "This way they're just wasted." Her hair was so wet that it lay flat on her head, and she did not look like herself.

"There's flowers on the other graves," said Laura. "Maybe they put more on later."

"They still wasted the ones in there."

"I wonder if Ted and Patrick saw the other side of the coffin," said Laura.

"And that's another thing," mourned Ellen. "It was so pretty; why did they have to bury it?"

"Milady," said Fence, behind them, "that you might remember that what they buried with it was infinitely more precious."

Ellen and Laura both jumped, and Ellen was silent. Fence went ahead of them through the gate and was submerged by the crowd.

It began to rain harder, and by the time they were halfway back to High Castle, the path had turned into a stream on which six-inch dolls could have canoed with great danger. Laura had scorned dolls for a long time; they were not nearly as exciting as playing the Secret Country with her cousins and brother. Now she wondered if she had made a mistake. Even if all your dolls came alive and began walking about, they could hardly land you in a situation like this one. She was soaking wet, and every now and then a branch would whack her in the face. She had the distinct impression that the forest was troubling them for their presumption in walking through it. She felt put upon and profoundly depressed because she was not unhappy enough about the King. Ellen was brooding too, probably because Fence had scolded her.

"That was a silly funeral," she informed Laura as they came through the clearing where they had feasted after the Unicorn Hunt. Laura thought of the exuberant people in their red and green; of the humorous, catlike stare of the unicorn; of the long head and gossamer mane laid like an apron in Ellen's lap. She said nothing, but followed the black-clad horde over Conrad's Bridge and through the garden gate.

"Maybe it'd have been better if we could have understood what they were saying," she ventured.

"Well, it was stupid that we couldn't," retorted Ellen.

Agatha caught them just inside the South Door and told them to go change for the feast. They dripped upstairs.

"Whoever heard of a feast after a funeral?" demanded Ellen, her head in their wardrobe.

"Funeral baked meats," said Laura, foggily.

"Heh," said Ellen.

They had a brief argument over what to wear; their only black dresses were the sodden ones they had on. Ellen favored white, and Laura yellow.

"We don't have to dress alike all the time, you know," said Ellen.

"It makes me feel safer," said Laura. "Besides, Agatha thinks it's cute."

"So what?"

"I think she's less trouble when she thinks we're cute."

"She'd be less trouble if she was at the bottom of the moat," grumbled Ellen.

Laura stared at her, and felt a mischievous impulse. "How do you know?" she said. "Have you ever known anybody at the bottom of a moat?"

Ellen threw a white dress at her. "Come on," she said, "before they eat everything."

Ruth, also in a white dress, met them at the door and dragged them briskly through the crowd to a corner, where they found Ted, Patrick, and an enormous collection of food. Ted and Patrick wore their usual dark-blue tunics, and Laura could see that they had been wearing these particular ones for longer than Agatha would like, if she found out.

"We have to decide what we're doing," Ted told them.

"First," said Ellen, "I want to ask you boys something. Did you look at your side of the coffin?"

"It had that same story on it," said Patrick.

"But was it the sun or the hole, at the end?"

Ted and Patrick looked at one another, and shook their heads.

"The last panel wasn't on our side," said Ted. "The last one we had was the young wizard pointing his staff at the hole."

"It couldn't be there, Ellie," said Patrick, with the patience that was far more exasperating than derision. "That tapestry had nine panels, and there were only four on each side of the coffin. Four and four is—"

"What about the end?"

"Flowers," said Patrick.

Ellen made an inarticulate growling noise and chomped into a chicken drumstick.

"Anyway," said Ted, "we have to decide what to do." He pushed his damp hair out of his face.

"Why don't you get your hair cut?" said Laura wickedly.

"Tomorrow is the coronation," said Ted, taking no notice. "The day after that's a council, where we make final battle plans, and have some sort of hearing about the King's death, and then we run around for three days doing this and that, and then we march."

"Do girls get to go?" demanded Ellen.

Ted looked taken aback. "I never thought of that," he said. "Ruthie has to or she can't do her sorcery on me."

"Why her, when there are so many better ones?" said Ellen.

"Green Caves sorcerers don't go to war," said Ruth slowly. She looked suddenly frightened.

"So why did Lady Ruth go?" Ted asked her.

Ellen snickered. "Probably because she's in love with Edward. You dress in men's array, Ruthie, and quickly heal his wounds."

"And you and Laurie can dress in men's array and carry the bandages," said Ruth, absently; she still seemed worried.

"We'll carry your books of sorcery," offered Ellen.

"Speak for yourself," said Laura, who had no desire to go to a battle if she could avoid it.

Ted sighed. "If we're all going," he said, "and if we can get the swords back from Fence, then we could make a break for it when we pass the Well and the House."

There was a long silence. The clatter of tongues and dishes surrounded them. Laura looked out across the crowd and saw Randolph, still in his black clothes, talking to Claudia. Claudia wore red, as always, and the smile she was turning on Randolph made Laura's stomach cold.

"*Ted!*" she said.

"She's been out for a couple of days now," said Ted. "I forgot to mention it."

"You are crazy," said Ellen.

Laura privately agreed with this. Ruth said nothing, but now she looked terrified.

"She wasn't at the funeral, was she?" said Laura.

"We're getting off the subject," said Ted. "Do we want to make a break for it?"

"No," said Ellen. "If I do get to go to the battle, maybe I can finally do something besides flounce around in frilly dresses and eat."

"You captured the unicorn," said Ruth.

Ellen was silent.

"It seems to me," said Ted, "that the only good we could have done around here was to keep Randolph from killing the King, and we didn't, so we might as well go home now. Randolph can run the war better than Edward, let alone me. They don't need us."

"Who's going to be King, then?" said Laura.

"Patrick's next, but if he's gone, I don't know."

"Fence told us once," said Ellen, scowling. "Patrick the

elder. Anna. Justin the Younger. Who are all those people anyway? I've never met any of them."

"They're in Fence's Country, I think," said Ruth. "And Benjamin's here."

"It's not our problem who'll be King," said Patrick.

"I don't know," said Ted. "Maybe it's our job to find the real Edward."

Patrick opened his mouth, looked at Ruth, and took a bite of apple.

"Shan's mercy," said Ellen, "we never thought of that."

"Ellie, don't say that," said Ted. "I think it means something."

"When are we going to have *time* to find the real Edward?" said Ruth. "We leave in less than a week. If I'm to get you back from the land of the dead, I'll have to study. That's advanced sorcery. I don't know anything about it except what Ellie and I made up, and how do we know that's right? I don't like this."

"*You* don't like it?" said Ted. "You aren't the one going to be stuck down there with all the ghosts."

"I used to be a ghost," said Ellen wistfully. "That was one of my favorite parts."

"I'll let you know how you compare to the real thing," said Ted tartly. "If we do go through with this story and everything works out, the game ends after we get back from the battle and I kill Randolph—which I won't—but anyway, the game is over then, so we should have more time to do things. We could look for Edward then. I'll be King: I could just order people to do whatever we think we need."

Laura doubted this. She could not imagine Benjamin and Agatha meekly obeying Ted's orders, even if he were King.

"If you come back alive," muttered Ruth.

"Maybe you won't even get killed," said Ellen. "Seems like nothing ever happens the way it's supposed to, unless we try to stop it."

"Yes, he will," said Laura. Ted looked at her, and she swallowed. "At the funeral, I saw it in Fence's robe."

"Saw what?" said Ted.

"You were lying on the ground with blood all over your chest, and Randolph was looking unhappy."

Ted looked more than unhappy. "I thought I was supposed to be killed by sorcery," he said. "That sounds like it'll hurt."

"Probably it'll be too quick," said Ellen.

"Are you sure it was the battle, Laurie?" said Ruth. "Maybe it was the fight in the rose garden."

"I didn't see any roses," said Laura, doubtfully. "It looked like a desert."

"I don't intend to have a fight in the rose garden, anyway," said Ted. "Well, we don't have to decide until right before we leave. Why don't you study what you can, Ruthie, and tell us on the night before the march whether you think you can do it? Let's all meet in the rose garden around midnight."

"What exactly have we decided?" said Patrick.

"If Ruthie thinks she can bring me back," said Ted, "then we go to the battle and go through with the story and, after it's over, try to find the real Edward—and the real Patrick and Laura and Ruth and Ellen, I guess. If she doesn't think so, or if Laurie sees something really awful, or if—well, if we decide it's not a good idea to stay, we go home when the army passes the Well and the House. We'd better figure out how to get those swords."

"Maybe we could get out using Shan's Ring," said Ellen.

"I'm not so sure I trust Shan's Ring," said Ruth, "not if it let Claudia out."

"I don't think that's the ring's fault," said Ted. "I think Claudia's a very good sorcerer. Fence acts like there's nothing *he* can do about her."

Laura thought that Fence acted far more as if he did not need to do anything about Claudia, but held her tongue.

"Well, then," said Ellen, "maybe we could use Shan's Ring to get Ted back? Isn't the Judge of the Dead an Outside Power?"

"Now that's an idea," said Ruth. "I always knew there was some reason for keeping such a brat around."

Ellen dropped a plum down the neck of her sister's dress, and the resulting wrestling match ended the discussion.

Laura, backed into a corner, wondered which would be worse: dressing in men's array and going to a battle, or staying behind at High Castle and not knowing what was happening. Then a stray grape, thrown by Ted, hit her on the nose. She hurled a meat pie at him and caught Patrick neatly behind the ear, and ran as fast as she could out of the hall and into the rose garden. It had stopped raining. Agatha was going to kill the rest of them, she thought gleefully. Then she sat down on a stone bench, sobered. It was not Agatha who would do the killing.

CHAPTER 6

THE coronation was to be at two in the afternoon. At seven that morning, Ted and Patrick, having been unable to sleep, sat on their bearskin rug, playing chess. It was one of Claudia's mornings. They had pulled the shutters over the windows to keep the fog out, and lighted a lamp. It looked and felt like the middle of the night, and their game had the flavor of conspiracy.

"Check," said Ted.

"Bishops move diagonally," observed Patrick.

Ted scowled in spite of himself, and put his bishop back. It occurred to him to wonder why there were bishops in the game when there was no Catholic church in the Secret Country. He did not care to ask Patrick. "Where's my knight, then?"

Patrick picked it out of the pile of Ted's pieces he had accumulated, and put on his face of exaggerated patience.

"Maybe if we played something that doesn't have kings in it?" said Ted. Everything seemed conspiring to remind him of the coronation, and the mere thought made him itch.

"Let's go practice fencing," said Patrick. "It's not long until the battle."

"You think we'll be going, then?"

"You see any chance of getting those swords before then?"

"*I* don't have *time!*" said Ted, his irritation rising. "I have to spend the whole blasted morning from nine o'clock having a lot of clothes made right on me, and the whole afternoon being crowned, and the whole night—"

"Do you think it's a good idea to be crowned here, when you're not really Edward?"

Ted stopped putting the chess pieces away. "You believe this now?"

"I'm just trying to play the game right."

"*That's* new," said Ted, and instantly regretted it.

Patrick's eyes narrowed, but all he said was, "Maybe this is a new game."

He picked up the chessboard. It looked like rosewood inlaid with ebony and ivory, and its border, wider than usual, was carved with scenes of court life and battle. Patrick tipped it toward Ted, smiling, and the lamplight slid down it like water.

"The props are sure better," said Patrick.

Ted closed the lid of their box, also carved, on the chess pieces, and he and Patrick put board and box away.

"So," said Patrick as they went downstairs, "do you think it's a good idea to be crowned?"

"Randolph thinks it is," said Ted, "and he's the only one who knows what's going on."

They nodded politely to Agatha, who passed them carrying a tray with two cups and a jug on it. She gave them a look of resigned suspicion, then smiled suddenly.

"Fence knows what's going on," said Patrick when they were several corners further on.

"That's not what I meant. Randolph killed the King, and he's the only one with real plans about what should happen after, because he's the only one who knew the King was going to die. Fence wanted to have the coronation after the battle, and I'd rather, but Randolph said we should have it before."

They clattered down the last steps.

"Did he say why?"

"He said that if they didn't crown me it would show doubt of me."

Patrick frowned at the wall. "Maybe they doubt you anyway. If *I* was Edward, *I* might kill the King. He was a terrible father."

Ted felt that this was unjust, but could not say why. Then the first part of Patrick's speech caught up with him.

"They *could* think I did it. They never did tell me what happened when Jerome got them all together and Agatha asked them questions, and Matthew wrote it all down."

"Well, Randolph won't let them hang you for it," said Patrick, starting down the hall again.

There was a guard at the open door to the practice yard. There had never been one there before. The ways from the yard to the outside were guarded, so another guard on this door was silly.

Ted wished he could feel more like a prince and less like a guilty child. He and Patrick had every right to come practice their fencing. They had been doing it for weeks. But let somebody with a sword and a leather cap and a mail-shirt show up, and he wanted to run for his room.

Patrick, after a brief pause, had marched on as if he were afraid he was going to miss the beginning of a movie, and Ted ran to keep up. The guard looked Patrick over until Ted came up, and then moved out of their way.

"Give you good morrow," she said. Ted looked at her in surprise. She was the woman with the scarred forehead who had sat next to Matthew at the Banquet and guarded the Council Chamber after the King was poisoned.

"Good morning," he said.

Patrick simply stared, and then pulled Ted out into the yard.

"I never saw a woman guard before," he said as they picked out their swords. Every rack and weapon had a patina of moisture, and Patrick frowned. "How come these things don't rust?"

"I saw some after Randolph poisoned the King," said Ted.

"Well," said Patrick, "if there are women in the army then I guess the girls can come to the battle."

"I don't know," said Ted, trying to imagine Laura in the middle of a fight. "It's not just that they're girls. They're only little kids, except Ruthie."

"So're we," said Patrick shortly, as he jerked a sword out, and danced away across the sand. "Come on."

Ted's fencing was better than his chess had been. But after less than an hour, Benjamin interrupted their labors by grabbing Ted's tunic collar and scolding him roundly for not having heard him coming. He then scolded Patrick for not having warned Ted.

"A milliard of years ye have had for swordcraft," he said when he had finished with that, "and ye needs must leave it all for coronation morning. Thou," he said to Ted, "with me, and thou," to Patrick, "to the West Tower."

The woman with the scar grinned at them as Benjamin hustled them through her door.

"My lord Benjamin," was all she said.

"Celia," said Benjamin, fixing her with his glare, "thy children have ridden Lord Conrad's new horses six times round the lake and done them no small damage."

Ted watched in fascination as Celia's face struggled to encompass worry, mirth, and respect all at once.

"My lord, you must speak to my husband," she said, her voice a little stifled. "I am at my work this fortnight."

"Oh, aye," said Benjamin, "and when, in all this hugger-mugger, I shall find time to catch thy husband, 'twill be, 'Speak to Celia, for I am at my work.' Meanwhile, those brats must take this castle stone from stone and use it to play at conkers."

"Are they worse than us?" asked Patrick.

"No fear," said Benjamin. "They are but three, and no twenty children are worse than ye. To the West Tower, go."

Patrick went.

Ted looked over his shoulder at Celia as Benjamin pulled him along, and was rewarded with a wink and a salute. He frowned, and suddenly remembered. Unless Celia were a common name at court, this was the person Matthew had wanted to ask about the fire-letters: the most accomplished musician.

"What's she doing guarding?" he said aloud.

"Who else should do't, all thy father's men being suspect?"

Comprehension dawned. The first women in mail, or with weapons, Ted had seen in High Castle: standing at the door of the Council Chamber after the King had been poisoned. Neither the King's, nor men. That explained it.

"Am I suspect?" he asked.

"Didst not spill the bottle from Randolph's hand, to Andrew's sorrow?"

Ted was too startled to lie. "Yes, but—" Now who had told them that? Andrew, perhaps.

"Cease thy foolish questions," said Benjamin. "Princes are foolish, but kings must be canny. Best begin now. Thou art as foolish a prince as I have seen."

Despite these dampening remarks, Ted felt more cheerful. Benjamin would rant, whatever happened. Maybe being king would not be so different from being Prince Edward.

Becoming king could, however, accurately be described as a royal pain. Ted had chosen to laugh at this thought at an inauspicious moment, and had a scratch from the tailor's shears for his trouble. The tailor had apologized, but without being in the least abject. It was clear from Benjamin's expression that, if he had thought there was time to spare, he would have spent it in making Ted abject instead.

The scratch was not a bad one, but the sweat caused by his coronation clothes made it sting. It was one discomfort too many. Ted was hot; the banquet hall was airless and crammed with people; they were all making a noise like twenty kindergarten classes let out to recess; and the musicians were making sounds like a restive zoo.

Ted held his arms out to his sides, hoping for some air to creep under the loose sleeves of his under-tunic. He had four layers of clothes on, two of them velvet and all of them cumbersome. The colors went together nicely, and he was pleased to have a white and purple unicorn on his front and a black and red dragon on his back instead of the usual running fox. But he felt more suited to Arctic exploration than to a formal ceremony.

"Except if I moved I'd fall down," he said aloud.

"If thou movest thou destroyest the ceremony," said Benjamin into his left ear. "They come to thee, not thou to them."

Ted looked out over the brilliant, shifting crowd and was not at all sure he wanted any of them to come to him.

Randolph appeared from their midst and sprang, like a child playing kangaroo, onto the platform where Ted and Benjamin stood. Despite his apparent energy, he looked exhausted. Ted thought he was thinner than he had been. He had blue smudges under his eyes. Ted stared at these for a moment. Ellen had managed to produce a very similar effect with the juice of smashed mulberries and a little cornstarch, to decorate a weary Lady Ruth after she brought Ted back from the dead. The rest of them had laughed at her, saying that nobody ever looked like that really. But Randolph did now.

"Benjamin," said Randolph, a little breathlessly. "Where are Matthew's children?"

Benjamin looked sour. "Seek them in the stables, or at the bottom of the lake."

Randolph pushed irritably at his hair, and Benjamin appeared to relent. "They need not attend; they are not of age."

"Margaret hath speech and reason."

Benjamin shrugged. "'Twill not be noticed in her."

Randolph went still, reminding Ted of Fence. "Benjamin," he said. "I will have every wight of useful age in this castle swear fealty to Edward if it is my last act."

Benjamin put a hand on Randolph's forehead, more as a calming gesture, thought Ted, then as if he were checking for fever.

"I will have no more like Melanie," said Randolph.

Benjamin sighed. "There was never yet coronation in this castle that began at its proper time. I will hold them 'til you come again."

Randolph slid down into the crowd and was gone.

"You mean all that rush was for nothing?" demanded Ted.

"It was not," said Benjamin.

Ted decided not to pursue this. "What did he mean about Melanie?"

"You need have no fear of Margaret," said Benjamin.

"I don't. What'd he mean?"

"Consider your history," said Benjamin, and Ted shut up and wished for Ellen. Some five hundred years ago, Melanie had spent her childhood in High Castle until she got into trouble with the unicorns, but he did not know what this had to do with coronation oaths.

Having nothing else to do, he considered his history further; and suddenly he had it. Melanie had not sworn fealty to the King of the Secret Country because she was so young; she had then gotten into trouble, and gone away for a time. When she came back, she was a powerful sorceress, and still had not sworn fealty to the King of the Secret Country, and caused a great deal more trouble than she had gotten into, because everybody assumed that she *had* sworn fealty. Randolph must think Margaret wild enough to do likewise. Ted was so pleased to have figured out anything at all that he grinned at Benjamin.

"Having this time at our disposal," said Benjamin, "we would do well to speak of thy counselors. Wilt thou keep all thy father's?"

Ted, having had no idea that there was any choice in the matter, goggled at him. "Well," he said, "I don't trust Andrew."

"Better to have him under thine eye, then."

"But I don't like being under his. Anyway, does that mean I should have Claudia, too?"

"If thou wilt so blithely break with tradition, 'twere better thou hadst Agatha."

"Agatha?" said Ted, thoroughly confused.

"She served thy mother well, a most astute tactician."

Ted shook his sweaty hands in the air and felt the beginnings of outrage rise in him. Every time you got used to this place it hit you with something new. "What's she doing carrying cocoa to little girls in the morning?" he demanded.

"What doth Celia guarding safe doors?" Benjamin mocked him. Ted felt himself growing redder than the heat in the room had made him. "What doth Suzanne spying in the South and Meredith waiting on late councils?"

"Did Wil—did my father kick them off the Council, then?"

"Every last one," said Benjamin.

"But he put you on? And what'd they do?"

"Thou hast had nose in thy books too long," said Benjamin. "I served thy grandfather, and thy mother also. She was not so great a fool as thy father, to turn her back on gathered wisdom."

"You think my father was a fool?" Ted was enthralled.

"In some matters, aye—take him for all in all, certainly he was not."

"Well," said Ted. He was torn between asking about his mother and deciding whom he wanted on his council. It sounded as though his mother had been Queen, and William had become King on her death, which was rather strange. But he found deciding about the council more appealing, as well as more likely to be useful. "I want you, and I want Randolph and Matthew. And Fence."

"Fence will be no counselor. He will advise thee at his whim, not thine. It was ever so with sorcerers, save Shan; and he rued it."

"Who else should I keep? Can I only have twelve?"

"Kings have had more," said Benjamin. "They proved but cumbersome."

"I'm not surprised," said Ted, thinking of the uproar only twelve could create.

"I favor Conrad and Jerome," said Benjamin. "Nor is Andrew without merit."

"That's only six. Maybe I should see what Randolph thinks. Is Julian good for anything?" Ted paused. "Won't the rest of them be mad if I get rid of them?"

"They have guarded safe doors before," said Benjamin.

"King or Queen's Counselor is the most uncertain of professions."

"I guess I'd better think on it." Ted felt a pleased excitement, as if he and Ruth and Ellen were devising some new twist to the plot. It had not really occurred to him before how many things he could now do as he liked.

Randolph came to the edge of the platform, flushed and panting. "Benjamin, you may begin. The stable it was." He wore his blue counselor's robe now, and used the steps to join them on the stage. His hand came down on Ted's shoulder for a moment. Ted's stomach clenched itself in answer.

"I will stand at thy right shoulder," breathed Randolph. "Shouldst thou forget aught of thy speeches, but pluck me by the sleeve and thou shalt have the words."

Ted, who had found memorizing speeches while having clothes made on him less than easy, was swept by a fierce gratitude. By the time indignation had begun to overtake it, Benjamin had signaled to the musicians and he had no time to indulge his feelings.

The musicians were playing the minstrel-boy song. Ted sighed. How had that come to the Secret Country? It was all very well to say that the five of them had had the Secret Country put into their heads, rather than inventing it on their own. But that song was an old one. He supposed the Secret Country could have put it into the head of whoever wrote it, but that raised more questions than it answered.

The crowd before him shifted and parted, and Fence came up the newly opened aisle, his robe striking a hundred bewildering sparks, a crown in his hands. It was the same intricately twisted silver as Ruth's ring, Randolph's dagger and circlet, and Fence's key. But the five stones in it were red. Ted looked at it with dismay. Red stones meant Claudia to him, and he did not like to think what it might mean that they were in the crown. Crowns shouldn't have anything to do with magic anyway, he thought grumpily.

"Benjamin," he breathed, "is that crown magic?"

"Certainly not," said Benjamin. "Hush."

Ted was a little comforted.

Fence stopped before the stage and looked up at Ted. The crowd hushed as swiftly as if it had heard Benjamin. Benjamin and Randolph moved a little backward, and Ted felt suddenly idiotic, standing all by himself so high above them all. He hated looking down at Fence.

"Edward Fairchild," said Fence. "I am about to confer upon you the powers, privileges, and obligations of Prince of the Enchanted Forest, Lord of the Desert's Edge, Friend to the Unicorns, and King of the Hidden Land. Are you willing to be so invested?"

When Fence put it that way, Ted was not at all willing. What was the Hidden Land, anyway? It must be the Secret Country, but then why didn't they say so? Fence stood looking at him, unmoved, but he heard Benjamin make an impatient noise behind him, and gave up.

"I am willing," he said.

"Do you solemnly swear, in the tradition of John, by the mercy granted to Shan, in accordance with the laws of the Hidden Land and the dictates of Chryse, to honor and protect the people in your power; to deal lightly in the exercise of your privileges and straitly in the fulfillment of your obligations; to reward valor with honor, service with service, oath-breaking with vengeance?"

Ted was petrified. He did not know what he was doing. What tradition, what mercy, what laws and dictates? Oh, God, he thought, we've got to find the real Edward quick. Fence's steady gaze still held him, more daunting than any sign of impatience or bewilderment.

"I do so swear," he said.

Fence turned his back on him and addressed the crowd. "If any wight in this gathering knoweth of any impediment to this coronation, let him speak now or be forever silent."

No one said a word. Fence gave them a good long time, during which the sweat ran down Ted's neck and he refrained from fidgeting.

Fence faced Ted again. "My lord Regent," he said to Randolph, "knowest thou of any impediment to my performing this act?"

"My lord, thou art suited to't," said Randolph.

Fence nodded to Ted, who knelt down and began to shake.

"In the names of John and Chryse, I call thee King," Fence said, and set the crown on Ted's head. It was heavy, and too large. Fence tilted it back a little. "Move gently," he breathed. Ted did not dare to nod, but he raised his eyes to Fence and tried to look intelligent. Fence held out his hands to Ted, who stared for a moment and then took them between his sweaty ones. Fence's were like iron.

"I, Fence, sorcerer, of no land, within the confines of my judgment and the needs of my knowledge, do become your liege man of life and limb, and of earthly worship, and faith and truth will I bear unto you, to live and die, against all manner of folk."

Ted's eyes stung and his throat clogged. Behind him Randolph's voice said, "I, Edward, do become your liege lord."

"I, Edward," said Ted, wishing his name were anything else, "do become your liege lord of life and limb, and of earthly worship, and that faith and truth I receive of you, that I will requite." Well, he thought, you've done it now.

Fence kissed him on the mouth. Ted did not mind that particularly, but he had a fleeting hope that everyone in the room would not do the same.

"Stand up," said Fence, kindly. Ted did; and remembering his instructions now, he backed to the far side of the stage. Randolph knelt and swore fealty to him, with a grim emphasis on the words "faith and truth" that made Ted shiver. Randolph must have sworn the same oath to William, but his hands between Ted's were quite steady. Saying, "that I will requite," Ted thought of the rose garden and shivered again.

"Put thy mind at ease," said Randolph before he kissed Ted; "all may yet be very well." He dropped down from the front of the platform and joined the crowd.

Benjamin swore next; he seemed delighted, which was comforting, if not understandable. Then people began coming out of the crowd. Ted was glad it had not been his task to figure out what order they should come in. For some time he did not know any of them: men, women, children his age and younger. He began to wonder what Randolph had meant by "useful age." Most of them did not kiss him. In the midst of a group of girls who looked as if they would have liked to, Ruth showed up; she was grinning so hard she looked as if she might cry any minute. She did kiss him; the crowd chuckled a little. Over her bowed and braided dark head, Ted saw Randolph set his mouth, and wished she had not done it.

After Ruth, more and more of the faces were familiar. Ted's counselors—or William's, really, he thought—began to show up, most of them with people Ted took to be their wives and children. Matthew, Celia, and a yellow-haired girl around Ellen's age came together. She must be the notorious Margaret, and Matthew and Celia must be married. Ted felt like congratulating them, but restrained himself. He was getting a little light-headed. Andrew came and went, so quietly and gracefully that he was an insult, and Ted no longer found it hard to believe that he was Claudia's brother. He looked for Claudia, but she did not come. Ellen came after Andrew, doing everything with a demure flourish that made Ted grin, and saying her oath as if she meant it, which made him nervous.

Ted wondered where Laura was. Perhaps she was not of useful age, poor kid. Or maybe it wasn't "poor kid." She probably wouldn't take kindly to swearing to obey him; she would be sure that he would take advantage of it when they were back home. And it would, in fact, be tempting. Ted felt a little cold. He should not have let Ruth and Ellen swear fealty to him. No one except Fence had mentioned any titles in the oath: it was just, "I, Ruth, do become your liege man"; and he had not accepted the oaths as King of the Hidden Land, but only as Edward.

Walking very tall in his green tunic and white cloak, Ted's cousin Patrick came up the room, knelt, and bowed his head—which, Ted noted, somebody had made him comb—and held his hand up for Ted's.

Ted caught him by the wrists and said in an urgent whisper, "Don't do that!"

Patrick looked up at him with the startled and irritated expression of someone who has been interrupted in the middle of a good book. "What?"

"Stand up!" hissed Ted, pulling at him. He most emphatically did not want to be Patrick's liege lord.

Patrick got reluctantly to his feet. "What's wrong?"

"Shhh! I don't want you doing this!"

"I have to," said Patrick, practically, just above a whisper. "It'll look funny."

"I guess I can favor my younger brother if I want to."

"Younger brothers are usurpers," said Patrick. "I don't want to be poisoned for my own good."

Ted was furious. "Randolph wouldn't do that." He was acutely aware of Randolph and Benjamin, in the front of the crowd, staring.

"It wouldn't have to be Randolph."

"I don't want you swearing fealty to me," said Ted.

"I'm swearing fealty to the King," said Patrick, "and as long as you are King, I might as well swear it to you."

"You are not. Weren't you listening? Edward, that's me. This isn't just a king's oath. It's personal."

"Uh," said Patrick, noncommittally. "We better do something, they're getting restless."

"Why don't you kneel down and mumble at me?"

"No, they have to hear the oath or it isn't legal. Give me a minute. Okay." Patrick knelt down again, and Ted took his hands. Patrick looked up at him. "This oath that I am about to swear," he said in a whisper, "shall bind me only upon the business of the Secret Country, and only so long as thou art king thereof."

"It shall bind thee only under these conditions," said Ted, remembering what this summer had almost made him forget, how satisfactory it could be to play with Patrick.

CHAPTER 7

LAURA stood in a corner and wondered irritably how many banquet halls there were in High Castle. They had held the coronation in the same hall they had used for the Banquet of Midsummer's Eve. This hall was not entirely as it should have been, but was at least in the right part of High Castle—the innermost, oldest building of gray stone that looked from the outside precisely as they had imagined it.

The coronation feast, however, was being laid out in a rosy twin of the room where they had their everyday meals. As far as Laura could tell, it was in the outermost pink part of the castle, on the same side and with the same orientation as the Dragon Hall. She hated the pink marble far more than it deserved; it was the most obtrusive reminder of their dilemma. The prospect of suffering it all around her for an entire banquet was almost the last straw. If Laura had thought anyone would notice, she would have skipped the coronation feast and sulked. She was not sure whom she was angry at, but she was certainly put out. She had found the ceremony awesome. Even Ellen had made not one snide remark. Laura would have been happier if she had. It was not so bad to be left out of a ceremony that Ellen made snide remarks about.

Laura pressed herself against the wall to let by two boys carrying a tray of fruit. Not only had she been left out of her own brother's coronation, but Ellen had not returned after her part in it. People were already beginning to sit down, and no one had come to find Laura. Sitting through a formal feast with strange grown-ups would be worse than having been left out of the ceremony.

Laura backed tighter against the wall to let by someone with a pile of napkins. A fold of tapestry landed on her head. Laura ducked frantically away from it, narrowly missed upsetting a tray of cheese and its bearer, and looked up. Sure enough, the tapestry hung crooked now, showing a bare space of gray wall. Laura got away from the evidence, taking the easiest route through the crowd. This put her too far from the doors. She began a course calculated to take her to the front of the hall but on the other side, and came face-to-face with someone in a page's costume who seemed to know her.

"My lady, the King requests your presence at his table at supper."

Laura, after one frozen moment in which "King" still meant the old man buried up on the hill, beamed wildly and followed the page.

Ted, Ruth, and Benjamin were standing in a tight group beside the head table. Patrick and Ellen lurked around its outskirts, making loud remarks and being ignored.

"What can he say to her with all these people around?" demanded Ellen.

"I tell you I'll not have it," said Benjamin to Ted. His back was to Laura, but she had no trouble hearing him.

"If you didn't mean I could sit with anyone I wanted to, why did you say it?" said Ted.

"Benjamin," said Ruth, "I give you my word of honor—"

"Those who kiss in public," said Benjamin with deadly calm, "need no speech in private."

Laura's page chose this moment, while both Ted and Ruth were gathering their indignation into speech, to say loudly, "My lord the King, the Lady Laura."

Benjamin turned. He, Ted, Ruth, Ellen, Patrick, and a number of random strangers all looked at Laura, who would gladly have been back under the tapestry.

"Thank you," said Ted to the page, who bowed and went away. Laura looked longingly after him. "Laurie," said Ted, "will you sit with us at supper?"

"Sure," said Laura, and recovered enough to do him a courtesy.

"Benjamin," said Ted, and Laura stared. The change in his voice was frightening.

"No," said Benjamin.

Laura took this to mean that Benjamin would not sit with them at supper, and was relieved.

"Ted," said Ruth, in her most ordinary voice. "It was a dumb thing for me to do. Just forget supper, okay?"

"This one time," said Ted, looking at Benjamin.

"My lord Benjamin," said Ruth. "I crave your pardon for my behavior at the coronation. 'Twas lack of thought, not malice."

Benjamin said, "Lack of thought in a sorcerer is like unto lack of weapon in a battle. For thy manners I pardon thee. Look well to thy thoughts."

Ruth swept him an impressive courtesy and walked away.

"May I have the rest of them?" Ted asked Benjamin. Laura could tell from long experience that he was furious but wished not to show it.

Patrick shook his head at Ted. When Ted frowned, Patrick touched the dagger at his belt and jerked his head upward. Ted's face cleared, and then he looked irritated.

"For heaven's sake," he said to Benjamin, furiously, "what difference does it make? Get Fence and Randolph and Matthew. I don't care!"

"I'll sit with you, Ted," said Ellen.

Patrick turned to leave, and Laura, momentarily abandoned, panicked and trailed after him. She was not sure Ted wanted her, and Benjamin obviously didn't. Patrick was better than strangers.

She was so busy following him that she did not realize he was leaving the hall until they were both outside it. Patrick stopped to take off his cloak, and Laura bumped into him.

"What're you doing here?" Patrick said. "You're supposed to be eating with Ted."

"Benjamin doesn't want me."

"No, he doesn't want Ruth."

"Well, I'm not going back there now. I bet they didn't save me a seat. What are you doing?"

Patrick drew her into the nearest stairwell and whispered, "Stealing our swords while Fence is eating."

Laura suddenly found supper with Benjamin more appealing.

"You can't get in," she said after a moment. "Fence keeps it locked."

"Yes, I can," said Patrick, and he held out to her on a grubby palm Fence's twisted silver key for the lower door, and the plain one for the upper.

"How'd you do that?"

"Bumped against him in the crowd," said Patrick loftily. "Well," he added, when Laura only stared, "I had to watch him for a month before I found out where he kept the key."

Laura was irked. "Ellen and I could've told you."

"And I tried three or four times before and couldn't get it because there wasn't enough of a crowd."

Laura was further irked. "Did you plan this for a long time?"

"Ever since the swords were stolen," said Patrick. "I wanted Ted to help me, but he's busy now and we're out of time."

Laura's feelings finally found vent. "Why didn't you tell us? We've been worried to death and you had a plan all along!"

"I didn't even tell Ted until today," said Patrick. "It was my idea, wasn't it?"

Laura gave up being angry. Made brave by one of the few feelings of pure admiration she had ever had for Patrick, she said, "I'll go with you since Ted can't." Ted had been meant to go on this adventure. This was what he got for leaving her out of his coronation.

Patrick hesitated, and then he grinned. "Sure," he said. "You can be my lookout, and distract the intruders with your childish blandishments."

Laura looked at him. No, he was not making fun of her. His tone of voice was maddeningly familiar but so out-of-place that it took her a moment to recognize it.

"You're playing," she said, half accusingly.

"D'you want to come, or not?"

"Yes," said Laura, wondering what blandishments were. She followed him up the steps.

In the hall before the stairs to Fence's tower, the purple torches burned. The yellow torches of High Castle smelled like turpentine; these gave off a damp scent of moss, and well water, and cold rock. How could anything burn that smelled like that? Sorcery, thought Laura grimly, that's how.

The lower door with its enigmatic carvings was shut. Laura kept an eye out for beasts, but saw none. Patrick put his shoulder to the door, and it swung inward without a sound. Another purple torch glared across the darkness at their feet, where the steps went down, not up. They looked at one another. A cold air came up the stairway and stirred their hair.

"What the hell?" said Patrick, leaning forward.

"Wait a minute," said Laura, trying to remember. The day Fence had come back seemed as long ago as the summers in Pennsylvania, when Patrick played Fence and torches, sorcerous or otherwise, burned only in their imaginations. Fence, covered with dust and looking just as he ought, had come along this hall with her and Ellen, and found that, contrary to his dispositions, the door was unlocked. Laura said, "Close the door and lock it. It makes the stairs go the right way."

Patrick frowned. "Well, it can't hurt." He pulled the door to and locked it, after a little trouble with the silver key.

"Now you unlock it again and everything's all right."

Patrick did this, and opened the door. The purple torch hung over a pit of blackness.

"It worked when Fence did it," said Laura.

"Could I have gotten the wrong key?"

"That one looks right. Anyway, it fit in the door, didn't it?"

"Well, Fence is a wizard, and we aren't. Huh," said Patrick thoughtfully, and went back into the hall, where he stood on a stone bench and took a purple torch from its holder.

"What're you doing?" said Laura, who knew quite well.

"Maybe this is just to scare us. If we could prop the door open it wouldn't hurt to go down a little ways."

He tilted the torch. It did not give much light, but it showed the first two or three steps. Laura thought with despair that this would keep them from breaking a leg, which would be enough for Patrick. She was very sorry she had been so angry with Ted.

Patrick was trying to drag a stone bench over to prop

open the door. He made so much noise and roused so many echoes from the dark stairwell that she went to help him just to get it over with. They could not lift the bench, but with considerable scraping of hands and floor they inched it along until it would block the door if the door should blow shut.

"Come on," said Patrick.

Laura wondered why he had forgotten about the blandishments, but she was past speech. She stood next to his free hand, and they started down.

It was cold and very quiet.

"Pat," said Laura, remembering how far it was to Fence's chambers when the stairs went the right way, "do we have to go *down* two hundred and eight steps to get anywhere?"

"I hope not," said Patrick, "though it would make sense. Ted is supposed to keep Fence busy after the feast, but we can't take too much time. And if too many people have left I can't sneak the keys back."

"Feasts are always long," said Laura.

They went down and around and down and around. On the ninth or tenth landing, Patrick's torch struck dim watery gleams from something spread on the stones. Laura stopped dead. The gleams grew to a great burst of light, then steadied to a long, winged shape of bright red, beating its way over a plain. It stooped upon a house. Laura had one moment to recognize the Secret House, and then it was fire. From its sparks another vision swelled. She saw a blackhaired man who looked like Fence and was not, for he also looked like Randolph. He sat robed in red, with a book open on his lap, and the book showed the long scarlet shape of the dragon, smiting the Secret House with flame. From the lettering below the picture one word leapt out at her.

"Belaparthalion," said Laura, trying it out letter by letter. The light died, and she stood with Patrick on a cold stair. At their feet was another purple beast.

"What?" said Patrick.

The beast made noises like a kettle about to boil. Patrick poked the torch at it, cautiously. It hissed and steamed up around them in a purple mist, and sifted away, smelling like damp stone and, a little, like the Well of the White Witch.

"Well," said Patrick, "now we know they don't like fire."

"If that's fire," said Laura, looking dubiously at the torch. They went on.

"Two hundred and eight," said Patrick at last. They looked along the ghostly sphere of the torch and past it into darkness.

"Pat," said Laura, without any great hope.

"Well," said Patrick, "it would make sense to have it be the same number of steps down, but when did anything about this place make sense?"

"Can we go back now?" Laura felt oppressed by the layers of darkness above them. She did not like looking into the dark, and she was afraid to look at the torch lest she see more visions. She hated them more every time she had one. They must mean something, but she could not tell what. She was beginning to feel that they, too, were laughing at her.

She looked at Patrick instead. He was not a comforting sight. The torchlight dyed his unremarkable brown hair a vivid purple, and his rosy face a pale yellowish violet. He wore what Ruth called his mad-scientist expression.

"Well," he said again, "it could be a multiple of the number going up."

"It could go down forever," said Laura.

"Sounds just like something Fence would do," said Patrick sourly. He started down the steps again. "Look," he said, when Laura stayed where she was. "Just two hundred and eight more, okay? Except, hell, in magic things go in threes."

"I am *not*," said Laura, "going down two times two hundred and eight more steps." Her legs ached as if she had been bicycling up hills all day.

"Well, come down one times two hundred and eight, okay? We don't really have time for any more anyway."

Laura strongly suspected that once he had gotten her down the second two hundred and eight he would try to talk her into the third. But he had not suggested leaving her there in the dark, and she was grateful for this. "All right," she said.

"Remind me," she added, as she followed the purple blotch of Patrick's light, "to tell Ted I saw something else, okay?"

"You did? When?"

"When the torchlight shone on that watery beast."

"You didn't see anything else about Ted getting killed, did you?"

"No. I didn't see anybody we know."

"Did you ever see me?"

Laura thought. "No. Nobody but Ted, that I knew."

They went on.

"Couldn't you count out loud?" said Laura after a while.

"I have to breathe, you know. I'll tell you every tenth one . . . sixty."

"Is that *all*?"

"And one hundred," said Patrick eventually, as they crossed another landing. "Hey," he said. "Jackpot. One and a half times as many steps."

Laura's hair prickled even before she crowded up beside him and saw what he saw. Down four steps on the last landing, a muted crowd of colored streaks lay across the stones, cast through the open doorway by things she could not see. The purple in this faded rainbow was the same color as the torch. Laura knew the green and blue at once as the colors of light given off by Shan's and Melanie's swords.

Patrick pounded down the last steps, passed stripedly across the landing, and said, "Laura!"

Laura followed and stood in the doorway with him. The room was full of weapons: swords, knives, spears, bows and arrows, a myriad of odd and ugly objects that Laura did not recognize. Some were hung neatly on the walls, some scattered across the floor. They all glowed, palely in purple, blue and green; in sickly orange; in pallid gold; in moony white; and with a vigorous red that reminded Laura unhappily of Claudia.

As her eyes adjusted to the light, like a jigsaw puzzle done in watercolors, she saw that the far wall of the room was lined with trunks. Their lids were open, and out of them spilled dim jewels. They drew her eyes into them; misty shapes began to form within them. Laura took a step forward, and another. Foggy, starlit spaces opened around her. She saw five figures standing by the bank of a stream. She strained to see them more clearly. One of them waved to her. They seemed familiar, but, like almost everything else here, not quite right.

Her breath was jarred out of her suddenly and pain shot up her right leg from her knee. Patrick called her name from a far distance. She blinked. She had tripped on a bow: her foot was still tangled in it. She had fallen and cut her knee on something. Laura moved the knee, and blood ran down her leg. She picked the sword up. It was small. The hilt was black, and set with blue stones, not like sapphires. A prickling went down her arm, as if a cold breeze had blown on her. The blade glowed blue.

"Here it is," she said to Patrick.

"You think so?" he said.

Laura looked at him. He held a sword like hers. They laid the hilts together and examined them. They were not alike. The patterns of the stones and the shapes of the hilts were different.

"Well," said Patrick, nastily, "which one is it?"

"How should I know?" said Laura. "Can you find yours?"

"There's at least three that color of green," said Patrick.

"Maybe they all do the same thing," said Laura. Her knee twinged, and she decided not to look at it. "Have you got a handkerchief?"

"Didn't you cut your knee on Shan's sword, too?" Patrick put the sword down and rummaged in his cloak.

"I can't help it."

"No, I just meant, since we don't have any other clues, why don't you take the one you fell on?"

"Which one will you take?"

Patrick tied a handkerchief around her knee. Ted would have wiped the blood off first, but this was not the time to say so.

"Well," said Patrick, "I know Melanie's had three stones in it, so I'll take a green one with three stones."

"You think they'll work the same?"

"A magic sword is a magic sword."

A battery is a battery, thought Laura, looking at him with exasperation. A transistor is a transistor. Was that even true? Impossible to argue with Patrick on his own terms if you didn't even know what they meant. She stood up and tried her knee. "We should go before I get all stiff," she said from experience.

Patrick looked rebellious for an instant. "Oh, well," he said, "I should get these keys back to Fence before he misses them."

They took up their swords and stood looking at the dim colors of the room.

"I bet they're *all* enchanted," said Laura. Enchanted weapons might be useful in a battle against monsters; she wondered if anybody knew this room was here. Fence had seemed amused, more than anything else, when he had seen the stairs going down instead of up. He had seemed to think this was a joke that Randolph might play. No doubt they knew all about it.

"Too bad we don't know what it all does," said Patrick. He took the torch from where he had stuck it in a tangle of swordbelts, and then looked thoughtfully at the tangle. "Wait a minute. If we get belts for these things we won't have to carry them."

This accomplished, they began their climb.

CHAPTER 8

TED got through his coronation dinner by repeatedly reminding himself how much worse the Banquet of Midsummer's Eve had been. In the intervals of this, he wondered whether he ought to have stood up to Benjamin more. Even allowing for his grief and perplexity at the King's death, Benjamin had been overbearing and rude. Edward would certainly have put up with this: his sudden acquisition of a real personality, in the game, did not happen until just before he killed Randolph. But Ted had already shown a real personality. Perhaps he should have gone on showing it.

Smitten by a sudden thought, Ted found that he was staring at Celia, and quickly smiled instead. He could not remember ever having shown a real personality to Benjamin. Something in Benjamin's manner made it evident that he expected to be tolerated and to be obeyed. Ted remembered how, at the first Council meeting, Benjamin had with a touch kept an enraged Randolph from speaking, and how he had sat at the King's left hand. Benjamin had not been at the Banquet when Ted attacked Andrew. All Ted's other defiances had been flung at Fence or Randolph. But Fence and Randolph put up with Benjamin, too.

Ted looked down the table at him. He was haranguing Matthew's wife and family. Celia grinned at him and occasionally said something. The three yellow-haired children sat stiffly, their noses almost in their plates and their faces solemn. Only when Celia said something would they slide their eyes sideways at one another; and then they looked as if they were battling what Ted's mother called interior mirth. Benjamin must have invited them on Ted's behalf, to make up for having forbidden Ruth and scared off Patrick and Laura. They did not look either pleased or honored.

Ted gave up on Benjamin and Matthew's children both, and looked at the rest of his dinner guests. Ellen sat next to Matthew and across from the two boys, and every time Ted glanced her way she made a face at him. Fence and Matthew were talking about music, with occasional appeals to Celia. Randolph, while everyone else had gotten to dessert, was still looking at his soup, and as if he expected to find worms in it.

Ted, staring absently at Margaret and thinking about Benjamin again, realized that she was speaking to him.

"Are you in the play, your Majesty?" she asked.

"No," said Ted firmly, fighting his stomach's lurch of panic.

"Why, what a pity."

"Are you?"

"Most certainly. I am the cat."

She was so obviously pleased that Ted ventured to say, "That's a good part."

"You may have it again next year, my lord," said Randolph, letting a servant take away his soup. "Being the New King's play, Margaret, 'twere foolish to ask whether he be a player."

Margaret shrugged. "And being a secret play, my lord, 'twere foolish to let out the cat from's bag."

Randolph laughed.

"Margaret," said Celia, "speak not so pert."

"She hath the right of me," Randolph told her.

"The more reason she should speak it meekly."

Just like a parent, thought Ted. Celia had spoken pert to Benjamin when *she* had the right of it.

Someone somewhere blew a trumpet, and everybody looked at Ted. No doubt he was to lead them to wherever the play would be performed. All my imperfections on my head, he thought wildly. He stood up, started to hold out his hand to Margaret, and hastily offered her his arm instead. "As one cat to another," he said, hoping he did not sound too idiotic, "will you walk with me?"

This seemed to please everybody except Celia, who raised her eyebrows at her daughter. Margaret raised hers back and smiled at Ted.

"Good King of Cats, I will," she said.

He had been right: she knew where to go, and he had only to follow her. They were obliged to parade the length of the Banquet Hall, stared at by everyone in the place. Ted could not think of another word to say; Margaret, luckily, did not seem to expect it of him.

When they had passed through the doors he heard the scrape of chairs as the rest of the company began to follow them.

Margaret led them to the fountain in the rose garden, did him a courtesy, and said, "By your leave, my lord."

"My best thanks to you, good cat," said Ted. She went on past the fountain and into a clump of bushes, and Ted stood waiting for someone to show him where to sit.

The feast had been a long one; it was early evening. The fog was gone, but the air was still chilly. The stone seats looked uninviting. Ted felt more kindly toward his coronation clothes.

The rest of the feasters began arriving behind him, gabbling and giggling. In their elaborate and no doubt costly coronation garments, they sat themselves down on the grass and flagstone paths and stone seats of the rose garden. Ted supposed that if you kept your finery in a dusty, clovey tower, you might as well sit on the grass in it. He was irritated with them all, without knowing why. He spotted Ellen and beckoned to her. She came to him readily.

"Do you know what's going on?" she demanded of him.

"*I* was going to ask *you*."

Randolph came up to them. "I'd forgot," he said to Ted, "thou hast never seen this form of the play. For this thou sittest on the edge of the fountain, not in the chair of state."

"Can I sit with him?" said Ellen.

Randolph scrutinized her for a moment and nodded. "Thou shalt be a page," he said, and made for the other side of the fountain, where another crowd of people had appeared.

Ted and Ellen stared at each other. Randolph came back with two velvet caps, a purple one for Ted and a gold one for Ellen. Ellen was delighted. Gold for faithfulness, thought Ted, that's right for a page. And purple—purple is kingliness. He tugged the hat on over his disordered hair. Ellen's hair, never orderly at the best of times, flared out beneath the tight rim of her cap like a cloud of soot. She looked, as she had looked on the last day of their game, like a witch, not like a page.

"Come on," Ted said to her. They walked over and sat on the edge of the fountain.

The crowd, seating itself, had left empty a wide round space before the fountain. Two pages, with gold caps like Ellen's, came from Ted's left, each carrying a torch, and took up places in the middle of this space, with perhaps ten feet between them. The last murmurs and laughter died down, leaving only the faint splash of the fountain. Randolph, with a red velvet cap on his head, walked out of the crowd into the space between the torches, bowed, and spoke.

His walk was not his usual swift and easy stride, but a sort of flat-footed, swinging affair; his bow, that could speak volumes of private history, was brief and clumsy. His voice was, if anything, more clear and compelling than usual, but Ted could not understand a word he said. The language Fence had used at the second council meeting, the language Fence and Randoph had used at the King's funeral, for the third time teased him with its almost-understood cadences, its words that stopped just the wrong side of the threshold of meaning.

Ellen tugged at his sleeve. *"What language is that!"* she said in a ferocious whisper.

"I don't know. Hush up."

Randolph, having finished his speech, sat down cross-legged on the flagstones, again with an abrupt and ungraceful motion unlike his accustomed behavior. It occurred to Ted that the effect of these different mannerisms was to make Randolph seem very young, perhaps not much older than Ted. The red cap meant, presumably, a Red Sorcerer; which was funny, when you thought of it, because Randolph was apprenticed to a Blue Sorcerer. The only Red Sorcerer Ted could call to mind was Shan, who had started out as one before taking his own strange path. But there was no guarantee that this play dealt with matters Ted knew anything about.

Out of the crowd on Ted's right came the vast figure of Conrad, with his black beard. Another red cap sat on his bald head, and he carried a staff. As Randolph's easy walk had become clumsy, Conrad's clumsy but vigorous stride had become halting; he moved like an old man. He stood over the seated Randolph, his shadow eclipsing the red cap, and said, in words Ted understood plainly, "Would you so?"

"I would," said Randolph, brisk and blithe; and Ted, for no reason he knew, shivered.

Conrad put three fingers into his mouth and whistled. A small form in a black-and-white checked cap bounced out of the middle of the crowd and clattered up to Conrad, grinning. It was one of Matthew's sons—Mark, Ted thought; and it was quite clear, though he walked on two feet and wore no costume, that he was a dog. Conrad tousled his checked cap and presented him to Randolph.

"This is your dog, child. Dog, guard him well. Child, this is the essence of faith; if you betray it, all the world else will betray you. Do you take this one as your fellow?"

"I do," said Randolph, his voice pleased, careless, and confident, as if he were agreeing to read a story to Laura after dinner. Ted shivered again. Shan, a young wizard, proud, and o'er-hasty, might have greeted so solemn-sounding an undertaking in just that tone.

The dog-boy sat down behind Randolph. Conrad whistled again. Margaret, in an orange-and-white cap, came gliding out of the crowd, sleek and serene, a very creditable cat. She bumped her forehead into Randolph's knee.

"This," said Conrad to Randolph, "is your cat. Cat, inform him well. Child, this is the essence of subtlety; if you betray this one, all your stratagems will be clear as glass to your enemies. Do you take this one as your fellow?"

"I do indeed," said Randolph, cheerfully.

Conrad whistled a third time, and the tall, lanky, solemn Jerome, wearing a brown-and-white cap, came nimbly out into the torchlight and bowed his head before Randolph.

"Horse," said Ellen, in tones of considerable approval.

"This is your horse," said Conrad. "Horse, bear him well. Child, this is the essence of swiftness. Betray it, and all your journeys will bring you too late to your desire. Do you take this one as your fellow?"

"Of a certainty," said Randolph, and the complacence in his voice started a pain in Ted's chest.

Conrad whistled. Matthew's other son, gray and white on his head, swooped in from the left, his arms outstretched.

"This is your eagle. Eagle, feed him well. Child, this is the essence of cruelty; betray it, and there will be no mercy for you. Do you take this one as your fellow?"

"This one most of all," said Randolph, and under the careless confidence of his tone Ted heard a grim amusement that almost choked him.

"Page!" called Conrad, turning to Ted and Ellen.

Ellen got up quickly and went over to him. "What service, my lord?" she said, which was probably safe enough.

Conrad took two round objects from his belt; they sparkled and glinted in the torchlight, but Ted could not make out what they were.

"Do you take these to your master and bid him choose between them, what path the Hidden Land will take during the years of his reign. Bid him remember well the choice of Shan, and all its consequences."

"My lord," said Ellen, made him an excellent bow, and carried the two round objects to Ted.

They were medallions of some sort, about three inches across. One of them was inlaid with a golden sun; the other was dark inside its thin gold border.

"It's the tapestry!" whispered Ellen urgently, bowed, and moved aside so the crowd could see Ted.

It was the story of the tapestry, all right: here he was,

choosing between the hole and the sun. On the surface, the choice was obvious. All the animals had run away from the hole in the tapestry; and from what Ted knew of Shan's story, all the world had indeed betrayed him, and all his stratagems had been laid bare to his enemies, and his most vital journey had been made too late, and no one had had mercy on him when he stood before his judges.

But then why did everybody in the Secret Country swear by Shan's mercy? It was too obvious, it was too easy, to choose the bright sun and shun the dark places. The sun could burn you as easily as the dark could trip you up. Ted closed his left hand on the cool dark disk, and stopped. He was not choosing for himself; he was choosing the path of the Secret Country, not just during his reign, short as he hoped this would be, but during Edward's, if they found him. You couldn't play games with other people, with a whole country and a whole history, because you thought the symbol of the sun was too obvious. In the ceremony this afternoon, he had promised not to do so.

He held up the glittering golden disk in his right hand.

"I choose this," he said.

There was a profound stillness in the garden. If they were waiting for something more, Ted could not give it to them.

But they had been waiting for Fence, who came forward with his moons and stars around him, his round face blurred in the torchlight so that only the bright hollows of his eyes were clear. The cap on his head was white. He passed the line of animals, and Randolph, and the stooped form of Conrad. Only Randolph, sitting on the ground, did not stand taller than he.

He walked straight up to Ted, and took the dark disk from Ted's left hand. "Then I will keep the part thou hast not chosen, shouldst thou have need of it," he said. He turned around and moved to Ted's left; Ellen was standing on his right.

"Bow," hissed Fence, after a moment.

Ted bowed; Fence bowed; Ellen bowed; Conrad bent stiffly; all the animals pranced and dipped their heads. The crowd applauded. Conrad and the animals filed past the fountain and disappeared into the darkness. The crowd stood up and rustled and muttered its way back into High Castle. The two boys took their torches away.

Fence and Ted and Ellen stood in a row, looking at Randolph, who sat still in the empty darkness with his elbows on his knees and his head in his hands.

"What's the matter with him?" whispered Ellen to Ted.

She had actually learned, sometime in the past year, to make a whisper that could not be heard for yards around. But Fence heard her just the same.

"The play's not over," he said. He touched Ted lightly on the arm. "What did Shan choose?" he asked, a note of ritual in his quiet voice. He sounded just as any one of them might sound in playing the Secret.

"He chose glory," said Ted, and stopped.

"Then do you give him length of days," said Fence.

Fence had the dark disk that apparently represented length of days, and the speech he had made when he took it had not sounded like something you would say if you were going to give it up again. Ted was thoroughly bewildered. Melanie had given Shan length of days, just how Ted didn't know, though Ellen might. He was also having trouble with the fact that Randolph was playing Shan, so that, in some wise, what he did to Shan he did also to Randolph. Of course, giving Randolph length of days was what he earnestly desired to do. How, then?

He remembered his talk with Randolph in the West Tower.

White was for health. He snatched the cap from Fence's head, ran across the flags to Randolph, and dropped to his knees.

"Your cap, I pray you," he said.

Randolph took his head out of his hands and pulled the cap off. His wild black hair, so like Ellen's, sprang up around his head again. Ted took the red cap from him and held out the white.

"Your health, my lord," he said; he could not help the faint malice that showed in his voice.

Randolph put the white cap on, absently; even in the dim evening his eyes held Ted's. Then he took hold of Ted's cold hands with his own colder ones, and they stood up together.

"All may yet be very well," said Randolph; and in his voice, as in Fence's, Ted heard the tone of ritual.

Randolph let go of him, turned, and walked away.

"*Well!*" said Ellen.

"Very well," said Fence.

Ted, turning Shan's red cap over and over in his fingers, wondered what he had done.

"Fence?" he said.

"Oh, thou didst choose wisely," said Fence. "But consider, didst thou so out of wisdom, or for that thy father's choice was the other?"

"Edward's very wise," said Ellen, with every evidence of sincerity. Ted suspected her of making a joke that only the members of the Secret could appreciate: Prince Edward was indeed wise, whoever and wherever he was; but Ted was not Prince Edward.

"So was Shan," said Fence.

Neither Ted nor Ellen chose to respond to this. The three of them went silently inside.

CHAPTER 9

THE day after the coronation found Ted hustled by Benjamin from one council to another. Most of them consisted of endless reports from officers and artisans of what they had been doing to get ready for the battle. Ted wondered fleetingly why they always spoke of a battle rather than of a war. Then, with a jolt like coming to the end of a flight of stairs one step sooner than you expect, he remembered the Border Magic.

It became clear to Ted that what Randolph called the mundane army had been mustering for weeks. Probably the old King had ordered that; he had believed that *something* was happening down on the southern border. The sorcerers, on the other hand, were in a state of vast disarray. Some of them had been quietly persuaded by Fence or Randolph to prepare as they would for a battle with monsters, and the division this had created between those who agreed with Fence and those who did not had cut right down to the apprentices and made a tangle of political and personal grudges and alliances such as Ted had never imagined in his wariest moments. And even the mundane army was not entirely ready for this battle: the great strength of the old King's army had been the cavalry, and horses, said Fence, were afraid of all sorcerous creatures. Ted found himself hoping Randolph had killed the King in time, and was appalled.

Nobody asked for Ted's orders. He found this both a relief and an irritation. He would not have known what orders to give, but, being King, he ought to have been allowed to give some. Besides, it would be a poor present to the real Edward, if they found him, to turn over to him a bunch of minions who always got their own way.

He was therefore rather testy when Benjamin told him, in the early evening, after five councils but before supper, to come along to the armory and choose his sword.

"Fence has my sword," said Ted.

Benjamin's face darkened. "Thou art not trained to an enchanted weapon," he said, "and it is overlate to change thy choice. Now come."

Oh well, thought Ted, following him, it was worth a try. Fence must have told him all about it.

The armory was under the Banquet Hall, and seemed even larger, for it was half underground and its slits of windows let in little light. Dim aisles, lined with racks of swords, spears, shields, stretched into darkness. Ted thought at first that there were enchanted weapons there; everything was so well polished that it glowed even in so little light. But he remembered Patrick's description of the room under Fence's Tower: weapons shining with their own light in every color. No, these were only mundane weapons. He could smell the polish that kept them so bright.

"They are making shield and helmet for thee," said Benjamin, "but for thy first battle thou must choose thy sword."

Ted wondered how. Quite apart from wanting to get Shan's sword back from Fence so they could go home, he remembered the bout he and Patrick had fought in the rose garden. Shan's and Melanie's swords had known what they were doing. It would have been a comfort to have them for

114

the battle. He put no particular trust in the swords Patrick and Laura had stolen. Those were magical, but not, he would bet, *that* magical.

He wandered down the long aisles, Benjamin at his heel. He fingered a grip now and again, but was not moved to do more. Perhaps he could find the sword he had had in his dream, the one that had fit his hand as one piece of a jigsaw puzzle fits into another. That would be a comfort, too. He wished he knew what it looked like. The dream-Edward had been thinking of other things.

In the middle of the third aisle he found it. It slid into his questing hand—the right hand—as if it had been waiting for him. Ted pulled it from the rack, saluted no one, and lunged with it down the empty aisle. Oh, yes, this was it. He stopped in mid-lunge, wrenched his knee, recovered, and stood staring. He had, in the dream, used this sword to try to kill Randolph. He had failed in the dream, but now he knew why, and if in fact they did fight he would not make that mistake. He looked along the blade. Should he play so into the dream's hands, into the game's hands? Did taking this sword mean he would kill Randolph?

Ted parried an imaginary attack and sighed. With this sword he might not fall in battle. He could save himself a trip to the land of the dead and Ruth a great deal of worry. That part had been fun to act out, but he saw no prospect of fun in the reality. After all, he thought, in the dream I was surprised at the mistake, so maybe I'd make it anyway. And I can refuse to fight Randolph. I do refuse.

He turned to Benjamin. "This one," he said.

Benjamin came closer and looked without touching. "Ah," he said. "That was John's."

"I thought he was a sorcerer," said Ted.

"Not he. He but knew when to employ them. Well, come: this may be a good omen. This sword was a curse to the Dragon King when last he came." Benjamin's voice was not as pleased as his words, and Ted looked at him thoughtfully.

"Benjamin," he said, "I've been meaning to ask you for ages. What are the Outside Powers?"

Benjamin shook his head. "That question meeteth a different answer in every mouth. I will say only, their color is red, their power beyond sorcery, their hearts not kindly."

"Claudia," said Ted.

Benjamin laughed. "No need to jape with fogs and daggers, were she such." He turned to go.

"What does it mean if they're rising again?"

Benjamin did not answer him directly. "When last they rose, the Border Magic kept them from us," he said. "They are not our sworn enemies, as the Dragon King is, but are yet inimical to us by their nature. I can tell thee no more."

"But I thought you said, at the council before Fence came back, that they *made* the Border Magic?"

"Wherefore should it not therefore keep them from us? I say again, their nature is inimical to us. They might hurt us as a man in a hurry trampleth the grass. And they might undo the Border Magic as a man in desperate need will destroy his own fences to get at his foe."

"Who's their foe?"

"I have said, I can tell thee no more."

That tone brooked no argument. "Benjamin," said Ted, struck with a sudden thought, "what about my dwarf-armor?"

"Randolph," said Benjamin, dangerously, "hath told me it did fit thee but by a trick."

"Oh, well," said Ted, wondering whether he had grown

since Randolph measured him, but not caring to make an issue of it. "We march tomorrow, then?" he said.

"At dawn."

Ted thought he would take a nap after supper, to prepare and to compensate for the midnight meeting with his relations in the rose garden.

The nap made him late, of course. He found the others by the blue and green glow. For an instant he thought they had their swords back. Then he remembered the ones Patrick and Laura had stolen.

"We're trying to decide who should have these," Patrick told him when he joined them.

"We haven't even decided if we're going yet!" said Ted. He sat down by Laura on a stone bench, brushing a wet spray of roses aside. Petals drifted down the sword-beams, dyed purple and orange. "And put those things away; what if somebody sees the light?"

"Well," said Patrick, sheathing the green sword with an uncharacteristic lack of argument, "I think, if we can do it without being noticed, we should try these swords and see if they get us home. But we shouldn't count on it."

"Ruth," said Ted. "What do you think? Can you bring me back?"

Ruth nodded, and her hair swung in the sword-glow. "It's a very simple spell," she said. "They call it advanced sorcery because they don't want just anybody doing it. You're supposed to save it for special cases. The sorcerers don't want the Lord of the Dead mad at them."

"Laurie, will you put that thing away? Are kings special cases?"

"Well, not any king. But a young one, who doesn't have an heir yet, and dies fighting the Dragon King, yes. It sounds like the Judge of the Dead and the Dragon King are enemies from way back. The Judge of the Dead made the Lords of the Dead let John come back to life, Meredith says."

Ted stumbled for a moment over the idea of having an heir, considered the rest of what Ruth had said, and nodded. "I'm okay, then. What about everybody else?"

"Sorcerers of the Green Caves don't fight," said Ruth, "and Meredith says I'm to come along to watch, so I guess they won't try to make me do anything I can't."

"Did Benjamin take you to choose your sword, Pat?"

"Younger sons don't get taken," said Patrick, without rancor. "He just told me to go and choose, and not, in my overweening ambition, to take one too long for me."

"I didn't know Prince Patrick had any ambition," said Ellen.

"He said he didn't altogether like my conduct at the coronation," said Patrick.

"Well, it *was* weird," said Ellen. "What were you doing, anyway?"

"We were discussing the oath," said Ted, "and I want to know about Patrick's sword."

"Well," said Patrick, "I'd like an enchanted one, but then I thought, maybe we should give them to the girls."

Ted looked at his sister, who looked away, but did at last sheathe the blue glow of the sword she held. "Are they going to let you guys come?"

"Agatha's been packing for us," said Ellen after a moment. "We even get to wear boys' clothes." She paused. "I want to take our jeans."

"Don't," said Ted. "I don't know what they'd say around here if they got a good look at those zippers."

"They have running water," remarked Ellen.

"So did the ancient Romans," said Patrick.

Ted said to Ellen, "Are you and Laurie supposed to fight?"

"I'm going to," said Ellen. "And take the jeans."

"We'll need them to go home in, anyway," said Ruth.

Laura pulled a ribbon from one of her braids and addressed the ground. "Agatha says we should see war in case there's a change in fortunes and we get to be more than door wardens. Whatever that means."

"I'm going to fight," said Ellen.

"If you wanted to fight," Ted told her, "you should have been out in that yard every morning with Patrick and me. You don't know how. You'll get killed."

"I will not."

"Ellen. I forbid you to fight."

"Who do you think you are?"

"I'm Edward," said Ted. "You swore me an oath."

"Now look," said Ellen, and paused, and said, "now look," and was quiet.

Nobody else said anything. The fountain bubbled like one of the purple beasts, and thin in the background some night insect creaked. Laura snarled the ribbon up, and Ted untangled it and tied it back onto the braid for her. She still would not look at him.

"If you can do *that*, how come you wouldn't let *me* swear to you?" Patrick said.

"You did swear to him," said Ruth. "I heard you."

"Yeah, but he made me qualify the oath first, so I was really swearing to the King of the Secret Country."

"*What?*" said Ellen. "You whoreson dogs!"

"Ellen!" said Ruth.

"The undercooks say it!"

"They don't insult their own mother when they say it!"

"What?"

"Well?" said Patrick.

"You wouldn't keep the real oath if you didn't want to," said Ted, "because you'd think it wasn't serious. And then you'd get in trouble for breaking an oath. But if I made you *think* about it, and swear a limited oath, then you'd keep that."

"There, Ellie," said Ruth, "you and I have been complimented."

"And I've been insulted, I suppose," said Patrick cheerfully. "Now, who gets these swords?"

"I think you're right; we should give them to Laura and Ellen," said Ted. "Not to fight with, but just in case things go wrong."

"Wish I'd thought to steal more," said Patrick. He made a figure eight in the air with the green sword, and sighed. "You're right, I guess. They'll need all the help they can get." He put the sword away as Ted drew breath to yell at him. "Come on down to the armory with me," said Patrick in his friendliest tones, "and help me pick out a normal one."

They left at dawn. The morning was clear again. In the mill before everyone was organized, Laura looked for Claudia. Laura and Ellen and Agatha were to walk behind Ruth and the other students of the Green Caves, among the pages and cooks. Claudia, if she were coming, would hardly be with them.

Laura climbed up the wall that overhung the moat, and watched High Castle empty itself, but she saw no one with black hair and a weasel's walk. As she began to climb down, she saw a group of women with spears, standing on the bridge over the moat. They were talking to Ted and Benjamin and Patrick. Laura was not sure she was speaking to Ted yet, but when the three of them came by she scrambled down the wall, tore her tunic, and caught Patrick by the sleeve.

"Who were those people?"

"Ted thinks they were the Queen's Council when there was a Queen," said Patrick, "and now they hang around waiting for another Queen and doing what nobody else wants to do. Like staying home from the battle."

"Claudia wasn't there, was she?"

"No."

Trumpets blew around them.

"I have to go," said Patrick. "Have you got your sword?"

Laura nodded, and went back to Ellen and Agatha to be scolded for tearing her clothes.

It took much longer to march to the Well of the White Witch than it had taken to ride there. Laura began by being grateful that they were not riding horses, but a few hours into the morning her knee began to bother her.

"Why didn't they bring the horses?" she snarled at Ellen.

"Horses are afraid of dragons," said Ellen.

Laura, thinking that that was very sensible of the horses, put her hand to the hilt of the sword and wondered if it would take them home.

They reached the Well of the White Witch at around breakfast time, according to Laura's stomach. The Secret House sat lumpily on its hill in the sun, and the light gleamed off its many windows.

Laura blinked and was caught. The spark of sun on glass shrank to a pinpoint surrounded by shadows. The pinpoint came closer, bobbing oddly. Claudia's face sprang up behind it, and Laura realized that she was carrying a candle down a flight of steps. She had something over her shoulder. She came forward, and the candlelight showed a cellar. Its floor was of great blocks of stone, like the floors at High Castle.

Two of these had been propped up. Darkness gaped below them. Claudia tumbled her burden onto the floor and turned to set the candle on a shelf.

"Shan's mercy!" said Laura. As Claudia moved the candle, it had shown Laura her own face in a tangle of hair on the cellar floor. She looked like a rag doll.

"What, what?" said Ellen's voice beside her. "Don't say that, Agatha'll hear you. Did you stub your toe?"

Patrick came up behind and took each of them by an elbow. Laura screeched, and then stood dumbly shivering.

"Shhh!" said Patrick. He drew them behind a supply wagon, out of Agatha's range. She was unpacking something from another wagon, but kept glancing around for them.

"Ted says Randolph says we have to stay here long enough to tell the Well what we're doing—"

"What?" said Ellen.

"That's what he said. And eat some breakfast. So look. Ruthie has to help with the Well. But the minute that's over, you guys slip away and meet us by the wooden bridge, over in the trees, remember? Don't forget the swords."

"Are we going home?" said Laura. Oh, God, she thought, let the swords work.

"Well, I don't think we decided. But we have to find out if it's possible."

Ellen jogged Laura's elbow. "Come on, let's get close to the Well so we can see Ruthie."

Laura came with her, hugging her elbows. *Mother, mother, make my bed/Make for me a winding sheet/Wrap me up in a cloak of gold/See if I can sleep.* They didn't play that when they thought she could hear it, and they didn't sing it at all. But she had heard. Patrick tagged along with them. They sat in the dry brown grass a few feet from the Well, and examined it.

"Still looks wrong," said Ellen. "I can't get over that pink."

Laura looked up the hill she had rolled down, and then squinted sideways at the house. In case they were not going home, she had better see just what Claudia was up to. *She set him in a golden chair/She gave him sugar sweet.* Laura stared at the mullioned windows, the odd sprouting round towers with their drapes of ivy, the red-tile roof going in humps like somebody's drawing of the ocean, until her eyes watered. But she saw nothing except what was there. *She laid him on a dressing-board/And stabbed him like a sheep.*

A trumpet blew, and Laura jumped. There was a solid circle of people around the Well now. The trumpeter stood on the other side of it from them. Behind him came a line of people in white, mostly women, but with one or two boys. They blocked Laura's view, and everyone else was standing formally, so she stood up, too. After a moment Patrick and Ellen joined her.

Each person in white carried a wooden bucket with a rope. The first three took the lid off the Well and leaned it against the side. Patrick and Ellen and Laura looked at each other, remembering their first meeting in this country. The first woman lowered her bucket into the Well and then spoke for some time in the infuriating, almost-sensible language Laura had heard at the King's funeral. She heard Ellen's indignant muttering beside her.

The woman took a ring from her finger and dropped it into the Well, talked for a little longer, and raised the dripping bucket.

"Ruthie can't do that by herself," whispered Patrick.

"She has to," said Ellen.

The woman peered into her bucket and seemed satisfied. She carried it over to a group of pages, who dipped into it with a silver dipper and began to fill silver cups and hand them around to the crowd.

One by one the people in white walked over the short dry grass to the Well, and lowered a bucket, tossed in a ring, said a phrase or two, peered into the bucket, took it to the pages, and became part of the crowd. Ruth did all these things as if she were buying a box of cookies at the corner grocery: except that when she peered into her bucket her eyes got big and she made a muffled and not very dignified squeak. After the pages had emptied her bucket she put her hand down into it, brought it up with the fist clenched, and searched the crowd with her eyes.

She found Laura and Ellen and Patrick, and came toward them as fast as her long skirt would let her. Nobody else seemed to notice her.

"Where's our water?" demanded Ellen.

"They'll get to you," said Ruth. She breathed as though she had been running. "Look at this." She opened her hand. On her damp and grubby palm there lay, its gilt flaking off to show dull gray and its stone scratched and cloudy, the little dime-store ring she had given the Well on their first day in this country.

Laura's breath went out of her. Even before the dull gleam of the cracked gilt blossomed into vision, she felt a swift conviction of disaster. The vision did not comfort her. She had a brief frozen glimpse of Claudia, and the man who looked like both Fence and Randolph, fighting with knives in a swirl of wet leaves. Then Ellen pulled at her and they were all pushing through the crowd to the woods.

"Laurie, have you got your sword?" said Patrick, in the tone of someone who is not asking for the first time.

"Sure," said Laura. "Ruthie, what does that ring mean?"

"I don't know," said Ruth, viciously pushing between a plump man in leather and a tall woman in white. "But," she added as they gained the edge of the woods, "I feel kicked out."

"Yes," said Laura; and she was not sorry. She patted the hilt of the stolen sword, and wished there had been a way to say good-bye to Fence and Randolph.

They tramped hollowly across the wooden bridge and scrambled along the edge of the stream toward the house. Laura tripped twice—the sword's weight put her off balance—but did not fall into the water.

"Where's Ted?" she said after the second of these mishaps.

"Randolph was talking to him," said Patrick. "Ellie and I can test our sword anyway. Our bottle-tree is just the other side of the house."

They went along through the coolness to the clump of bottle-trees. Even in her horror and bewilderment, Laura was fascinated by them. They looked as if they had been made, probably by a mad sculptor, rather than grown. Patrick and Ellen floundered about under their bulging trunks and got thoroughly scratched, but the sword took them nowhere except to the other side of the clump. They made Laura try with their sword, and then with her own, and got nowhere still. Neither sword made her arm prickle, but even in the sunlit forest their blades glowed faintly.

They went back to the bridge and found a highly irritated Ted awaiting them. He took the news about the swords and the bush with equanimity, but when Ruth showed him her gimcrack ring he looked appalled.

"Something here has found us out," he said.

"Well, I don't suppose it can tell anybody else," said Patrick, "and anyway, it wouldn't have to know anything except that that isn't the right kind of ring. Look, let's see if either sword will get anybody through the hedge."

"I guess we're lucky it's not worse," said Ted, as they slithered along the bank again.

"What's not worse?" said Patrick.

"Well, Ruthie isn't really a sorcerer of the Green Caves, and she did draw water from that Well. Could have been a lot worse."

"I did lose my Ring of Sorcery, though," said Ruth.

Ted stopped dead. Ellen bumped into him, and Laura fell over Ellen. "Oh, God," he said, ignoring the indignant cries and scrabblings behind him, "does that mean you can't bring me back from the dead?" Laura stopped trying to get up, and listened.

"I don't think so," said Ruth. She scowled. "Of course not," she said, more strongly. "I've never seen any of the Green Caves people use theirs to do magic. It's a symbol, and it can be a defense against—well, it can be a defense. But nobody uses it for any of the spells I've been taught. It's like an ID card. We have to show it for a ceremony."

"Well," said Ted, "there won't be any ceremonies 'til after the battle and we'll think of something by then. Come on."

No matter who crawled under the hedge with which sword, it was still the Secret Country on the other side. These swords would take nobody home.

"Well," said Ted, "that's that."

They stood looking at one another. Patrick seemed indignant, Ellen cheerful, Ruth thoughtful, and Ted worried. Laura found herself wanting to try the swords again, in the way she would want to look again for a lost shoe which just had to be there. She wondered if she could sneak away and go back to High Castle. She would probably get lost, and it would be galling to have to ask for an escort, not to mention explaining herself to all the people back there who had wanted to go to the battle but were obliged to stay home. Besides, Claudia was at High Castle. Better to be as far as possible from Claudia and the Secret House.

Nobody had anything to say, and they began to drift back toward the camp. Oh, well, thought Laura. Maybe Ruth can bring *me* back if Claudia kills me. And that was not part of the story, so perhaps they could go home before it happened. Tripping on the first plank of the wooden bridge and catching herself with a hand on the rail, she thought that she would not like to be killed even if Ruth could bring her back. She wondered if Ted felt the same way.

They had missed their breakfast, and were all five scolded by Agatha.

"Well," said Ruth, as the army reformed itself and they had to return to their places, "at least she didn't say anything about Ted and me."

"Maybe she's on your side," said Ellen.

The army swung a little to the west to cross a larger bridge than the wooden one. They took an amazingly long time to get across. Then they settled down to walk the lumpy and thinly forested lands behind the Secret House. There was a road of sorts, not as good as the one that led north from the Well to Fence's Country. At first Laura saw houses and fields of grain and cows grazing, but as they went on south the signs of habitation dwindled and vanished, and the land grew hillier and wilder-looking.

Laura's knee gave out completely after a few hours, and Agatha put her in a wagon among the bedding and tents, with Ellen for company. Most of the army was ahead of them, which made it rather dusty where they were. But to see the long line glinting with color and sun on metal was worth a little dust. Laura and Ellen looked at one another, and Ellen grinned.

"This," said Ellen, "is an adventure."

And for all her fears of what might happen after, Laura thought so, too.

CHAPTER 10

THEY came to the end of the hills that evening, and made their first night's camp just outside the last forest, on the edge of a plain that seemed to Laura to go on forever.

Supper at Agatha's fire was dull. Ellen tried to get her to talk about being Queen's Counselor, but Agatha acted as if the request were an insult. Laura could not see how anyone who had ever been a Queen's Counselor could sit around a fire at the edge of the woods and talk about sewing, but Agatha did it. Laura and Ellen gave each other speaking looks until that was boring, too. Before they could fall asleep or do something desperate, a boy about their age came to say that the King wanted them. Laura still went cold when she heard that. She and Ellen got up and followed the boy to Ted's fire. He and Patrick and Matthew and Randolph and Fence were there.

Fence turned out to be a good storyteller, and Randolph could play something like a recorder, which sounded much better than most of the instruments in High Castle. Matthew, to Laura's immense surprise, could sing, which he did at Fence's request when, after six stories, Fence's voice began to give out.

The first song he sang, she did not know. But at the first notes from the recorder, she saw Patrick, on Ellen's other side, shoot upright from his lounging position, scattering

Ellen and Fence with dry leaves. Laura looked quickly at Ted, who was on her other side, but almost on the other side of the fire as well, next to Randolph. He was frowning.

The song's tune was sprightly; its words otherwise:

Fear no more the heat o' the sun,
Nor the furious winter's rages;
Thou thy worldly task hath done,
Home art gone, and ta' en thy wages.

Patrick poked at Ellen and whispered.

"Shut up," said Ellen, a little too loudly.

Fence, sitting cross-legged in his wizard's robe just beyond Patrick, gave them all a quelling glance. They subsided. Laura wanted to hear the song, in any case; Patrick would have to wait.

Fear no more the frown o' the great;
Thou art past the tyrant's stroke;
Care no more to clothe or eat;
To thee the reed is as the oak:
The scepter, learning, physic, must
All follow thee, and come to dust.

The whistle piped obediently its flourish, and in the pause between verse and verse Matthew said, "Randolph?"

Randolph, on the other side of the fire, lowered the instrument to his knee; the ring on his hand flashed, and then the silver curve of his circlet sparked in the firelight as he turned his head to look at Matthew.

Matthew sang, *"Fear no more the lightning-flash,"* but Laura only half-heard him. It was happening again. The first blue glint from Randolph's ring blurred and widened, and in place of the red fire and the sharp-shadowed faces of her brother, her cousins, and her inventions, she saw Lord Andrew. He stood in a bare, round room through whose windows showed only the high and empty sky. He leaned his hands on a plain wooden table, staring at its surface, on which lay a scattering of splinters and colored glass. The splinters came from a vicious gash in the tabletop, as if somebody had hit it with an axe—or a sword. You could not tell from looking where the bits of glass came from, but Laura knew. This was how the room in the North Tower had looked, after Patrick broke the Crystal of Earth. Except that Andrew had not been there.

Randolph's circlet gleamed again as he moved his head, and the vision was swallowed in firelight. Randolph was singing now, in a voice lighter than Matthew's, and one that sounded somehow less trained, but was very clear.

"Nor the all-dreaded thunder-stone."

"Fear not slander," sang Matthew, *"censure rash."*

"Thou hast finished joy and moan." Randolph's voice faltered a very little; perhaps he had been out of breath from his playing. Laura looked at Ted again. He was staring at Randolph as if he expected him to begin doing cartwheels.

The next lines Matthew and Randolph sang together, as Laura's mother and father did, as though they were used to it:

All lovers young, all lovers must
Consign to thee, and come to dust.

Laura wondered where Ruth was; Ruth, whose lover Randolph was supposed to be, except that Randolph had seemed to prefer Claudia.

Then Matthew, *"No exorcisor harm thee."*

And Randolph, *"Nor no witchcraft charm thee,"* and his

voice cracked on the word "witchcraft" and barely recovered for the end of the line.

Matthew, his face anxious, went on, *"Ghost unlaid forbear thee,"* and Fence's voice rose and mingled with his.

"For the love of heaven, Matthew, something cheerier."

The stories he told had been funny ones, thought Laura. She did not understand what was happening. She looked from one to another of them. Matthew was obviously upset. Fence's face was quite calm, and Randolph's hidden in shadow as he bent his head to the recorder again.

"Patrick Spens," said Matthew, quickly, and they began it.

Laura knew this one, and was pleased. It did unsettle her, a little, to hear a Scottish song in the Secret Country. She smiled at Ted, but he was still staring at Randolph.

The King sits in Dumferling toune,
Drinking of the bluid-red wine,
Oh, where shall I find a steely skipper
To sail this gallant—

The music of the recorder wavered, squawked, and fell silent. Matthew was silent also.

"I cry you mercy," he said after a moment.

"No, I cry you," said Randolph. His voice was steady. "My skill is someways rusty. Fence?"

"Not, I think, the whistle," said Fence, cheerfully. He looked around. Laura saw that the boy who had brought her and Ellen had disappeared.

"Patrick?" said Fence. "Of your courtesy, will you go to my tent and bring me the lute you find there?"

"Gladly," said Patrick; he sounded excited.

He got up and walked off. Randolph unscrewed the two

pieces of the whistle and began to dry them carefully, as Laura's mother would do with her recorder. Ted watched him as if he had never seen anybody do such a thing. Matthew and Fence, looking at one another, might have been holding a long conversation by telepathy, if there had been telepathy in the Secret Country. The fire popped and rustled. In the otherwise utter quiet that had overtaken them, Laura could hear laughter and singing at other fires, and a discreet chinking that puzzled her for a moment. Then she saw, dimly in the trees behind Fence, the two armed and mailed men who stood watch there, one facing the camp and the other the dark woods.

Laura's sense of happy adventure was beginning to suffer. She was disturbed, as always, by any anxiety or discord among the grown-ups; and the guards had reminded her what she had managed to forget: that they were going to a battle, not to a picnic. She looked at Ellen, who was scowling at the fire.

Ellen looked back at her, and leaned over. Her sense of adventure seemed to be suffering, too. She looked worried.

"Maybe I was wrong," she said in Laura's ear. "Maybe he *is* sorry."

Then Laura understood. No witchcraft charm three, and Randolph had killed the King with a magical poison. The King sat in Dumferling town, drinking of the blood-red wine. And Randolph had put the poison in the wine.

"What will they *think*?" she whispered back. The song's the thing, she thought wildly, wherein we'll catch the conscience of the counselor.

"Just that he misses the King and doesn't want to be reminded of what happened," said Ellen, serenely confident as always.

"Well, he'd better watch out."

"They think he's wonderful," said Ellen, a tinge of the usual scorn returning to her voice. "They'll never guess."

Laura, whose other self, the Princess, had loved Randolph almost as much as she loved Fence; who would have loved him that much herself had not what she knew made her afraid of him, opened her mouth and closed it again. Even if arguing with Ellen would make Ellen change her mind, which was not often the case, she could not do it here. She said instead, "What's the matter with Patrick?"

"He thinks the song proves something."

"What?"

"It's Shakespeare."

"So what?"

"He thinks," said Ellen, exasperation in her voice as she struggled to explain Patrick's thoughts, which were never either simple or pleasing, in a whisper, "that it doesn't mean anything if they *sound* like Shakespeare, or even if they say some *lines* from Shakespeare once in a while, but if they sing a whole *song* from Shakespeare, then we *did* make all this up."

"He's crazy," said Laura, automatically. She had other things to worry about.

Patrick, looking no crazier than usual, came back with Fence's lute, and after an amiable period of argument during which first Fence and then Matthew tried to tune it, and Randolph was finally obliged to take a hand, they settled into an uneventful evening of music. They gathered gradually a large audience and a number of helpful voices, trained and untrained. Agatha could sing, so could Conrad, so could all Matthew's family, so could Andrew. Benjamin could not, but nobody seemed to care.

Laura, a disappointment to two musical parents, kept her mouth shut. Patrick's argument was gaining force as the songs followed one another through the dark hours of the evening. She knew almost all of them. Her father had records full of them. *"There lived a wife in Usher's Well/A wealthy wife was she."* Her mother sang them around the house, baking bread or bathing the dog or painting the ceiling in the back hall that cracked every spring. *"A lady lived by the North Sea shore/Lay the bent to the bonny broom."* Her parents sang them together in the evenings, when she and Ted were in bed. *"A holiday, a holiday, in the first month of the year/Lord Donald's wife rode in to town, some holy words to hear."* Her mother sang them to her when she had the mumps. *" 'Twas in the merry month of May/When green buds all were swelling/Sweet William on his deathbed lay/For love of Barbary Allen."* She sang them to Ted when Ted broke his wrist. *"O what can ail thee, knight at arms,/Alone and palely loitering."* Her father, who very seldom sang by himself, could occasionally be heard warbling one or two when engaged in some particularly vexatious duty, like fixing the fence where Laura had run into it with her bicycle. (The bicycle had been beyond fixing.) *"Young women they run like hares on the mountain."*

Laura sniffed hugely, and then swallowed hard. Ellen knew these songs, too; she was singing them, grinning, her anger at Patrick and her misjudgment of Randolph no longer troubling her.

> Oh, tell to me, Tam Lin, she said,
> Why came you here to dwell?
> The Queen of Fairies caught me,
> When from my horse I fell.

Laura's parents had not seen her for perhaps two weeks, if she understood what Ruth and Ellen had meant to do with Shan's Ring, and if they had really done it. Actually, she had not seen her parents for three months. She had been furious when they parted from her, going callously off to Australia to visit Ruth and Ellen and Patrick and their parents, as they always did in the summer—but leaving Ted and Laura at the mercy of the cousins on the other side of the family, the wrong cousins, who watched television and played hide-and-go-seek.

Oh they will turn me in your arms
Into a naked knight.
But cloak me in your mantle
And keep me out of sight.

In that fury and frustration, there had been no time to miss them. And then she had fallen over Shan's sword, the scar of which she had still; and they had found the Secret Country, with Ruth and Ellen and Patrick waiting there already. Her parents were living in the same house as Ruth and Ellen and Patrick, but neither she nor Ted thought for a moment of asking after them. They had too much else to do.

Oh, had I known, Tam Lin, she said,
What this night I did see,
I had looked him in the eyes
And turned him to a tree.

"Oh, God," said Laura, and burst into tears.

"Laurie?" said Ellen, who hated people who cried but had learned, after a fashion, to manage Laura when it happened.

"I want to go home!" said Laura, in a wet and strangled whisper.

"Fence, for shame!" said the vigorous voice of Agatha, that only a moment before had been singing better than Laura's mother. "You've kept these children hours beyond their bedtime, and look at your reward."

She picked Laura up off the ground and stood there holding her by the shoulders. Laura was so horrified that she stopped crying. You didn't show a whole crowd of people that somebody was making a fool of himself. Agatha had, as her father once said about the high-school boy who drove the ice-cream truck past the farm every summer evening, the sensitivity of a deaf cow.

"And these soldiers also," said Fence, tolerantly; and everybody laughed and began to go away.

"Let go of her!" said Ellen furiously to Agatha. "She isn't a baby!"

"Let her not so behave, then," said Agatha, smartly; but she did let go of Laura. "And mind your tongue," she added to Ellen.

Ellen, perhaps mindful of the slap she had received the day of the funeral, said meekly, "Yes, mistress."

"Come your ways, then," said Agatha, and walked off in the direction of their own fire and tent and bedrolls. Laura managed a weak giggle.

"What's the *matter* with you?" demanded Ellen.

"I want to go home," said Laura, drearily.

"Cheer up," said Patrick behind them. "You *are* home. Didn't you hear those songs? Right out of our heads, every one of them. Or do you think somewhere in the Secret Country people talk in Scottish accents?"

"Patrick," said Ellen, "shut up. You promised Ruth."

"But there's new *evidence*."

"I don't care."

"You'd make a terrible scientist," said Patrick, in his most scathing tones.

"Thank you," said Ellen, and did him a courtesy.

"You *deserve* this!" said Patrick. "You deserve to be stuck in a crazy hallucination. But why me?"

"I don't know," said Ellen, in a tone Laura had very seldom heard her employ. "*I* could certainly do without *you*."

And taking Laura by the arm as if they were about to begin a dance, she walked her away from the fire.

The next day they came down out of the wooded hills, and began walking, with no great fervor, across the grassy miles and miles and miles before the mountains of the Secret Country's southern border. Every once in a while the land would fold itself around a stream or spring, and there would be a few trees. But the army used these only for camping, not to walk through the shade of them. The sky was like a bowl of glass Laura had seen just before High Castle's glassblower cooled it, and all around them grasshoppers creaked and bounced.

Something in the weather or the landscape seemed to be having a depressing effect on everyone. Last night, everybody except Laura and Randolph had seemed to be having a good time. But this morning, said Patrick, who came back from wherever he was supposed to be and walked with Laura and Ellen, you would have thought everyone had been drinking too much.

He said Fence and Randolph were grumpy and had infected Ted. It was getting hot by this time, and Laura decided that Fence and Randolph must have infected Patrick, who was infecting her and Ellen. They had a few sharp exchanges, and soon became too disgusted even for that. They marched along in a glum silence. It got hotter and dustier, but somehow no nearer lunchtime.

"What's wrong with everybody?" said Laura to Ellen. "I thought in the old days when war was a good thing everybody used to go to it singing."

"I dunno," said Ellen.

"They're still going to get killed," Patrick said in his reasonable way, "and dead is dead, whether they get you with an arrow or an H-bomb."

"But for a good reason," said Laura.

"What's a good reason?"

"Defending the Secret Country from monsters," said Ellen promptly. She looked ready for argument, and Laura sighed. "Not to mention," added Ellen, "that weird Border Magic."

"Weird isn't the word for that," said Patrick. "We can't even wait until we're sure they're an enemy; we have to go fight them outside in case they are."

Laura was alarmed. She reminded herself that this was only Patrick.

"I've been reading up on the Dragon Wars," Patrick went on, "and one historian thinks that dragons aren't really evil, but ever since the Dwarves cheated them in that deal over the Fabulous Mines, they've wanted their revenge."

Laura thought of the dragon smiting the Secret House with fire. If Claudia had been in the house at the time, you could hardly call that an evil deed.

"Why should they go bothering us?" said Ellen. "We aren't Dwarves, and they don't have to come this way to get the Dwarves; the Dwarves live on the southern islands. Or they're supposed to," she added, with the caution that three months of unpleasant surprises had instilled in all of them.

"We probably look like Dwarves to the dragons," said Patrick.

"We don't look anything like them!" said Laura. She watched Patrick decide to bypass the chance for an insult.

He said patiently, "Dwarves and people look more like one another than like dragons; just like a mouse and a hamster look a lot alike to you."

"I can tell a mouse from a hamster!"

"Can you tell a hawk from a handsaw?" said Ellen, but both of them ignored her.

"That's because you've had a scientific upbringing," said Patrick.

"I have not! I just looked at them."

"Observation, that's the scientific method."

"Observation means looking?"

"Yes."

"Okay, that's how I said the dragons could tell us from the Dwarves!"

There was a dusty silence.

"What would you like to sing?" asked Patrick.

But Laura, on reflection, did not want to sing anything.

When they stopped for lunch, Ellen dragged Laura with her to ask Fence about the villainy, or lack thereof, of the dragons. They found him standing at the head of the army's line, looking southward and shaking his head.

"What's the matter?" asked Ellen.

"The spies have been withdrawn," said Fence, "but there is some presence here that mislikes me. Perhaps the Dragon King hath us in his looking glass."

"Wait a minute," said Ellen. "Why didn't all these spies set off the Border Magic? They're enemies, aren't they?"

"The Border Magic regardeth enemies in arms," said Fence, still looking south. Laura looked that way herself, but saw only the long green plains of grass, with a smudge on the very horizon that might be dust, or the mountains.

"Fence," said Ellen, "Patrick says the dragons aren't evil."

"Nor are they," said Fence, looking faintly surprised.

"Well, why do they fight for the Dragon King?"

"They do not."

"Well, who *does* fight for him if his own subjects won't? Why won't they?"

"I think I must speak to Matthew on the matter of thy education," said Fence, not smiling. "The Dragon King is the Dragon King; he is not King of the Dragons."

"Who is, then?"

"Belaparthalion."

"Oh!" said Laura.

"And why do you call him the Dragon King if he isn't—"

"He is a shapechanger, and the dragon's the shape that best pleaseth him."

"What do the dragons think of that?" said Laura, thinking of what dragons could do when displeased.

"Ask not a wizard for the mind of a dragon," said Fence.

"I don't suppose they'd help *us*, because they don't like him?"

"It is not their task to help us," said Fence. "It may be their task to destroy us at the end."

"Oh," said Laura, hollowly.

"Well, by what three things may the Secret Country be destroyed?" Fence asked her, a little impatiently.

"The Border Magic," she said, that being the only answer she knew.

"The Crystal of Earth," said Ellen, boldly.

"And," said Fence, smiling on them now, "the Whim of the Dragon."

"I hate that!" said Ellen. Laura suspected her of hating this sudden presentation of new and contrary information about the Secret Country, but Fence of course could not know what she meant.

"Think not, three things may destroy us," he said to her, "but rather, a milliard things may not: not flood nor earthquake nor plague nor sorcery; not even the jests of the unicorns."

"Are dragons terribly whimsical?" said Ellen, dubiously.

"Ask not a wizard," repeated Fence. He looked south again, and after a moment Laura and Ellen crept away. Ellen was furious, and Laura thoughtful.

"Let's go find Matthew," she said, "and get educated."

Matthew was with Randolph, arguing with him about the fire-letters they had found in Shan's journals. He wanted to cast them into the fire and play a piece of music traditionally associated with Shan, in the hope that whatever information was in them could be gotten out and thought about before the battle. Randolph, who seemed to have fewer doubts about the battle than did Matthew, wanted to save the fire-letters, do more research, and risk them to the wrong music only in a slow and orderly fashion. Laura and Ellen stood silently until this argument had begun for the third time, in different words.

Then Ellen said, "Excuse me!"

They looked around and smiled.

"Fence was criticizing our education," said Ellen, "so we thought we should get some more from you before we talked to him again."

"Well?" said Matthew.

"Are dragons terribly whimsical?"

"No; that is why we are in the keeping of the Dragon's Whim."

"And there won't be any dragons in this battle?"

"Only in seeming."

"Is it easy to break the Crystal of Earth?"

"How thy thoughts run on doom!" said Randolph, laughing. "Now, I promise you, that even though the Outside Powers rise again there shall be no dragons in the battle; that the Dragon King's army shall not breach the Border Magic, for we will be there before it; and that not Chryse herself could break the Crystal of Earth, even were half the Queen's Council not between it and her. Are you satisfied?"

"Thank you," said Ellen, so Laura had to go away with her, though she was not satisfied at all. She wanted to ask about Belaparthalion, King of the Dragons, and what might make him smite the Secret House with fire. She wanted especially to know whether he had done it already, or if it was still to come. She had seen somebody reading a book about it; but perhaps the book was still to come.

"So," said Ellen, as they went to find Agatha and their lunch, "Patrick couldn't have broken the Crystal of Earth because the Secret Country wasn't destroyed, and so what he did break wasn't the Crystal of Earth."

"It was something, though," said Laura, remembering that frozen moment when the Secret Country had faded around her and she had seen again the dusty concrete of the Midwestern town she and Ted had been exiled to. "We almost went home when he did it."

CHAPTER 11

FOR the next five days of the march, it rained. Sometimes it rained in a fine drizzle; sometimes in great sad drops that went down your back when you bent to lace up your boot, and hit the flint and tinder just as you were striking a spark, and plopped onto your wrist when you put your arm out of your bedroll in your sleep, and went into your eyes when you looked up to see if it was raining. Randolph put his whistle away because the damp was bad for it; Matthew got a sore throat; and Fence told worse stories, both in quality and in scariness, than any of them had ever heard in summer camp.

Whether from the stories or from some other cause, Ted began to have bad dreams. He would find himself on a vast plain where red eyes came at him out of the blackness and unseen things chuckled evilly. When he pulled his sword out they shrieked with laughter, and when he slashed at them they vanished. A wind came up with sobbing voices in it, and pulled the sword out of his grasp. He ran crazily after it through the howling air until he came upon a man in a dragon mask, gray and intricate with red eyes, who held the sword and cut with it letters in the ground. Ted could not read them. They were in the alphabet of the Secret Country, and he could not remember it.

After dreaming this dream four nights running, he could

remember their shapes, though he still did not understand them. On the sixth night of the march, when they had camped by a little wood, he got Ruth to come with him after supper to a patch of moss he had found, and he cut the letters in the moss with his sword and asked her to read them.

She knelt, looking, in her brown tunic and leggings, more like his cousin than she had in some time, and squinted at them. "The mask," she said hesitantly, "of a prince, on the face of a beggar. I think. That's in the older alphabet and I don't really know it very well." She looked up at him. "Where did you get this?"

"I dreamed it."

"What do dreams mean here?"

"I don't know."

"Maybe it's just a nice psychological dream," said Ruth consolingly. "It means you feel like an impostor. Which is silly, but perfectly natural."

"I don't know," said Ted. "The other dream I had here meant something. And the man with the sword had a mask on, too."

A drop of rain went down Ruth's back, and she shivered vigorously. "I almost miss Australian weather, " she said, standing up.

"Do you think I should ask Fence about the dream?"

"I don't guess it could hurt," said Ruth. She eyed him speculatively. She had been several inches taller than he was to begin with, and had grown this summer, so she could do this impressively. "Just don't go trying to confess to him. He has enough on his mind without thinking you're losing yours."

"I don't know," said Ted slowly. "I think he's the only person here who might understand what happened to us."

"What good would it do?" demanded Ruth. "We'd still

have to fight this battle. And we know too much for a bunch of strangers from another universe. They'd think we were dangerous and I don't like to think what they do with people they think are dangerous."

"I know, I know." Ted hesitated. "Do you suppose Patrick's right about us?"

"Sure," said Ruth. "Look at what a good time you're having. Look at how happy you are. Look at me queening it over the army and being carried in a litter and pampered to death. Patrick thinks too much; such men are dangerous."

Ted was unable to reply to a combination of sarcasm and Shakespeare, but he was not altogether reassured.

When they got back to the camp, the guards on its perimeter, and the boys carrying water, and the men putting up the tents, looked at them with surmise, and with unpleasant expressions. They looked at one another with shock.

"We forgot," said Ted.

"Fence'll kill us, especially after that kiss at the coronation."

"How long were we gone?"

"Half an hour?"

"Lovely," said Ted.

Fence bore down upon them with a terrifying expression. Ted refrained from clutching at Ruth, which would only have made matters worse. She took a step toward him and then away again.

"Fence, we forgot," said Ted desperately.

Fence stopped with his mouth open; in itself a sight to dare much for. The hopes this aroused were speedily squashed, however.

"Forgot," he said, as if he were cursing, and meant it to stick.

"Fence," said Ruth, "think how easy it would be for us to forget if we weren't really fond of one another."

Fence was caught again with his mouth open. Ted fought down a wild desire to giggle. "If you are not," said Fence at last, "why all this mummery?"

"What mummery?" said Ted.

"We *were* fond of each other," said Ruth, obviously hating it, "but we stopped being. It was—it was a childish fancy. But we would like to talk to each other occasionally."

"As you did at the coronation?"

"That was an impulse," said Ruth. "Because—because I was most marvelously moved at the ceremony. But if I were secretly in love with Ted, would I be so stupid as to give way to my feelings like that?"

Fence seemed beyond speech, but his mouth quirked.

"Couldn't you tell everyone," said Ruth, "so we can go talk in peace if we want?"

Fence looked as if he had had too much. He put the flat of one hand to his forehead and said, "If this is some stratagem—"

"Fence!" said Ted, before he knew he was going to.

"My lord, I humbly beg your pardon," said Fence instantly.

"I hope so!" Ted felt quite unreasonably enraged, not so much on his own behalf as on that of the absent Edward, for whose existence he might in some wise be responsible, and whose reputation he must uphold.

"Ted," said Ruth, in the tones of the sorcerer she was becoming. She looked both surprised and uneasy.

"Granted," said Ted to Fence, still irked.

"Ted!" said Ruth, in the cousinly voice with which she had always greeted his excesses. Ted remembered, suddenly and vividly, the time he had pushed Ellen into the pond because she let free all the frogs he and Patrick had laboriously collected.

"Never mind," said Fence to Ruth.

"Fence," said Ted, "will you come and look at something?"

"And leave me to deal with Agatha?" said Ruth, in a tone somewhere between scorn and panic.

"Agatha!" said Fence. "Agatha will take you by the hand and thank you heartily, that you have thwarted Benjamin's most untimely plans."

"Okay?" said Ted to Ruth.

"Of a certainty," she said.

Fence and Ted clambered in silence to the patch of moss. Fence knelt, as Ruth had done, and scowled. " 'The visage of a prince,' " he read, " 'on the soul of a villain.' That is from King John's Book."

"Oh," said Ted, wanting to comment on the difference between Ruth's translation and Fence's, but not knowing what it might mean.

"How came this here?" asked Fence.

"I cut it there," said Ted.

"Oh?"

"I dreamed it."

"Oh." Fence walked once around the patch of moss, twitched as a raindrop went down his back, and said, "What else dreamt thou?"

Ted told him. Fence, startlingly, whistled. "What, I wonder, augers that?"

"I hoped you could tell me."

"Great good or great ill," said Fence. He looked at Ted with curiosity. "Dost feel like a villain?"

"No," said Ted, "I feel like a beggar."

Fence was nonplussed, and Ted was not sorry. They paced aimlessly back in the direction of the camp. A cardinal sang suddenly in the wet trees above their heads. They craned their necks and got water in their eyes.

"I am weary of omens," said Fence, "even good ones."

"Why, have you had others?"

"A dream here and there," said Fence.

The bird sang smugly on. The wet black woods dripped. A clammy wind crept along and tugged at their hair. Fence sighed, and Ted tripped on a tree root and fell flat in a puddle.

"Good," said Fence briskly, hauling him out. "All will think I have knocked thee down for thy own good, and be satisfied."

Ted was not amused. Ruth was, and chortled, when she caught sight of them coming back, until Fence remarked that the whole army would be certain that Ted had tried to force her against her will and been suitably punished.

"At least it's a new lie," said Ted sourly.

Fence gave him a sharp look, but said nothing.

After lunch on the next day they came to the mountains, which rose quite abruptly from the flat land, holding up the sky with gray and white and purple cliffs. The army of the Secret Country wound and scrambled to the beginning of the pass they would use out of their domains, and stopped for the night earlier than usual.

Ted dreamed again. He dreamt that he and Lady Claudia sat in a summer garden and drank tea and fed the swans their biscuits. Claudia was offering him all the castles of the Secret Country, and the glory of them; but Ted seemed to have, running beneath his mind like the knowledge of fencing in his first dream here, an appreciation of her crimes considerably larger than his waking knowledge. He had no trouble refusing her. Claudia rose in a rage which did nothing to diminish her beauty, but did upset the table. Amid spilled tea and broken china, she spread her arms and wailed at him like the things in his nightmare of the letters. Her eyes grew red like theirs and the garden faded to a blank white fog. A cold wind blew the fog to tatters, and Ted saw what he took to be the ocean. Shapes began to rise from the crinkled surface of the water.

Ted sat bolt upright in his bedroll, cold with sweat, and kicked Patrick without meaning to.

"Have at you now!" shrieked Patrick, clutching at Ted. He flung himself, bedroll and all, upon his cousin and began to pummel him. Ted shoved a fist out of his eye and put his elbow into Patrick's stomach. The sword of the nearest sentinel hissed out of the scabbard, and he came running, a dark figure with the thin light of the fire in his eyes and on his sword.

"It's all *right!*" yelled Ted. "Don't hurt him!" He administered a soothing punch to Patrick's shoulder and demanded, "Wake up!"

"Uh?" said Patrick.

"Wake up and shut up."

"Oh, no," said Patrick. "Was that you?"

"Well?" said the sentinel, standing over them accusingly.

"Bad dream," said Ted, acutely embarrassed.

The sentinel's disgruntled look began to try to be a smile. "My lords," he said.

Fence strode up, tousled and perplexed. He was fully dressed, however sleepy he might look. "What's the matter now?" he said, in the precise tone of an exasperated parent.

"Bad dream," said Ted.

"Oh?" said Fence, in a different tone entirely, and sent the sentinel away. Ted and Patrick disentangled themselves and worked their ways out of their distorted bedrolls.

"Come to my fire," said Fence, taking each by a shoulder, and they came with him. He had built the fire under an oak tree which presented an alarming collection of shadows in the fitful glow and rustled ominously over them. This gave a certain color to Ted's story and a distinctly grim cast to Patrick's.

Patrick had dreamt that he, not Ted, was killing Randolph in the rose garden. Or at least, that he was trying to kill Randolph. He had dreamt that he was losing, not as a young prince, half-taught, might lose to his teacher, nor even as Patrick with only a few months' training might lose to *his* teacher, but as Patrick Carroll, who had mimed fights with sticks of wood, might lose to a Lord Randolph who never knew him—quickly and ridiculously. Except that Randolph would kill him, and that was worse than ridiculous. Patrick could not tell it to Fence just that way, of course, but Ted had no trouble at all divining what the dream had been and how Patrick had felt.

Fence was puzzled by both dreams. "Both have elements I cannot understand, wherefore I may not tell you what they signify. As with thy dream of the letters in the moss, Edward."

"Could Claudia have sent them?" asked Patrick. "You said she did things with magic that can't be done, so maybe she sends dreams that can't be read."

"Maybe," said Fence. "Maybe."

"Which elements don't you get?" said Ted.

Fence hesitated. "Ah, well," he said, "these are your own dreams, after all. In this of Patrick's, then: the loss of power should come never with the teacher of power. And in thine, Edward, those of the red eyes have naught to do with water, most particularly with the sea."

"And what about my dream of the letters?" said Ted.

"The dragon is not the mask of a prince," said Fence. "Although time was when a prince was the mask of a dragon."

Ted and Patrick exchanged resigned glances, and did not protest when Fence sent them back to bed. Always, always, they must stop asking questions before they understood the answers, lest someone realize how little they knew, how foreign they were, how tenuous their claim was to the powers and privileges they enjoyed daily.

"Wonderful," said Ted to Patrick when they were back in their restored bedrolls. "We can't hide anything around here!"

"You mean the elements he can't understand were from our—our other lives?"

"I think so. I didn't know what he was talking about, but I bet we dream differently than people here do." Ted thought. "We should have asked him what those of the red eyes are. Do you suppose they're the Outside Powers? Benjamin said red was their color."

Patrick was silent. "It felt like Claudia," he said at last.

"What did?"

"The dream. I kept thinking I heard her laughing. I bet she dreams differently than people here, too."

"Why didn't you tell Fence you heard her laughing?"

"Well, she was laughing because I couldn't fence. She knew. She knew about us."

They were silent for a moment. The trees dripped slowly, and over by the fire one sentinel relieved another.

"In my dream, Claudia turned *into* a thing with red eyes," said Ted. "Do you think *she's* an Outside Power?"

"Did we unfurl her when we used Shan's Ring, then?"

said Patrick. He concentrated, assembling memory and information as none of the rest of them was able to do. "Nobody saw her until the Banquet, which was after we used the ring."

"But things were going wrong before then," said Ted, "so she couldn't be responsible for them."

"Why?" said Patrick, bitterly. "Just because she wasn't there? Why should that mean anything? Why should *anything* mean anything? We can't figure out anything, Ted: we don't know the rules."

"I'll try to get more out of Fence tomorrow," said Ted.

It was a long time before he slept.

CHAPTER 12

THE pass through the mountains might have been disappointing to the truly adventurous, but it was a great relief to all five adventurers, none of whom had ever even pretended to be able to climb mountains. The paths grew rocky and narrow, but they were below the snow line all the way. The army came, finally, to the spot where things all went downhill instead of up, and saw a dizzying view of the land beyond the Secret Country.

Laura thought that it looked like a deserted sandbox stuck about with twigs and pebbles. Nothing moved from the end of the mountains to the horizon, except the air shimmering in the heat. Brown and yellow and black the bare land fell to the smudgy line between sand and sky. She could smell dust and rock and heat.

"They say," said Agatha at her shoulder, "that this land, too, once had a Border Magic. Through a double treachery the Dwarves were made to march across its borders, and so it is as you see it."

Neither Laura nor Ellen could find anything to say to this.

They camped in a round valley with a spring in the middle. The floor of the valley sloped back toward the mountains and the stream from the spring ran, seemingly perverse but really natural enough, back toward the mountains to disappear under a cliff.

Laura managed to collar Ted before supper and tell him what Fence and Matthew had said about dragons and the Dragon King. He seemed only mildly interested, and asked her what visions she had seen in things lately. Laura, feeling as though someone had jumped out of a bush at her, remembered the things she had seen in the windows of the Secret House.

"I saw Claudia burying me in the basement of the Secret House," she said, "and I saw five people standing by a stream, in the fog. They looked familiar, but not right. And—I saw Lord Andrew in the North Tower looking at the broken Crystal of Earth."

"Claudia *burying* you?" said Ted, with flattering concern.

"I thought we'd go home before it happened."

"I should hope so!" said Ted, still staring at her. People hurried by them carrying wood and tents. "Or wait," he said. "Maybe it wasn't you. Maybe it was the other one."

"What?"

"Princess Laura."

"I *am* Princess Laura."

"No, the real one."

"Now look."

"Never mind. Come and have supper with me, and bring Ellen. I'm going to ask Fence some things."

The five of them sat around Ted's fire with Fence, Randolph, and Matthew. Randolph and Matthew were still arguing about the fire-letters.

"Fence," said Ted, "could we ask you more about dreams?"

"You may ask, doubtless," said Fence, in a tone more encouraging than his words.

"First," said Ted, "Laurie, tell him about Claudia and the basement."

Laura was mildly put out. That had been not a dream but a vision. And yet she had had dreams also, and would have liked to know what they meant. On the other hand, she would be telling Fence her vision, and that should please the unicorns.

"I dreamed that Claudia was burying me in the cellar of the House by the Well of the White Witch," she said.

Matthew broke off his discussion with Randolph to say something like "Faugh!" in commiserating tones.

"Matthew," said Fence, "hast taught these younger ones aught of dreams?"

"Not yet," said Matthew.

"Know, then," said Fence to Laura, "that this may mean one, or some, or all, of five things. It may be that this hath happened, that it shall happen, that thou fearest it may happen, or that Claudia wishes 'twere so. It may mean only that she wisheth thee harm."

"Does that apply to the dreams Patrick and I had?" Ted asked.

"Not to thine," said Fence. "That was an allegory, I think. Thy brother's, perhaps."

"But couldn't Patrick and Laura's be allegories too?"

Matthew laughed.

"There is a school of thought," said Fence, "holding that all dreams are allegories. I myself have suffered true dreams both of past and things to come, and so I hold not with that school."

"Well, what was mine an allegory of, though?"

"I know not," said Fence, sounding thoroughly troubled, "because of those elements I told thee of yesternight."

"You mean," said Laura, having thought through what Fence told her, "that Claudia *might* kill me and bury me in the cellar?"

"I think we can prevent it," said Fence. He said this quite soberly, as if he were talking to another grown-up, and Laura was satisfied.

Patrick, however, snorted. Fence's head swung around toward him, but Randolph said, "Fence, in what manner have we thus far prevented aught that she chose to do?"

"Well," said Fence, "she hath not yet chosen to lay hands upon any of us."

"She doesn't have to," muttered Patrick. "Action at a distance."

"That is a skill of the Outside Powers," said Fence, very softly.

"She?" said Randolph; even in the firelight they could see him staring.

"If she is of that family, she would not harm a child," said Matthew.

"What if she's gone bad?" demanded Patrick.

"Forgive me; I spoke carelessly. If she is of the family," said Matthew, "she cannot harm a child."

"She'll wait 'til Laura grows up?" said Ellen.

"Were you grown up in the dream?" asked Patrick.

"No."

"Well, then."

"Fence," said Ted, exasperated beyond bearing, "what *are* the Outside Powers?"

"Hush," said Fence. "Speak not that name so loudly."

Patrick snorted again, but nobody heeded him.

"I tried asking Benjamin," said Ted, "but he just told me riddles. And what does it mean that they are rising again?"

"They are a riddle," said Randolph.

"I *know* you know more than that! Why won't you tell me?"

Laura saw Fence and Randolph look across the fire at one another.

" 'Tis a thing kings must know," said Randolph.

Patrick made an explosive noise of profound disgust.

"He said not that *thou* shouldst *not* know," snapped Fence.

Laura stifled a giggle as Ellen poked her gently in the ribs and whispered, "That showed him!"

"But it beareth not upon our present distresses," said Fence.

"But you said at the council that they were rising again, and everybody was upset. It sounded as if it had everything to do with this war!" said Ted.

Fence let his breath out. "Only in the same manner," he said, "that, if our weather-augurers were to tell us, during the month we propose to fight in the desert great dust storms will come. Now dust storms are a thing of nature; the Dragon King bringeth them not. But they have a most potent bearing on the battle: where and how and whether it shall be fought."

"But when you said at the council that the Outside Powers were rising, Benjamin said—"

"Benjamin," said Fence, with finality, "hath concerns past those of the Hidden Land."

Laura watched Ted decide to settle for this, and then tap Patrick on the knee when Patrick shifted and began to speak. She was impressed that Patrick did not go ahead anyway.

"Milady Ruth," said Randolph, "thou art silent."

"I was wondering," said Ruth, abstractedly, "if it was dry enough, my lord, for you to play the whistle."

"I think not," said Randolph.

Everyone else thought not also: there was neither singing

nor story-telling that night. But long after everyone was asleep, someone began to play a flute. It sounded eerie and everywhere, like a cricket in a quiet house.

Laura had been dreaming, again, the dream in which she hurried through an autumn forest listening for a tune. When she heard it, she began to sing to it. Slowly the noise of men starting from their blankets and calling for torches, of sentinels drawing their swords and Fence calling for some book, grew around her, but by the time she realized that she was awake, she had been singing loudly for at least one verse. Ellen and Agatha were sitting up and staring at her. Then they stared past her with even greater shock, and Laura turned around and saw what they had seen.

The musician came out of the woods at the foot of the mountains, glimmering like the moon behind a wisp of cloud. The night was still, but his long dark hair streamed behind him. His cloak flapped but made no sound, his pale clothes were flattened against him, and he walked with his head bent against some great force. The light that came from him did not show up the trees he came from or the ground whereon he walked. He looked like Ruth and Ellen and Randolph. He lifted the flute he carried, and although his face and clothes did not catch the light of the watchfires, the instrument did.

"Who claims this music?" he cried, in a voice so like Randolph's that Laura looked wildly around for him, half convinced that remorse and guilt had sent him mad. But Randolph was standing with Fence beside a fire a little way off. He looked, in the dubious light, perplexed and a little irate, like someone who will be able to remember something if everyone will just keep quiet.

"Who made the claim?" cried the musician.

"Laura," called Fence, gently.

"I know the *song*," said Laura. She felt as if she had spoken out of turn in a word game.

The musician looked across the fire at her. There was a light in his eyes, but it was not firelight. "Who art thou?" he said.

"Laura," said Laura, choked in time over her last name, and added, "Princess of the Secret Country."

"Who taught thee this music?"

Laura, panicked, fell back on the truth. Princess Laura was supposed to have a music master, but Laura had never seen him. "I can't tell you."

"Dimwit!" whispered Ellen. "His name was Nathan."

"Well said," the musician told Laura, "for I cannot tell thee whence came the flute."

He moved across the grass toward her, stepping right over or through the fire. She could not see it through him; it did not cast light upon him; and when it was behind him he cast no shadow forward. He brought a breath of cold air with him.

Laura, pretending valiantly that he was Randolph, stood her ground. He knelt before her on the grass, which meant she could look him in the face, and held out to her across his two palms the shining flute. He had a ring on his finger. The red stone in it was all the color he had.

Laura took the flute. It was cold. "Well," she said; she resented him enormously for so embarrassing her. Then she looked at his long hands and kindly face, and was ashamed of herself. "My lord," she said, "I humbly thank you." And she did him, as well as she could in the short boy's tunic, a courtesy.

The musician stood up and walked away into the forest. He faded through, and not between, the trees.

"*Who was that?*" said Laura, wishing they would not all stare at her.

"Cedric," said Randolph. "He was a wizard and his skill was with sounds. He was the only one of all the wizards in history to master music. He was my six-times great-grandfather." He had started on a pleased note, but he sounded a little shaken by the time he had finished.

Laura remembered the unicorns. They had said that she would play Cedric's flute. Well, here it was. Maybe Ruth could show her how.

"Fence," said Ted, "what does this mean?"

"Rather ask a musician," said Matthew. "The prophecies touching Cedric have come down not from wizards but from bards."

"Well, then?"

"It is said he will save us at the end."

"Is this the end?"

"No doubt," said Fence, dryly; "if it is, seemingly we shall be saved."

Randolph looked at the circle of faces. "Back to your posts and your beds," he said, cheerfully. They went as he bid them. Laura noticed how quiet they all were. They were not discussing what had happened. She wondered why.

Ruth and Ellen came over to her and looked at the flute.

"Can you show me how to play it, Ruth?" said Laura in an urgent whisper. Princess Laura probably knew how already.

"Well, I could try," said Ruth. "Isn't it beautiful?"

Randolph and Fence came over, trailing Ted and Patrick. Most of the others had dispersed; Agatha still lurked, waiting for Ellen and Laura, and Matthew stood beside her.

"May I see it?" said Fence to Laura. She held it out to

him. He took it from her, and she felt him jerk and stiffen as he touched it.

"Well," he said, and his voice caught. "If sorcery can save us at the end, then of a certainty there is enough here to do't." He handed the flute back to Laura. She wondered what he meant. It was very cold to the touch, but it did not prickle as the enchanted swords did. "Guard it well," said Fence.

Laura, accompanied by Agatha and Ellen, took it and put it in her pack. Then she took it out again and got into her bedroll with it.

Fence and Randolph stared at one another in the moon- and firelight, and Ted and Patrick fidgeted. Ruth stood still.

"Fence," said Ted, suddenly, "what about the fire-letters?"

"Well?"

"I mean—if this is a famous flute, and the song means something, if we used it on the fire-letters it might turn out to be right."

"If it were not," said Fence, as he had said to Randolph several times already, "it would be the end of the manuscript, which would burn like any common parchment."

"Couldn't you copy it?" said Ted.

"It would then not be sorcerous. Half its virtue lieth in the substance whereon 'tis inscribed."

"Fence," said Matthew. "It may be—"

"Speak to me in the morning, then," said Fence.

Ruth said in Ted's ear, "For pity's sake, don't get them to ask that child to play the flute! She hasn't any idea how."

"Good grief, I forgot," whispered Ted. "Sorry."

"I should hope so."

Ted turned to find Randolph's eye on them. He did not look angry. Ted was not sure how he looked, but he did not want to see it again. "Randolph," he said. "Could I talk to you for a minute?"

"Of course, my lord," said Randolph.

Ted took him a little way off into the dripping trees. "I just wanted to tell you," he said, "that I don't want to marry Ruth, and Ruth doesn't want to marry me. And," he added, feeling this too brusque, "you're welcome to be happy with her."

It was too dark to see Randolph's face, but he made a startled movement. "This is most convenient, my lord, seeing that I am betrothed to her."

"You don't act like it," said Ted, without thinking. Then he remembered Claudia.

Randolph was quite still. "Well," he said at last, "I am amazed. What is the Lady Ruth's desire?"

"That," said Ted, "you will have to take up with Ruth." He turned to go before he got himself—or Ruth—into any more trouble, and Randolph caught his wrist.

"My lord," he said, "why tell me now?"

"Because," said Ted, his fear coming unbidden to his tongue, "I might not be here to tell you tomorrow."

Randolph's grip on his wrist bit like a manacle. "Not while I have breath—in which case it would not matter."

"I know," said Ted, suddenly close to tears, "but still."

"Edward," said Randolph, "who art thou?"

Ted was too startled even to jump, but he was sure Randolph could feel the shocked blood pounding in the wrist he held.

"You know as well as I do."

"Maybe," said Randolph.

"If that's too little," said Ted, truthfully, "you can't be sorrier than I am."

"No?"

"What do you want?" cried Ted.

"That thou shouldst tell me who thou art."

"I'm the King," said Ted, desperately.

"And what am I?"

Ted's throat hurt as if he had been running.

"Thou knowest quite well. Now, is it meet that a king should give his cousin to a—"

"Be quiet!" shouted Ted. "I will not hear this!" So he had said, playing; so Edward would say when Randolph was finally accused of having poisoned the King. "I am the King and I give what I like."

Randolph let go of him. "And see naught but what liketh thee?"

Ted felt all the shame that ought to be felt by a king who was willing to marry his cousin to a murderer. In the damp dark of the woods his face burned. He still found it very hard to think of Randolph as a murderer, or of his treachery as wrong; but Randolph did think of these things thus. There was, of course, no question of Ruth's marrying anybody here; and Ted did not want to marry Ruth: so telling the truth had seemed a harmless way of making things easier. But he certainly could not say that to Randolph.

Randolph seemed to mistake his silence. He said, "Consider this. Fence squeezed from the napkins that wine you spilled from my hand." He looked at Ted's face, and his mouth twisted. "And he gave it to Matthew, who is something of an alchemist. And he did find therein, not a poison, but an antidote therefor."

"Andrew was mad because I spilled his antidote?"

"So 'twould seem."

"But how'd he know there'd be anything for it to be an antidote *for*? I mean, it makes sense he didn't want the King killed, because the King agreed with him, but—"

"I know not," said Randolph.

Ted barely heard this. Coldness had washed through him. "Oh, God," he said. "Shan's mercy, my lord. If I hadn't spilled the antidote the King would've drunk that with the poison."

Randolph nodded. His face was impassive. He watched Ted as if Ted were a pan of fudge about to lose its shine.

"This is awful," said Ted. He had killed the King. The one part of the game they had tried most earnestly to change, he himself had accomplished. He began to laugh, painfully and found that tears were running down his face.

"So close were we come to immediate salvation and final doom," said Randolph. "But see you that Andrew, on whom Fence would most quickly put the blame, is now safe from it?"

Ted wiped his eyes.

"So have a care," said Randolph, "that you use me not in your deeper-laid plans. I will not be here."

They turned and went in silence back to the camp.

CHAPTER 13

THE army of the Dragon King was two days late. This seemed to afford great satisfaction to Fence and Randolph, and to unsettle Andrew considerably.

"Maybe he *is* a spy of the Dragon King," said Ted to Patrick, in the middle of the second day. It was too hot to do anything in particular, even if their nervousness would have allowed them to be interested.

"I think so," said Patrick. "I've been talking to the Peonies—that's his company—and they're mad at him because he told them the army was leaving two days later than it did, and Conrad yelled at *them*, not Andrew, for not being ready."

They had learned a little about the organization of the army. Its smallest unit seemed to be called a company, to consist of twenty-four men, and to be named after a flower. The companies were collected into fellowships, which were named after jewels, and the fellowships into orders, which were named after trees. This was the mundane army; how the sorcerers were organized, how the two were to be combined, and who exactly was running things, they did not know. Most of the King's counselors commanded mere companies, Conrad being the notable exception.

"And who told Andrew?" asked Ted.

"I don't know, but I'll bet it was Fence."

"He did take Laura seriously when she said Andrew was a spy."

"Not seriously enough, or he wouldn't let Andrew keep that company."

"Couldn't he put it where it can't do any harm?"

"If he can afford to waste twenty-four men, sure."

"How big *is* the Dragon King's army?"

Patrick looked at him, and looked away.

"How'd you get the Peonies to talk to you?" said Ted hastily.

"Childish blandishments," said Patrick, grinning, and showed Ted a blue-eyed stare that made him look closer to ten than to thirteen.

"What?"

"Never mind," said Patrick, looking secretive.

There seemed no conversation possible that did not suddenly develop pitfalls.

"Let's go practice fencing," said Ted.

On the third day, the day they expected the Dragon King, Fence got them all up before dawn. Ted sat hunched over a fire, eating lumpy oatmeal brought to him by Agatha, and watched the clear red light chase the stars down behind the mountains. It was chilly. The mountains looked forbidding, and the bare land before them parched and miserable in the growing light. Ted had a cold knot in the center of his stomach, which the oatmeal did nothing to alleviate. He wondered how soon he would be killed.

There was a great deal of purposeful bustle going on, which no one had bothered to explain to him. Ted became irritated. Even if your minions had it all their own way, they might do you the courtesy of telling you what they were up to. Thinking of minions reminded Ted of Ellen, and he thought of going and telling her once more that she was not to fight in the battle. But if he insulted her by the reminder, she might go just to spite him.

In the end he found Agatha. She was wearing a sword, which suited her very well, and building up fires, which suited her equally well. I bet she *was* a good Queen's Counselor, thought Ted. I wonder why the King didn't want her.

"The Lady Ellen," he said to her, "has thoughts of fighting in the battle."

The moment he had said it he was sorry. This was the ultimate betrayal: going to a grown-up to solve a problem. Especially in the Secret, even if it was not the Secret they knew, it seemed reprehensible. But surely letting Ellen get herself killed would be worse. Agatha looked at him with resignation, and assured him that Ellen would be far too busy with carrying water and rolling bandages to sneak off to the battle. Ted thanked her and crept off to be collared by Fence and Randolph.

Both of them seemed perfectly calm, though Ted did notice, again, that Randolph was thinner than he had been and looked as if his head hurt. If it did, this did not stop him from giving Ted and Patrick a brisk and compressed lecture on how they were to conduct themselves during the battle. Ted was to fight with Matthew's company, whose badge was a bloom of lilac. He was to stay with the company. People wearing a yellow feather were messengers: if one told him to do something, he was to do it; and if he saw anything amiss, he was to find a messenger and so inform him. Patrick was to do likewise, except that he would be with Benjamin's company, whose badge was a daisy.

Ted, receiving these instructions silently, thought of his mother, when he was much younger, delivering him to a birthday party with mild reminder not to throw the present at Adam Simmons no matter what Adam said to him; to say "please" when he wanted something and "thank you" when he was given something, whether he wanted it or not; and to inform his hostess he had had a nice time even if he had hated every child there and his dumb sister Laura could have made a better cake.

These reflections made him feel worse rather than better.

They left a body of soldiers with the camp and moved the main army out a mile or so into the desert, since the surveyors they had brought were not as sure as they ought to have been about where the borders of the Secret Country were. Randolph, most uncharacteristically, snapped at them, and was rewarded with a lecture from Fence concerning the possible actions of sorcery upon geography. Patrick, whom Ted and Fence and Randolph had collected on their way, shut his mouth on the suggestion that this was because none of the five children who had made up this story knew the first thing about surveying, doing so in such a way that Ted knew exactly what he was not saying. This did not improve Ted's temper.

When the army was safely into the desert it sat down and waited. Ted saw people playing cards and dice and chess, and other things he did not recognize.

"They must be crazy," said Patrick.

He sounded so resentful that Ted stared at him. Patrick was scared, too. This was alarming. Ruth was the only one of his three cousins who had ever seemed to be afraid of anything. It was probably good for Patrick to be frightened, but Ted wished he had not noticed it.

"Cheer up," he said stiffly. "It isn't real, after all."

"There's nothing either good nor bad," said Patrick, venomously, "but thinking makes it so."

"Start thinking, then," said Ted, and walked away before

he could say something nastier, or be sorry he had said anything.

He almost fell over Randolph and Fence, who sat a little apart, drawing lines in the sand and putting pebbles on them and murmuring to each other.

"Those don't look like any battle plans I ever saw," said Ted over Fence's shoulder.

"This is wizardry," said Fence tranquilly. "I have neglected my apprentice of late."

Ted looked at the ring on Randolph's finger.

"What ails thee?" Fence asked him, without even looking around.

"I'm nervous," said Ted truthfully, and sat down in the sand.

"This will occupy your mind," said Fence, and shifted so Ted could see. "These are spells of opening and closing. When thou comest to cast them," he said to Randolph, "'twere best thou hold the patterns in thy mind. To draw the runes is to do much damage. The Dragon King draweth runes for them, and he shattereth mountains."

"Oh, wonderful!" said Ted. "Could he shatter us, too, if he liked?"

"No," said Fence crisply, "he could not—not in this manner. Where is thy scholar's abstraction? That is not the point."

"Fence, have some heart," said Randolph.

"That is neither for scholars nor for wizards," said Fence, with an austerity that seemed to chill the growing heat of the desert.

"And for friends?" said Randolph. Ted looked away from his searching and ironic eyes.

Fence flung his hands up. "You are both a trial," he said.

"No doubt," said Randolph.

Ted, seeing far away something even worse than the look in Randolph's eyes, sprang to his feet, scattering sand. "Look!"

They looked to the east, squinting at the early sun. Crawling across the desert were a line of black specks and a cloud of dust. Crawling across the sky was another line of specks. Fence and Randolph snatched up helmet and sword and were gone in opposite directions, shouting. Ted looked down at the pattern they had left in the sand, and shivered.

The Lilacs, when they came to fetch him, seemed rather preoccupied and subdued. Ted had somehow expected them to be pleased that theirs was the company chosen to fight with the King. A very little reflection, as they trudged to their appointed place in the desert between the Daisies and the Mallows, showed him that this expectation had been foolish. They might be blamed if anything happened to him. Even if his protection was delegated solely to Matthew, that would keep Matthew from doing whatever else he was supposed to do as captain of a company. Ted was a charge and a nuisance, that was all. Well, Edward wouldn't have been any better; he was much shyer than Ted and hated fighting.

Matthew, having arranged his men in a peculiar pattern that made no sense at all to Ted, came up to him and smiled the smile of a parent who was about to take you in for a tetanus booster because you could not remember what you had stepped on.

"Hast been told of shape-shifters?" said Matthew.

They were always harder to understand when they got excited or worried. "I don't think so," said Ted.

"To kill them once sufficeth not; thou must kill each of their shapes."

"How many do they have?" asked Ted, saw the face of

the scholar begin to overtake Matthew's soldierly mask, and added quickly, "Generally?"

"Seven or nine," said Matthew.

"Great."

"The spies say there are many."

"Great," said Ted, and was immediately sorry. This wasn't Matthew's fault.

Matthew looked down at him without anger. His fair skin was already red with the heat. "I wish for my books also," he said softly.

Ted found it easy to smile at him. This was what Patrick would call a lovely irony. The last thing Ted wished for was his books. He was in one of his books, in the most exciting chapter of all, and wished earnestly to be—where? Not back at the Barretts', being polite and watching television. Not even on the Pennsylvania farm, playing at war in the meadow. He was extremely frightened; but while he wished he was somewhere else, he could not think where.

"All may yet be very well," said Matthew, as if he wished it were something better.

"My lord," said one of his men, in the tone of somebody asking for the salt. "They come."

The battle was not like a riot. Ted could not see what in the world he was doing, nor very much of what anyone else was trying to do to him.

Matthew's carefully laid-out pattern disintegrated within ten minutes. In that time, three squat scaled things came at Ted, who swung at them all and missed, and were dispatched by Matthew.

"Aim lower!" shouted Matthew. He was two feet away and Ted could barely hear him. The din was unbelievable, worse than the tornado that had flattened the old barn three years ago. It had that huge rattling sound like a train, compounded with the sound of six hundred three-year-olds beating on pots with spoons, shrieks, growls, and hisses as of a record-breaking cat fight, and other screams that were like nothing Ted had ever heard and that obliterated instantly what little levity he had left in him.

He swiped the sword at another scaled creature, obediently aiming lower, and succeeded in changing it into an enormous snake. He managed to cut off this one's head, but not with any of the moves so painstakingly taught him by Randolph. He used the good, solid motion his mother had shown him when he demanded to be allowed to chop wood.

The snake fell into two pieces and the churned sand around it darkened with green. Somebody else must have killed it several times already, or else the Dragon King was using cut-rate monsters.

"Edward!" yelled Matthew.

Ted stopped staring and backed up hastily while Matthew killed the wolf that had sprung at him. Matthew actually did use a fencing move, except that he had altered it by— The wolf disintegrated quietly into a shower of stones, Matthew shouted again, urgently, and Ted stopped thinking.

Once he had cleared his mind, the sword seemed to come to life; or more likely, that undercurrent of knowledge from Edward was able to work its way up and direct his arm. Every time he tried to analyze what he was doing, he missed his aim and had to be rescued by Matthew. After the third rescue, Ted stopped trying to analyze anything. The day grew hotter. What Ted remembered best of the morning was just the acute discomfort of sun and sweat and thirst and the irritating way his helmet-strap rubbed his ear.

Fence found him at noon, said six short words which disposed of the snaky thing he was fighting, and made him come back to camp and have something to eat. Laura brought it to him, staring at his sword and clothes.

"Who's winning?" asked Ted through a mouthful of dust. It was the first thing he had said since, "Look!"

Fence shrugged, scattering sand and debris from his shoulders. Thin in the background against the vast silence of the desert the noise of the battle went on. Ted felt a reluctance to go back to it akin to the reluctance one has to go on hiking after a rest stop. He felt torpid. Fence got up and went away.

"Where's Ellie?" Ted asked Laura.

"Washing bandages," said Laura to the ground.

"You'll stop her, won't you, if she tries to go fight?"

"Agatha won't let her," said Laura, but this seemed to have been the right thing to say. At least she looked at him.

"She's too quick for Agatha," said Ted, and Laura smiled at him.

Fence came back with pen and paper and a writing-board. "The enemy's sorcerers being for the moment discomposed," he said, "and Conrad having the soldiers well in hand, 'tis time for thy challenge to the Dragon King."

"What?"

"Who hath conducted thy education?" said Fence, despairingly.

"You can't mean challenge the Dragon King to single combat?"

"Thou needst not fight thyself," said Fence. "Thou hast a champion, my lord."

"Well, who?"

"I for the arcane, Randolph for the mundane."

"Great," said Ted, but he took the materials. In the end Fence, having explained that the single combat was to spare any more slaughter than had already taken place, and having failed to explain why it was not issued before any slaughter had happened, had to dictate the letter to him. He wondered what Fence would think of the Roman alphabet, but Fence, scanning the paper when Ted had done, seemed not to think it strange. He went off to arrange for its delivery.

"Laurie," said Ted, "do you remember anything about a challenge?"

"Only once or twice," said Laura. "We had to stop having the single combat after you stuck Patrick in the shoulder with the branch, because the Dragon King got to choose the weapon, and Patrick wouldn't choose anything smaller. And then for a while we said that *Edward gave* the challenge, but the Dragon King didn't care about honor so he refused it. And then it seemed dumb to give it if we couldn't have the fight, so we just stopped."

"But nothing about a king's champion?"

"Uh-uh."

"Oh, well," said Ted, "I should give up expecting things."

"That's easy," said Laura. "It's the unexpected things that are the trouble."

"Have you been seeing things again?"

"No. But there was one I forgot to tell you." And she told him about the dragon burning the Secret House, and about the man with the book, reading about the dragon burning the Secret House, that she had seen on the steps leading to the enchanted armory below Fence's tower.

"Belaparthalion," said Ted. "I've heard that before."

"They did a song about it the other night. And Fence said Belaparthalion was the King of the Dragons."

"No, before that. I've got it. At the council after Fence came back. Andrew said he couldn't accuse Fence of treachery because anybody could have told somebody something, I forget who or what. And Fence said not just anybody could, and he asked Andrew if Belaparthalion had honored us with his presence."

"Huh," said Laura.

"And that's not all. Randolph and Belaparthalion had to be raised or consulted or something before the coronation. But we had the coronation all right, and there certainly wasn't a dragon there. I think that's what he said." Ted scowled. "Yes, that's right. He said that we had to wait for Chryse and raise Belaparthalion."

"Chryse?" said Laura.

"What's the matter?"

"I know Chryse; it's a unicorn; I talked to it the day of the Hunt."

"You what?"

"That's why I started telling you all these things I see; Chryse said to."

"If I'd known *that* I wouldn't have waited so long to tell Fence about them," said Ted. "We'd better do that right away."

Lord Randolph, looking as if someone had emptied a flour sack over his head, came back to them and sat down heavily upon a stump. "Thy challenge hath been delivered," he said. "Stay yet a while for the answer."

"Where's Fence?" said Ted.

Randolph's mouth twisted. "Battling some kitchen-wizard. Better he left such work to his apprentices."

Ted and Laura looked at one another. Ted shrugged, and Laura shook her head.

"What do you know about visions?" Ted asked Randolph.

"More than I care to," said Randolph.

"Well, Laurie's been having them."

Randolph looked at Laura, who looked at his foot.

"Of what nature?"

"If I look at a light or a fire, or something reflecting off something, then I see things."

"What manner of things?"

Laura, sounding as if she were reciting a list of the principal exports of Brazil, reeled off the things she had seen. Ted noticed that she did not mention the sight of him covered with blood on a field of battle.

"All the stars in heaven," said Randolph, staring. "First that, and now the flute. Child, what art thou?"

"What do they mean?" said Laura, her voice quavering.

"Thou hast seen naught bearing on this present battle?"

"No," said Laura, firmly. Ted opened his mouth and closed it again. Maybe she had a good reason.

"We must tell Fence of this, when all is done," said Randolph, "and he can tell thee, better than I, what these things purport." He looked thoughtfully at Laura, who appeared ready to cry. "Thou art safer having them than not," he said, and pushed a loosening ribbon back up on one of her braids. Ted, who had heard Agatha scolding Laura for doing that very thing instead of retying the bow, grinned.

A page came up calling Randolph's name, and he excused himself to them and went off.

"Why didn't you—" began Ted.

"Because we can't tell him we know you'll be okay, and he'd just worry, or not let you go back."

"Which might not be such a bad thing," said Ted.

"Don't you want to finish the story?"

"Good God!" said Ted. "Doesn't anybody but me take any of this seriously? Why should I want to get killed and go to the land of the dead?"

Laura looked at him soberly. Her braids, as well as losing their ribbons, were coming undone, and her face was dirty. "Is it really awful?" she asked him.

"How should I know. I've never been there."

"No, I mean the battle."

"I don't know," said Ted, slowly, "there isn't time to think about whether it's awful."

"Because the people we're taking care of, some of them are hurt, and it *is* awful; but most of them act more like they're crazy. They sound like we did in that grass, yelling about things that aren't there."

"I guess the mundane part is doing better than the arcane."

"What?"

"The unmagic part of our army is doing better than the magical part."

"So Fence will have to fight the challenge?"

"I don't know."

They sat in silence until Randolph came back with a message from the Dragon King. Ted could not read it, but it was clear from what Randolph said that the challenge had been refused, and not politely.

"Well," said Ted, handing his cup to Laura and standing up, "I guess I should get back." You sound like an office worker, he told himself.

Randolph looked at him thoughtfully and came with him without a word. From a distance, the battle looked different. The army of the Secret Country appeared to have driven the Dragon King's some way back into the desert and seemed to be herding the Dragon King's soldiers in the direction of a great outcropping of rock that stood up above the sand like a spoon in a bowl of cornmeal mush. For somebody who had been able to choose his ground, the Dragon King was not doing very well. But no; he had not been able to choose his ground, because Fence had gotten here first.

Close up things were the same as ever, except that it was hotter now and everything seemed to move much more slowly.

Ted had been dimly aware, in the morning, that Matthew was saving him from any number of unpleasant fates. But now he could examine every stroke. Randolph was much faster than either he or Matthew was, and, obviously, much faster than most of the enemy, too. Ted felt a sudden acute fear for Patrick, with no one to protect him and less reason to fight well. But someone came at him, and there was no more time for thought.

The monsters had dwindled. It was mostly men now. The sword was more use against them, and Edward's knowledge in the back of Ted's mind grew stronger. Ted put the sword through the face of the third person who attacked him, and stared horror-struck at the result.

"Young fool!" said Randolph, pulling him behind a rock. "An he were but a little quicker, such a stroke had left thee open to be gutted."

Ted, the image of the man he had killed still before his eyes, looked away from Randolph's wrathful, dusty face to what he had thought another rock, saw that it was someone who had in fact been gutted, and threw up.

"I know," said Randolph, offering him a filthy rag with which to wipe his mouth, "but 'twill do thee no good neither to make thyself weak and dizzy." He hauled Ted to his feet. "This is no time to stand chattering. Guard thyself better in future."

They came out from behind the rock again and found themselves in the midst of a mixed group of Mallows and Peonies. The men themselves were filthy, their helmets scratched and dented and covered with sand, their sashes slashed and thick with a mud composed of dust and blood rather than water. But on each helmet and each sash the little embroidered flower shone clear and clean. The badges must be magical. Ted thought of all those women, warriors and counselors in their own right, and probably sorcerers too, sitting in High Castle sewing because the ruler was a man. It seemed a very odd way to run a country.

He shook his head sharply and tried to attend to what was going on. They were in a little pocket of quiet, but the sound of the battle was still immense. One of the Peonies wore a yellow feather and was talking so fast to Randolph that Ted could not understand him. He plucked the nearest Mallow by the sash.

"Please, what is it?"

"Conrad," said the young man. His look at Ted was compounded of curiosity, reluctance, sympathy, and speculation. "He's sore hurt."

"Oh, God," said Ted. He stood very still and did not try to remember whom the game had killed. Then he took three steps and stood as close to Randolph as he could get.

"I will serve better where I am," said Randolph to the messenger. "Do you find Jerome—and you, Stephen, go as quickly as you may to the camp and bring Agatha. I weary of this waste."

"Aye, my lord," said the messenger, a little dubiously, and made off into the desert.

Stephen, the young man whom Ted had asked what was going on, frowned, looked at Ted, looked back at Randolph, and followed the messenger.

"Randolph," said Ted, in a tone of voice he had not known he possessed. "Go where you're needed."

The hovering Mallows and Peonies melted away from around them as cats leave the room when people began to quarrel. Randolph's green eyes regarded Ted calmly from out of his sweat- and dust-striped face.

"I am there now," said Randolph. "Use me while yet you may." And he caught Ted by the wrist and pulled him toward the retreating Peonies. A yelling crowd of little pale men in red rose up suddenly out of the rocks, and it was not possible to argue. Ted gave his mind back to Edward's impulses and let the sword do what it would.

Laura watched Ted and Randolph walk away, and put the cup down on the ground. She thought of the coronation, of Claudia and the cellar, of Ted in the land of the dead, where he did not want to go after all, and of Ellen grumbling and fingering her sword-belt as she washed the bloody bandages. She drew the stolen sword from its scabbard. It blazed like a lightning bolt even in the bright air before the desert. The prickling previously absent shot up her arm and shoulder, and suddenly she felt that she knew all about fighting.

"I'll show you," she said to all of them, and went after Ted and Randolph.

The shrieking cacophony of the battle would have frightened her into going back, had it not seemed to have an almost magnetic effect on the sword. Laura had to run to keep it from pulling her arm out of joint; it was like being run away with by a very large, energetic, and invisible dog whose leash you held. The sword did not seem to care whether there was a path for Laura, as long as the space it had to go through was clear; but she managed to keep her feet until it zipped over a rock almost as tall as she was, which caught her painfully in the chest and left her breathless.

"Wait!" croaked Laura. The sword, more obedient than such a dog, promptly stopped pulling, although it quivered in her hand.

"What are you *after?*" said Laura; she could hardly hear herself in the din, nor see more than a few yards for the dust.

But in those few yards she saw more than enough. Ted and Randolph were battling five or six very tall men with braided yellow hair, and bare chests, leather trousers, and high boots. For a moment Laura thought everything would be all right, seeing Randolph deal three of them wounds that certainly looked as if they ought to be mortal.

But as each man went down he blurred and wavered and became a small dark woman in leather armor; and as those were injured they turned into large fox-like creatures; and when they crumpled up bloodily they became inky shadows with red eyes, hugging the ground. Ted's and Randolph's swords went into them and came out smoking, but the shadows seemed none the worse for that.

The sword tugged at Laura. "All right," she said to it, "and we'll show those visions, too."

She came out from behind the rock, and thrust the sword at the nearest red eye. The creature made a bubbling noise horribly like one of the purple beasts', shriveled up, and sank slowly into the ground, like spilled motor oil. Laura slashed at one that was pulling itself up Randolph's leg, and it followed the first. The sword wrenched her around and did in two more. Randolph shouted behind her, and she spun and dispatched the last one. It did not seem to matter in the least where the sword touched them.

"Laura Kimberly Carroll!" said Ted. "What the hell are you doing here?"

"*I* didn't swear you an oath," said Laura, and was satisfied.

"Edward!" said Randolph behind her, and thrust her against the rock. She heard more than felt the crack of her head against it, and doubled over, clutching her head in her arms. It took some time for the pain to wear off. When she looked up again, Randolph was fighting a tall man in green, and Ted lay sprawled in the sand with blood all over his front.

Laura screamed, surprising herself.

Randolph finished his opponent off somehow; Laura did not care to look at them. He crouched down over Ted, put a hand to Ted's throat, and shook his head. He shook it several times, as if he were warning Ted from a distance not to talk with his mouth full. Then his look slid into something worse than unhappiness but different from anger. They seemed frozen before her eyes, exactly as she had seen them in the vision.

CHAPTER 14

TED opened his eyes, or thought he did. He could not see anything with them, not blackness, not anything. He did not seem to have eyes, or anything else. Randolph, he tried to say, but he had nothing to say it with. It was like dreaming, and knowing you were dreaming, and trying to wake up by remembering the bed, and the pillow, and the color of your pajama sleeve: it was like the time just before the trick worked and you woke up.

"Randolph!" said Ted, and jumped. He had a voice, and ears to hear it, and a nervous system to make him jump when he was startled.

He stared into grayness, and blackness, and mist, and a hundred shadows suggestive of nothing familiar. He looked down at himself. The sourceless light was not strong enough to show colors, but he knew well enough what the blackness caked over the whole front of him was. He decided not to look more closely. He held out a hand and looked at it instead. His fingernails were black. He was as grimy as he had been in the battle. He stared around him again, and a few yards ahead of him the shadows took on shapes that might have been the foam and waves of a swift river. Ted stood up. Everything worked and nothing hurt, but there was a curious emptiness in the region of his chest. He took a step toward the river.

A voice spoke out of nowhere. It had a clear and piercing sound, like a flute heard from a distance. Its tone was neutral.

"Such water is not for you."

This did not sound promising. Ted decided to find out the worst. "Is this Hell?"

"This is not."

Not Hell, or not anything? thought Ted, and realization smote him. He had given the Secret Country neither Heaven nor Hell, only a shadowy, dim, pathetic sort of place, like Hades in the *Odyssey*. What had anyone else done? Patrick didn't believe in an afterlife; he wouldn't have bothered making up what type the Secret Country had. But people in the Secret Country said, "Dear heaven," or "For the love of heaven."

Ted looked around again and thought that it was clear that nobody besides himself had so much as considered the matter. Nobody in the game or out of it, he thought grimly. This looked to be the one place where there were no unexpected changes. Then he wondered whom he was talking to. In the game Patrick had done well at being a bent and twisted figure in black robes; but here there was nobody to be seen.

"Why is the water not for me?" he asked.

"The living cross it to become the dead. You are neither. There is a bargaining for you."

Well, Ruth had managed to get their attention, at least.

"I hope they remember their lines," said Ted.

The voice did not answer that.

"Who is bargaining?" asked Ted.

"Ruth of the Green Caves, Fence of no land, and Lord Randolph, King's Counselor of the Hidden Land."

"What is the bargain?" His lines came easily to him.

"What must it be? Life for life."

That was wrong. Ted, Ruth, Fence, and Randolph were all supposed to promise to do certain labors for the Lord of the Dead. Once or twice Ted's family had spent Christmas at the farm, and those labors had come in handy then.

"Whose life?" said Ted.

"That concerns you not. Only the outcome concerns you."

"Is the one whose life is to be exchanged engaged in the bargaining?"

"Tricks will not avail you," said the voice, but its neutrality had given way to amusement. Ted found a sense of humor to be a disconcerting quality in the Lord of the Dead. If this *was* the Lord of the Dead.

"Who are you?"

"I am the Guardian of the River."

"What's the river?"

"If the bargaining is not concluded, you will know. If it is, you will not need to know."

"Isn't it my right to know the terms of the bargain?"

"Who art thou, then?"

"Edward," said Ted, "King of the Se—the Hidden Land." After all, he had been crowned. It would be a lie to say, "rightful King," but what he had said was probably all right.

"What power hath the Hidden Land over the Lords of Death?"

The question had a quality of rote about it; the voice clearly expected that Ted would know the answer. As a matter of fact, he did not. He stared into the mist until his eyes ached, but neither memory nor logic gave him an answer. Then he was distracted. Like an aerial photograph of familiar country, the mist came into focus and he knew what he saw.

It was ghosts, hundreds of them, crowding down to the opposite bank of the river and staring at him across it. Their voices came across gradually louder, like the television warming up.

"Living man, hast thou brought blood?"

"He is not living man, he hath had his death's wound."

"He is not dead man, for his substance is solid."

"Hast thou brought us blood?"

"Only mine," said Ted, wryly.

"Come across, that we may drink of thee and be for but a brief while what we were. Let us remember."

Too bad I don't have a sheep handy, thought Ted crazily. Not that I'd want to cut its throat anyway. He put a hand to his chest. It came away sticky. Maybe that blood would do; it seemed a pity to waste it. He stood up.

"I'll give you what blood I can," he said, "if you'll tell me, what power hath the Hidden Land over the Lords of Death?"

The voice said, again with a faint note of amusement, "You cannot cross with the blood of life yet in you."

"Well, they don't want me without it!"

"This is the doom of men," said the voice, not sepulchrally, but with the glee of someone making a particularly complicated pun.

Ted took a step toward the river, and another. The river and the ghosts stayed the same distance from him.

"You cannot cross," said the voice.

Ted had been staring steadily at the ghosts, and their outlines had become clearer. He saw creatures like the ones he had killed in the battle. He hoped only the newly dead were here. He did not want to see the King. Then he froze, and the breath went out of him as if someone had hit him. Down at the very edge of the river was a group of children. Ruth,

Ellen, Patrick, and Laura. Oh, God, thought Ted, were we all killed, did we lose the battle? And then, are they all dead but me?

Then he saw himself. He was taller than Ruth; but it was he. Ted felt the hair prickling on the back of his neck. He had always thought it would be terrible to meet one's own image walking in the garden; but that would have been a charming surprise compared to meeting it in Hell.

"Hey," he tried to call, but his throat was dry. He swallowed, and tried something more dignified.

"Hark!" he shouted. "You five children! Who are you?"

"We know not," said the figure of Ruth. Her voice was perfectly identical to his cousin's, although she had a trace of accent.

"Well, I bet *I* do. Are you Lady Ruth of the Green Caves, and Princesses Ellen and Laura and Prince Patrick of the Secret Country—of the Hidden Land?"

Four of the ghosts stirred and leaned together, whispering; except Edward, who came a step forward, his head tilted. "I have seen thee before."

"In the mirror," said Ted. Edward's voice was not familiar to him, but they did say that nobody really knew what his own voice sounded like. It was still a boy's voice, not a man's, despite Edward's height. The strange voice made things easier.

"Truly?" said Edward.

"Think about the mirror," said Ted, with no very clear idea of what he was doing, but possessed of a burning desire to make Edward remember who he was. "What can you see in it, behind you?" He felt he sounded like either a psychiatrist or a dishonest hypnotist, but it was the only thing he could think of.

Edward looked at Prince Patrick, and laughed. A wavering like that of water into which a stone has dropped went through the other ghosts, and most of them backed away from the five children.

"My brother Patrick," said Edward, "coming privily with a wet towel to make me late for supper."

"Edward!" said Prince Patrick, exactly like someone in a bad romance; and he and Edward hugged each other. "Laura!" cried the ghost of his sister, gleefully; "Ellen!" yelled the other small girl, and then they hugged each other and shouted, "Ruth! Ruth!" whereupon Ruth hugged them, and Edward, and Patrick.

Ted, who had never considered hugging Laura, let alone Patrick, was nonplussed.

"We thank thee," said Edward to Ted, formally, "for giving us back ourselves. What power is in thee to do this thing?"

"Who are you, then?"

"Edward Fairchild, Prince of the Hidden Land. And thou?"

"My name's Edward, too, Edward Carroll. But they all think I'm you. What happened to you?"

"Treachery," said Edward, grimly.

"Was it Claudia? Andrew's sister?"

"Verily, by that guise were we slain."

"How'd she do it?"

"A stratagem and a potion," said Edward. "What art thou?"

"I don't know," said Ted, "but look—they think they're bargaining for your life—"

"They haggle for a pig with no poke," said Edward; "there is no life in me now."

"But I'm talking to you!"

"That is not life, but spirit. Besides," said Edward, "Melanie waits at the gates of death and of a certainty I could not pass her. Nor," he added, "might I leave my brother and my cousins in this place."

"King Edward!" said the voice.

"King!" said Edward. "What of my father?"

"King Edward!" said the voice, imperatively.

"That is no name of mine," said Edward, in a way that made Ted wish it was none of his, either.

"Answer or forfeit," said the voice, delightedly.

"Well?" said Ted.

"You may go back to life if you will kill Lord Randolph."

"What infamy is this?" demanded Edward.

Ted, who fully intended to say No, opened his mouth and was shaken with sudden fear. What would happen if he didn't agree? Did the negotiators get more than one chance? The voice had sounded hideously pleased with itself. But if he said he would kill Randolph, he would have to do it; and it seemed to him at that moment as if he had spent all his time in the Secret Country plotting to avoid that very action. He would just have to hope that Ruth would not abandon him.

"No," he said.

The ghosts were silent. Ted put a hand to his chest and it came away wet. He pinched at his ankle, and the flesh was there. His substance was still solid.

The voice spoke again; it held a clean and vigorous glee. "You may go back to life," it said.

"I won't kill Lord Randolph."

"We are assured that he will die; how is the business of those who covenanted for you. You may go back."

"I won't!" said Ted, seized with perversity.

"This is not your place."

"Edward!" said Edward. "Go. Avenge our foul and most unnatural murder."

The place wavered and went out, and bright light hurt his shut eyes. He blinked them open. He was lying in the sand, in the sunshine, under blue sky. Randolph was hunched down beside his shoulder, bloody and dirty and bespattered, but very pale underneath it all. Laura was standing beside Randolph, with enormous eyes, and she looked one degree worse than he did: she had as much dirt and blood and grime on her face as he, and tear streaks on top of that.

Ted put up a shaking hand and pulled at the remnants of one braid. Laura smiled at him. He looked back at Randolph, who was also smiling.

"How could you?" said Ted. "How dare you?"

"Necessity dares all things," said Randolph, lightly, but he gave Ted a look which meant that Ted had better be quiet. Ted looked at his sister and decided to shut up for the moment.

He sat up and wiped his sweaty hair out of his eyes, looking over Randolph's shoulder. "Where's the battle now?" he asked, and stopped.

The sand was red, and there was a great deal more red that was not sand: mounds and huddles of things he did not want to look at. Just beyond Randolph were a hand and outstretched arm clothed in green. Ted looked quickly back at Randolph's face.

"The end passed while you were yonder," said Randolph. "We have the victory."

"And," said Ted, reluctantly falling back on his lines, "at what price?"

"A very high one," said Randolph. He had stopped smiling. "Many of the best are gone."

Ted could not remember whom of their characters he and the others had so blithely killed. Now was not, in any case, the time to find out whether the reality had followed the game. He remembered that Conrad had been hurt, and did not ask about him. "Is any of the enemy left to treat with?"

"We do not treat," said Randolph, "with the likes of those that are left. If their master wisheth terms, no doubt he will so inform us. His immediate army is destroyed, and Fence saith that his sorcery is vanished from the desert."

"I hope there aren't any prisoners?"

"No," said Randolph. "My lord, none of those we fought were men."

"You mean there wasn't any mundane army on the Dragon King's side?"

"If you mean by that, was there then no need for our own, there was great need. The greater part of those creatures had only to set foot over the border to leave us without a home to go back to."

"What was it that got me?" said Ted, wiping his face again.

"I have never seen its like," said Randolph. " 'Twas a shape-changer, yet it seemed held to but several shapes."

"What happened to it?"

"I got it with this sword," said Laura.

"Who told you you could fight?"

"Who told me I couldn't?"

"You little brat," said Ted, heatedly, and stopped. A number of things he had been almost too busy to notice, let alone think about, fell together in his mind. "Oh, well," he said. "A lot of good most of my liege men did me when I needed them. Do you think you'd like to be one, too? Maybe you could show them something."

Laura looked as if she thought he was making fun of her; then she shrugged suddenly and grinned at him. "Sure," she said.

"Do you know the words?"

"Certainly."

"Well, kneel, then." Laura obeyed him, and Randolph sat where he was; he looked bemused. Ted took his sister by the hands. "Put your title in," he whispered.

"I, Laura, Princess of the Secret Country, do become your liege man of life and limb, and of earthly worship, and faith and truth will I bear unto you, to live and die, against all manner of folk. So help me God," added Laura, startling both Ted and Randolph.

"I, Edward, King of the Secret Country, do become your liege lord of life and limb, and of earthly worship, and that faith and truth I receive of you, that I will requite. Rise, Sir Laura," said Ted, in his best Prince-Edward tones, "Knight of the Secret Country."

Laura seemed as delighted as he had ever seen her, but all she said was, "Does this mean I have to ride a horse?" Then she looked in alarm at Randolph, but he had stood up and was staring out over the battlefield; you could probably have burst a paper bag under his nose without making him jump.

"Now what about this sword?" said Ted.

"It wanted to come here," said Laura, "and when you stick it into one of those black things with the red eyes, they shrivel up." She held it out to him. "Hey!" she said. "What happened to the stones?"

"What stones?"

"It had those blue stones in the handle—in the hilt, but now it's all smooth." She tilted it to catch the sunlight. "And the blade used to be blue and shiny, and now it's just ordinary."

"Well, maybe you used up its magic."

"Whence came that?" demanded Randolph, returning from his abstraction.

"Fence's armory," said Laura boldly.

"As well for us that it did," said Randolph. "What brought him to give it thee?"

"Well . . ."

"Shouldn't we be getting back?" said Ted. "I want to thank Ruth and Fence. And do they even know it worked?"

Randolph smiled. "They have the word of the Judge of the Dead. But that is always a slippery thing. Come, then."

Randolph led them through the remnants of the battle in a random zigzag; probably, thought Ted, guiding them away from the worst sights. The ones they passed close by were bad enough. Ted looked aside at Laura, struggling along with the heavy sword, and was visited by an unexpected emotion.

"Would you mind holding my hand?" he asked her.

Laura gave him an astonished look and did as he asked.

When they were out of the area that had been fought over, Randolph asked Laura, with a grave politeness, to do him the favor of running ahead and bespeaking some stew for all three of them, "for, although thou hast fought most bravely this day, yet we two have fought longer."

Laura bowed to him and went on ahead.

"My lord," said Randolph, stopping Ted with a hand on his shoulder, "for all that she did bravely, and for all that her sword seemed made to deal with such shape-changers, I know the sorcery to deal with them; and had she not turned both our sights away from the battle, thou hadst not been killed and this dilemma would not now be upon us."

Ted laughed, before he knew he was going to. "That *would* happen," he said. He heard himself giggle, and stopped quickly. "I think it's my fault," he said, "because she didn't swear fealty to me, you see, and I didn't notice. And then I told El—the Lady Ellen that she couldn't fight and bound her not to by her oath of fealty, you see, and so the Lady Laura got mad." He snickered again.

Randolph's mouth had fallen open somewhere in the middle of this speech; when Ted had finished, he blinked and closed it.

"So how can I scold her?" said Ted, laughter giving way to helplessness. It was one thing to have the story go differently than you expected. It was one thing, when you tried to make it go differently, to have that very attempt make it go as you had expected but hoped it wouldn't. But this business of having something that never did happen in the original story, and that had not been done to stop something in the original story, be responsible for the occurrence of something that did happen in the original story, was another thing, and one thing too many.

"My lord, in some wise the fault is mine," said Randolph. "I charged myself to see that all of useful age did swear to thee, and methinks I was mistaken in useful age."

"I didn't think of it either," said Ted. "But look—however it happened, how could you let them take you instead?"

"Because it is in the nature of things that they will take me very soon," said Randolph, looking him straight in the eye. "Thy use for me is drawing to its conclusion; and Fence, though he knoweth not what he knoweth, doth draw near to his conclusions touching the King's death."

"Why'd you try to get me to agree to kill you, then?"

"I did not," said Randolph; "that was a condition made by the Judge of the Dead. It is also," he said, dropping his hand from Ted's shoulder, "a condition made by the laws of the Hidden Land, whereof thou art King. Think on it." And he went on ahead of Ted into the camp.

CHAPTER 15

THERE was a great deal of cheerful confusion in the camp. Ted was swept into his share of it by Ruth, Ellen, and Patrick, who did not actually run and hug him, but did surround him, talk at him, and show a disposition to tug at his sleeves and help him take off his corselet. He wondered briefly why this garment had not turned the sword-thrust that had killed him. Probably the sword had been magic; certainly its wielder had.

Out of the usual tumble of their conversation he managed to discover that Patrick had a slash on his leg from some horned creature, and a bruise on his side from he was not sure what. He seemed both exultant and subdued; at least, thought Ted, many of his most Patrick-like qualities were subdued. He had gotten through the battle so well largely because Ellen, at the last minute, had insisted on his having her magic sword.

"But you weren't used to it!" said Ted.

"I took it *and* the ordinary sword," said Patrick, "and lost the ordinary one in the first five minutes. But the magic one seemed to know how to fight all the strange creatures by itself. And Benjamin," he said, grimacing, "stuck to me like a piece of gum and took care of all the normal soldiers." On his dusty face was an expression compounded of glee and puzzlement. Ted wondered if he could possibly have enjoyed the battle. Now was not the time to ask; it would only remind Ellen that she had been prevented from fighting.

"Matthew and Randolph did the same to me," said Ted.

"Did the stones come out of your hilt, too?" Laura asked Patrick.

Patrick showed her that they had not; Ellen demanded to know what Laura had meant by "too"; and Ted was just as pleased to be dragged by Randolph away from the rising tide of Ellen's indignation and into a brief Council about what councils should be held.

He was not glad for long. He wanted most desperately to collect his fellow-imposters and discuss with them what Randolph had done about the bargaining, what Claudia appeared to have done to their other selves, and what they proposed to do about it all. It was galling to him to be saddled, on top of these burning responsibilities, with innumerable kingly duties that could far better be performed by others.

Fence and Randolph wanted to leave half the army behind to deal with any strays from the Dragon King's; they wanted it decided whether to bury the dead where they were, or take them back, or bury some and take some back; they wanted to settle whether an envoy should be sent to the Dragon King's court, and if so, who it should be and what he should say.

Ted could not find fault with these wants, but he wished they would leave him out of it. Just when he could have done with being ignored, they had to bring him in on everything. He knew nothing about the army, but he had to sit for hours listening to Fence and Randolph and the pitiful remnants of his own King's Council wrangling over which pieces of it should be left behind and with what precise instructions.

No doubt it would be good for a new King. But Ted had no patience with it when he had not decided to be King. It now seemed impossible to him that, knowing where Edward was and being able to talk to him, they should be unable to get him back where he belonged.

Besides, it was almost unbearable to sit and look at all the empty seats. Of the counselors he had lost, he remembered only Conrad well; he had not lost any of the game's favorites. Nor, perhaps unfortunately, had he lost Andrew, who had not so much as a scratch. But along with him, he had only Randolph (with his arm in a sling); Julian (who limped); Jerome, Matthew, Benjamin (all of whom had their heads bandaged); and Fence (who seemed very gloomy and was not a proper counselor anyway). He missed the cheerful temper and practical mind of Conrad. So, he found, did everybody else. With the exception of Benjamin, of the erratic temper and anomalous position, Conrad had been the only counselor of very great age or experience; nobody else seemed to be over thirty. Ted no longer found the idea of appointing new and untraditional counselors quite so appealing.

Except for Fence, Randolph, and Benjamin, who acted toward him precisely as they always had, the counselors did not seem to find Ted very appealing either. The answer to the puzzle of their constraint and odd glances was obvious once he thought of it; but it took him a day and a night and half another day to think of it. It was, of course, hard to act normally around someone who had been brought back from the dead by sorcery. As far as he could tell, only his Council, his sister, and his cousins knew about that.

Randolph told Ted that, with his gracious permission—that part sounding like an order, not a request—they were to camp three days and four nights in the round valley between the desert and the mountains.

On the first day after the battle Ted found out who had been killed, and was taken by Randolph and Fence to visit those who appeared to wish they had been. The Secret Country seemed to have remarkable methods for curing bodily wounds, but the wounds inflicted by the Dragon King's minions must have been mostly mental. Those who had been hurt had dreams worse than any of Ted's. Fence, however, seemed more at home with these dreams, interpreting them handily and offering numerous methods, from potions to poetry, of preventing their return.

Ted stayed close to Fence during this visit; at first, because he had been braced for horrors of one sort, and then because he began to be visited by those of another. He knew quite firmly, if vaguely, that hospitals had been terrible, verminous, filthy places before the advent of modern medicine. You could hardly expect modern medicine in the Secret Country; therefore he had been steeled for filth and vermin and the stench of gangrene. He found nothing of the sort. Agatha grumbled about the desert dust and sand that crept into everything, but all this did was give the hospital tents the air of a slightly neglected but very tidy attic. For the most part things were clean, airy, and decorous.

But nobody was happy, or even restful. Fence, who had flung off his gloom like an old cloak when he ducked into the first tent, could make people smile, but the moment he moved on they stopped smiling. There was an atmosphere of dread such as Ted had never known and would not, perhaps, have recognized had it not been for that part of his mind which knew some of what Edward had known. That underlayer of his thoughts was not susceptible to search; he recognized the feeling of the hospital tents without for a moment knowing what he recognized, or what had happened to Edward to make this state known to him.

"What's the *matter?*" he exploded at Fence, the moment they were outside again.

"They have bad dreams," said Fence.

"Yes, I know, but for heaven's sake!"

"Those are the war wounds of sorcerers," said Fence. "Be glad thou hast chosen another way."

The evening of that day and most of the next were taken up with the disposition of the army. Then everyone wrangled over what to do with the bodies of the dead. Ted, during a break for food, took Randolph aside and asked if they could not all be brought back, as he had been. Randolph asked him if he cared to choose who should die in their stead. Ted, his suspicions satisfied and his conscience hurting him, apologized. The Council finally decided to bury in the valley those who had no families, and to take back with them those who did, so that the families could have the consolation of a funeral. Ted thought that if he were a family he would not find a funeral consoling.

That evening they discussed whether they ought to send an envoy to the Dragon King. They held their councils in the pavilion that had been set up, before the battle, to keep the rain off the cook-fires. It still smelled of woodsmoke and a batch of burnt bread. They sat on folding stools of wood and canvas, the ingenuity of which had both delighted and enraged Patrick; and leaned their shabby elbows on a series of long, narrow tables that also folded, but were less ingenious. To them clearly from outside came the smells of the stew the ousted cooks were making; a few tired voices and a few vigorous; and distantly the sound of a lute, two recorders, and an indeterminate number of voices singing mournfully a shapeless tune.

Phlebas the Phoenician, a fortnight dead,
Forgot the cry of gulls, and the deep sea swell
And the profit and loss.

"The best you may hope for," said Benjamin in his abrupt voice, "is to waste yon villain's time and patience as he hath wasted ours. You'll stir in him neither regret nor fear."

Agatha's voice sang alone:

A current under sea
Picked his bones in whispers. As he rose and fell
He passed the stages of his age and youth
Entering the whirlpool.

"But leave him alone," said Randolph, "and you'll stir contempt."

"We have that already," said Fence.

All the voices rose:

Red Mage or Blue
O you who turn the wheel and look to windward,
Consider Phlebas, who was once handsome and tall as
you.

Ted, not wishing to consider Phlebas, and made courageous by impatience, said, "Isn't it a little late to send him a protest? We should have done that when Fence came back and told us about all the signs of his spies in the South."

"Certainly we should have," said Randolph, "but your father forbade it." His face and his bandage were both dirty, and his eyes narrowed as if his head hurt him, but his voice was as usual. "Besides, we should send more than protest. We have won a great battle, my lord, and we should press upon the Dragon King terms such that we need not fight another."

"How can you make terms with somebody who has no honor?" said Ted, bewildered.

Fence looked up.

"By force, how else?" said Randolph. "In this matter, force sorcerous."

Ted saw Fence wince and look troubled. Randolph looked over at him, apparently expecting him to give details, as if this were a plan they had worked out between them. He caught the end of the wince, and his face set as if the headache had gotten worse. Fence's eyes widened suddenly and he leaned forward. Randolph's gaze dropped before the wizard's: not quickly or sneakily, but with considerable deliberation. Fence's face flushed, and he turned to Ted.

"If Belaparthalion and Chryse did but give him a moment of their thought—" he said.

"Why didn't they come to the coronation?" said Ted, thoughtlessly; but Fence did not seem to take the question amiss.

"No unicorn will come under a roof," he said, "and thou knowest well that Belaparthalion fitteth not under any roof ever devised. We had not the time to travel to a place of their choosing. Fear not; thou hadst their blessing on thy accession."

Ted was not sure he was comforted by this.

"What have we to offer them?" said Randolph, and once more looked expectantly at Fence.

Fence grinned. "I have certain weapons," he said, "for which those two indeed have no use, but whose presence in hands such as ours makes them to sleep most uneasily."

Ted thought of the armory below Fence's tower.

Randolph frowned. "Have such hands as ours no use for them?"

Fence gave him a long, thoughtful look that to Ted seemed to say something like "I thought as much." "Less use for them than for the good will of Belaparthalion," he said, a little reprovingly.

"And Chryse?" said Matthew, without looking up from his writing.

"The good will of such as she is more perilous than the malice of the Dragon King," said Fence, "but if history speaketh aright, she hath a fondness for Belaparthalion that we might turn to our own account."

"Wilt thou speak with them, then?" said Julian.

"If the Council and the King so desire."

The Council murmured that it did so desire, and Ted nodded.

"Granting that we have that to force him to our demands, then," said Randolph, "whom will we send?"

"Lord Andrew?" said Ted, actuated half by mischief and half by curiosity.

"A most astute thought," said Randolph, holding Ted's eyes in a manner half reassuring and half alarming. "A true test of your philosophy, my lord," he added to Andrew. "Whom do you desire to accompany you?"

"Julian," said Andrew. He was a little red, but seemed less discomposed than Ted had hoped. He had thought it a nice irony to send Andrew as an envoy to the master he had failed; apparently Randolph thought so as well. Ted supposed he might have given to Andrew only an opportunity to make his excuses, whatever those might be.

"My lord?" said Randolph to Julian.

"Gladly," said Julian; but he looked as alarmed as Andrew

should have. "Might you spare Lord Jerome as well, your Majesty?"

Ted looked at Randolph, who gave him no sign. "I think so," said Ted. Fence had said he must learn to speak for himself. What was galling was that he was speaking for Edward.

"You must choose you a party of soldiers also," said Randolph, and wandered off into a maze of diplomatic complications that Ted did not bother to follow.

He busied himself instead with the exchange of looks between Fence and Randolph. At first he thought that Fence had not considered sorcerous force the way to keep the Dragon King honorable. But the rest of the discussion showed that he thought it a fine way. He must, then, have been disturbed by something in Randolph's attitude. Perhaps saying "How else?" about sorcerous force was somehow wrong.

Ted scowled, caught Matthew's amazed glance, and composed his face again. Fence had been unhappy with, but not surprised by, what Randolph had said. And Randolph had expected this reaction and had set himself to ignore it. Now *that* had surprised Fence; and from Fence's surprise Randolph had looked away.

Ted, in a burst of illumination, thought, why, Fence kept expecting Randolph to—to deny, or apologize for, or at least be ashamed of, what he said and the way he looked; and Randolph kept not denying it, and Fence looked as if that made him remember something, or realize it. And when Randolph asked didn't *we* have a use for the weapons, then Fence thought that proved he was right. About what? He shook his head, wishing he knew what in Randolph's original statement had been so distasteful to Fence.

He sat revolving the rest of the conversation in his mind,

looking for a clue there, and when he remembered Fence's saying, "I have certain weapons," he knocked over his untouched wine-cup, and sat without apologizing while they sent for a page to clean it up. How could he have been so stupid? Those weapons had to be Shan's and Melanie's swords.

If Fence gave them to a dragon and a unicorn, that would be the end of that; or at least, Ted and his relatives could spend years questing around for them. The idea of such a quest flamed up briefly in his mind, and was pleasing to him; then it was drowned in a flood of fear, and he turned his attention back to the Council, trying to discover when Fence planned to give the swords to the creatures.

He was a little comforted by a number of intimations that dragons always talked over everything for a long time and that unicorns would not do anything to please you unless you could convince them that it would hurt you more than you knew. He probably had some time to work in. But this was one more reason to talk to the others.

On the third day the Council met again, but Randolph told Ted that he did not need to attend; he could read over Matthew's notes later. Randolph sounded a little strained as he said this; but Ted would have let the Council plot his own murder if it would have given him an hour with the others. He scrambled around the camp, dragging Patrick from watching a competition with throwing-knives, interrupting Ruth and Laura in a flute lesson, and summoning Ellen away from Benjamin, whom she was making late for the Council by demanding fighting lessons of him.

"It's Randolph who gives fencing lessons," Ted told her as they made for a little fir-wood on the mountain side of their valley.

"Randolph already said no," said Ellen. She was the only one who seemed angry with Ted for the interruption; Patrick had said "About time," and Ruth, "Thank goodness." Laura, as usual, said nothing.

Arriving at the edge of the fir-wood, they sat down in a drift of pine needles, leaned their backs against convenient trees, rooted a few cones and sticks out of the way, and looked expectantly at Ted.

CHAPTER 16

"ALL right," said Ted, "first, Ruthie, thank you very much for getting me out. I didn't like it down there."

"What was it like?" asked Ellen, but Ruth interrupted her.

"I didn't," she said.

"What?"

"I didn't get you out." Ruth began shredding a pine cone. "Randolph came and got Fence and me and took us back to where you were. You looked horrible. Ted, if I'd known it would be like that I don't think I'd have agreed that we should come to the battle. Did it hurt?"

"Never mind," said Ted, putting a hand to the solid substance of his chest; something had lurched inside him. "I wouldn't have agreed either, believe me. Just what do you mean you didn't get me out?"

"I said the spell—that's all you do, just say it. The trick is to know where to find the spell, and to know what to do once you've said it. A voice answered, coming out of nowhere, and said we must choose a ground whereon we might have speech of one another. It told us to choose between the sea and the Well of the White Witch. I figured we should stick to what we knew, so I said the Well."

"I don't know," said Ted, "the Well doesn't seem to like you."

"I said the Well," repeated Ruth. "A wind came up and blew sand in our faces, and when it died down we were standing right where I was when Ellie and I were using Shan's Ring to change the time, and I got into the place that looked wrong. Remember, I told you about it: with the army camped by the Well, and the sky the wrong color and the air all shimmery?"

"Go on," said Ted.

"And you were gone," said Ruth. "It was just Fence and Randolph and me. We went through the woods, and across the bridge, and up to the Well. Randolph didn't like it at all, walking right up to an army like that, but Fence kept telling him it was all right. And a unicorn came out of the army and stood on the other side of the Well."

"What'd it look like?" said Laura.

"It had gold eyes," said Ruth, promptly, "but otherwise it looked like the one we hunted."

"That was Chryse," said Laura.

"Chryse's the one you talked to?" said Ellen.

"It told me that was its name."

"It didn't like me," said Ruth. "Or maybe it thought I was funny. They're very strange creatures, those unicorns. I told it we wished to bargain for the life of Edward Fairchild, King of the Hidden Land. That's the last thing that went according to the game. It knew I had Shan's Ring, and it asked me if I'd give it up to have you back. I said I would, and it said that the willingness took away the value of the gift, and we'd have to give something else. So Randolph offered his life—and Ted, the unicorn said exactly the same thing, that the willingness took the value away." She gave him a sharp and anxious look from the green eyes like Randolph's.

"Well, what do you expect?" said Ted, a little irritated. "We always said that Randolph wanted to die after he killed the King. He figured it was what he deserved, and worth it to save the Secret Country." Ted paused, thinking. "He was probably tickled to death at the chance."

"Ted!" said Laura. "He was! After you got killed," and she swallowed hard, "he said, 'This is not so foul a chance as it appears, so take heart'—to me, I mean, when I told him to get Ruth."

"I'd forgotten that about Randolph," said Ruth. "Well, it's nice to be right occasionally, except we always seem to be right about the things we'd rather be wrong about. Anyway. Randolph asked if you could take part in the bargaining. The unicorn said we couldn't talk to you, but it would apprise you of what was happening, and it tilted its head and pitched its voice a little oddly, and said, 'King Edward! You may go back to life if you will kill Lord Randolph!'

"Well, Fence and I both objected, and Randolph said to the unicorn, 'Here is thy unwillingness,' and the unicorn said, 'I have one will serve me better,' and told us that if we would return to the place whence we came, we would find you alive."

Ted supplied them with his side of the conversation with the Guardian of the River; a little discussion of the quality of the Guardian's voice made them decide that it had been the unicorn's.

"What'd it mean, it had one that would serve it better?" asked Ellen.

"Probably that my unwillingness was more fun than Ruth and Fence's, because it was my life Randolph was saving," said Ted, sourly.

"Ted, what are we going to do about that?" asked Ruth.

"Well, I won't kill him. I didn't ask him to die for me. He can damn well do it himself. Do they have hemlock here?"

Ruth looked appalled, and Ted, a little shocked himself,

scowled at her. She did not seem impressed. "No, all right," said Ted, "of course I don't want him to kill himself. I need him if we can't get Edward back. If we do get Edward back, Edward'll need him. And anyway, he did save the Secret Country, so why should he suffer for it? I mean," said Ted, overcome by a helpless feeling as he remembered the King, "even if it was wrong, what else could he have done?"

"A tragedy," said Patrick, in a most peculiar voice. He fixed his untender blue gaze on Ted, in the way he used to do when he was playing Fence. "That's what you get for reading Shakespeare so young."

"I don't think Randolph *can* kill himself," said Ruth, sparing Patrick not so much as a glance. "He and Fence stood there in that peculiar air under that wrong sky, with the army writhing all over the plain, and argued about it. Fence was furious with him; I mean, quite apart from being his friend. He told him he'd offered what was no longer his to give. It sounded as if magicians aren't allowed to kill themselves, and Randolph is Fence's apprentice. Also, Fence convinced Randolph that he would have to be killed by someone unwilling or the unicorn wouldn't accept the death and would take you back."

"Hell!" said Ted, without knowing he was going to. "I have to kill him or I'll die, is that it? My God, do you know what's happening to us? If I hadn't tried to stop it the King wouldn't have died; if Laurie hadn't tried to stop it I wouldn't have died; and if you hadn't tried to bring me back I wouldn't be under an obligation to kill Randolph, which is really the one thing I've been trying to avoid all along!"

"What, what?" said the rest of them, and Ted had to fill them in. Laura seemed to shrivel up.

"It's not your fault, Laurie, Randolph said it was all his." Laura looked unconvinced, but less unhappy. "Furthermore," said Ted, "when I was down there in the land of the dead I met the real us. I met Prince Edward and Princess Laura and the rest of them."

Patrick, who had been tapping a dead branch on the ground, sat very still. Ruth stared, and so did Laura.

"They're *dead?*" said Ellen.

"They didn't remember who they were at first, but after they did remember, they said Claudia killed them."

"Oh!" said Laura, with such profound relief that Ted gaped at her.

"It *was* the other one she killed," said Laura. She seemed to pause and hear what she had said. The relief drained out of her voice, and she hunched her shoulders. "Claudia's awful."

"Laura!" said Ted. "Have you told Fence about those visions?"

"No . . ."

Ted put his head in his hands, feeling that he knew why Hamlet had called his head a distracted globe and had seemed to doubt how long memory could hold its seat therein. "Now look," he said. "No matter what happens or what we decide or what time it is, even if we have to burst in on the blasted Council, when we're done here we are going to tell Fence about those visions."

"Randolph should have told him by now," offered Laura.

"Should's," said Ted, "shoe no horses. All right. The real us told me that Claudia killed them and that it was treachery, and Edward said, 'Avenge our foul and most unnatural murder.' "

"Isn't it nice how all these people keep quoting Shakespeare?" said Patrick.

"How do we avenge them, kill Claudia?" said Ellen. The idea seemed to please her.

"Fat chance of that," said Ruth. "Even Fence can't seem to do anything with her. But wouldn't it be a fine revenge to get them all back? Then they could testify against her."

"That's what I was thinking," said Ted, "but now I don't know. Can you think of five things you're unwilling to give up? Also, Edward said Melanie wouldn't let them by the gates of life. I don't know what that means, but I'd hate to tangle with Melanie."

"Isn't *she* dead?" said Ellen. "Seems to me the dragon killed her because Shan couldn't fulfill his word to the dragon without her, and she broke *her* word to Shan."

"Well," said Ted, "around here that wouldn't stop her from standing at the gates of life, I bet, not if she were on the side of death, keeping people there. Besides, from what the voice said to me and from some things Randolph said when I asked him about bringing the dead counselors back, I don't think they'll take anything but somebody else's life."

"Chryse did ask about Shan's Ring," said Ruth.

"Well, that's true. I wonder if Chryse would take that for the five of them. Or for the counselors?"

"They won't take anything you want to give them," said Ruth. "Or at least, that's what it sounded like."

"Do you really want to give them Shan's Ring?"

Ruth shrugged, and one of her braids fell down. "Chryse thought I did. And I don't see what use it is to us. We used it to change the time, but it doesn't seem to do anything else. Except to combine with the sword to take me somewhere I'd just as soon never go anyway."

"How do you know you don't want to go there if you don't know where it is?"

Ruth sighed. "I guess you're right."

Ted looked at her thoughtfully. "You sound disillusioned."

"Well . . . the Well took my ring away, and I didn't bring you back from the dead, and the worst part of the story is all that's left, and—"

"And we won a great battle but there's something missing," said Ted, identifying the source of his own unease with considerable astonishment.

"Well, you were dead," said Ellen, practically, "you didn't see the end."

Ted looked at Patrick. "You did, didn't you?"

"I know what you mean," said Patrick, slowly. "It wasn't— it wasn't spectacular at all. We did what we were told, and Randolph and Fence's plan worked, and Benjamin kept me from being killed, and Randolph almost kept you from it, and we won, that's all. Wouldn't you think the Dragon King would have figured out King John's tactics in four hundred years? I expected this Belaparthalion they keep talking about to swoop down from the sky and save the day or something. But the day didn't need saving. Which ought to be fine, but—"

Ted thought of five hundred and forty-three dead men and uncounted dead creatures, and Conrad, and the haunted faces of the people in the hospital tent.

"For pity's sake," said Ruth to her brother, "what's the matter with you?"

"The same thing that's the matter with you!" said Patrick, very red in the face. "Now that you can't do anything you don't like it. Well, Ted and I couldn't do anything about winning the battle; and we didn't even make *up* anything spectacular *about* winning the battle, so we're disappointed. And so are you."

"I don't dislike it because I can't do anything!" flared Ruth. "I fear things are getting out of control, wherefore I am afraid."

"Things have been out of control since we got here," said Patrick.

"Not like this."

"Yes they have. It just took a while for everything to come together. We're just puppets of our damn plot—"

"Whose damn plot?"

"Well, all right. Maybe it's Claudia's damn plot."

"Stop it a minute," said Ted. "Before I forget what else I have to say. Do you know what Fence and Randolph are going to do with our swords?"

"How could we?" said Ellen. "This is no time for dramatics."

"They're going to give them to Chryse and Belaparthalion in exchange for their keeping the Dragon King in line."

He wished he were in a better frame of mind to appreciate their reactions. Laura and Ellen looked blank, Ruth horror-struck, and Patrick desperately thoughtful. A cardinal whistled over them, and they all jerked their heads back and gaped at it.

"And those stupid birds," said Ted, remembering that it was one of them that had sent Laura blundering into the hedge in the first place.

"They're Green Caves servants," said Ruth. "They're all right."

"Well, but they're red, and Benjamin said that was the color of the Outside Powers."

"Well, that doesn't mean that everything red is from the Outside Powers, does it?"

The cardinal whipped away toward the mountains.

"I feel spied on," said Ellen.

"We stray from the point," said Ted.

"Which one?" said Patrick.

"All right. First, we've got to get those swords back. And when we do, we had better go home."

"Leaving everything all up in the air?" cried Ellen.

"If we stay I'll end up killing Randolph."

"But now that we know Claudia killed the real us—"

"What are we supposed to do about it?" said Ted, wishing she would not so accurately reflect half his own mind on the matter.

"But I want to know *why!*" said Ellen.

"When did she do it?" Patrick asked Ted.

"They didn't say. We didn't have very long."

"Well," said Patrick, sitting forward, "remember the first day we were all here together, and Benjamin found us? He was mad because you and Ruth were together, and you were late to the Council. But we didn't seem to have been missing for very long. What if she did it then, because we were all here?"

"Why should she want us here?"

"I think we should ask her."

"If we could find her," said Ted. "I agree that we should give Claudia her just deserts. But what we try to do doesn't seem to have much connection with what happens; or else it has the wrong kind of connection."

"What if we left a note for Fence?" said Ruth, abruptly.

"*That's* an idea!" said Ted. "I wouldn't feel so responsible then. And I wouldn't kill Randolph."

"You'd still owe him your life," said Patrick, "and leave him in a mess. Not to mention—"

"Well?"

"I don't think I'll mention it," said Patrick, looking secretive.

There was a pause, full of the rustle of pine needles and

the distant trickle of water. Ted considered the debt he owed Randolph, and remembered the land of the dead. A great burst of clarity overcame him.

"Wait!" he said. "Randolph didn't want *me*. He wanted Edward Fairchild. Well, Edward Fairchild's still dead; he's still down there. Chryse didn't fulfill its bargain, so why should Randolph fulfill his?"

"You think Chryse'd let you get away with that?" said Ruth.

"I bet it'll have to. Magic and bargains with the devil and things like that are always very—what's the word—"

"Literal," said Ruth, brightening.

"What?" said Ellen.

"Literal," said Ruth. "That's when someone says to you, 'Make me a chocolate milkshake,' and you turn him into one."

Ellen gave a delighted chortle.

"We can point that out to Fence in the note," said Ted.

"If Randolph really wants to die, he'll find a way," observed Patrick.

"But look," said Ted. "The whole point of what he's been doing has been to save the Secret Country. Well, once we're gone and he knows what's really happened, saving the Secret Country will mean getting Edward back. And maybe by the time he's done that he'll feel better about having killed the King."

As he spoke, Ted saw again the shadowy Council Room, the King's candlelit, agonized face, and the way Randolph looked as if he had been poisoned himself. Ted, who had tried to stop it, did not feel any better about the whole thing: how could he expect that Randolph, who had done it, ever would?

This did not seem to occur to the others.

"Well," said Ruth slowly, "let's see. If we get the swords and go, and leave a note, we'll have to put Fence and Randolph on Claudia's trail and given them a chance to get the real us back, and we'll have kept Ted from killing Randolph and perhaps given Randolph something to live for."

Ted groaned. "And we'll have taken away the bribe Fence was going to give to Chryse and Belaparthalion to keep the Dragon King in line."

"If the Dragon King's out of line, won't Randolph have more to live for?" asked Ellen.

Ted could not help laughing. "Maybe," he said, "but it hardly seems fair."

"If you throw the sword back through the hedge," said Patrick, in his most superior tone, "it should take itself back here. Then they could come get it, if we put that in the note, too. And the same with ours."

There was a long silence.

"That would be it, then," said Ellen. "We'd be stuck home for good."

"We can always stay here and kill Randolph," said Patrick.

"Oh, all right. But—oh, well," said Ellen.

"You could have cornflakes for breakfast," Laura said to her, tentatively.

Ellen shrugged.

Ruth sighed heavily.

Ted looked up through the wavering green and black of the trees to where another cardinal was beating lazily across the illimitable sky. There was one round cloud that looked as if it had been cut out of cardboard. A fierce possessiveness clamped down on him: he wanted to hold the entire Secret Country in his two hands, as if it were the Crystal of Earth. He felt that it was his, and not even its shadowy Hell nor the inhuman humor of the unicorns nor the ugliness shortly to erupt when Fence discovered the treachery of Randolph could make him want to give it up.

"Ted," said Ellen, "now can you tell us what the land of the dead was like?"

Ted sat up, staring. The Secret Country was not his. It was not even the Secret Country. It was the Hidden Land, and it was Edward's. Every act he had performed as its King had been disastrous. Randolph could rule it; Edward could rule it. Ted would ruin it.

He began to tell Ellen about the land of the dead, and the conversation drifted off into what the rest of them had been doing while Ted fretted in councils. Nothing extraordinary had happened, except to Ruth and Laura.

"She can play that flute," said Ruth, "and I can't."

"What do you mean, you can't?" said Patrick.

"Well, you know what happens when you let an ignorant person play around with a flute. He can get a few squeaks and whistles out of it, but he probably won't hit on the right fingering or the right way to blow into the mouthpiece. That's how it seems with that flute when I try to play it, even though I know what I'm doing. But Laurie, who doesn't know what she's doing, and who had to give up piano lessons because she was so uncoordinated—"

"Hey!" said Ellen.

"I'm sorry," said Ruth, looking abashed. "But it's a significant detail, even if it is rude to mention it. She can play all sorts of complicated things without even thinking. And it's not that the proper fingering for that flute is unusual, because I can tell by looking at her playing that it isn't."

"How does it work, Laurie?" asked Ted. Something in Ruth's description sounded familiar.

Laura, red in the face, looked up from the tree-root she sat on. "I just know, somehow, underneath."

"In the back of your mind?"

"Yes."

"That's how I knew how to fence," said Ted to Patrick.

"Huh," said Patrick, in his most noncommittal tones.

"It's too bad I can't remember how to ride a horse that way," said Laura.

"Maybe it's only the important things that stick," said Ruth.

"No," said Ted, "because I remembered the names of the flowers we saw on the Unicorn Hunt the same way, and that wasn't important."

"Well," said Ruth, "it might have been important to Edward."

"Ruth Eleanora Carroll," said Patrick, in a scandalized tone that Ted recognized as an imitation of Patrick's mother's, "is that how you do your sorcery so well?"

"Only some of it," said Ruth, growing as red as Laura had been. "That's how I could read the alphabet. But I had to work hard, too, Patrick!"

"I knew it!" chortled Patrick. "You wanted us to think it was all your own cleverness, and all the time—"

"Patrick," said Ellen, "how did you get those keys out of Fence's pocket?"

"Prince Patrick was a prestidigitator!" cried Ruth.

Patrick was not at all embarrassed. "What a bunch of fakers," said he.

"Ted's not," said Laura.

"Neither are you," said Ted, promptly. "Must run in the other side of the family."

"*I'm* not a faker," said Ellen.

"Only because you didn't get the chance," said her brother.

Ellen threw a handful of pine needles at him, and Ruth began helpfully to stuff them down the back of his tunic.

"Wait!" said Ted. "What does it mean? What kind of connection is there between us and the real us, that we can remember things they knew how to do?"

"That's nothing," said Patrick. "I've got a whole list of hard questions. Why didn't breaking the Crystal of Earth work? Why is Laura having visions and what do they mean? How did Randolph poison the King's wine after Ted spilled the bottle? What's the story that they've put all over plates and doors and coffins? Why did Shan's Ring hold Claudia? Why did it stop holding Claudia? What's Claudia up to? Why—"

"Stop!" begged Ellen. "You know we're leaving and we'll never know."

"Speaking of Laura's visions," said Ted, "let's go root Fence out of the Council and tell him about them."

The bell rang for the noon meal, and they abandoned this pleasing plan, to plague Fence's appetite instead.

"Ted," said Ellen, as they walked back to the camp, "did you see the King down there?"

"No," said Ted, looking sideways at her alert and inquisitive face. Ellen never failed to amaze him. She sounded as if meeting the King in Hell would have been a nice thing, somewhere on the level of strawberries for breakfast.

"I wonder if he's met the real us yet," said Ellen.

"They wouldn't recognize each other," said Ted.

"I wonder," said Ellen.

CHAPTER 17

BEING hungry themselves, they did not really try to drag Fence from his meal, but only asked to speak with him afterward. Laura could hardly eat. She felt as if she were about to take a test she had not studied for.

They took Fence, who seemed mildly puzzled and considerably amused, to the place where they had spoken earlier. He sat down on a tree-root and looked expectantly from one to the other of them. Laura could not look at him and remain apprehensive. His round face, his big eyes, the disorder of his hair and robes after march and battle and three days of councils, even the four days' growth of beard that could make her father look so formidable but lent Fence only an absent air: all these made him seem pleasant and harmless.

"Did Randolph tell you about the Lady Laura's visions?" Ted asked.

Fence sat up straighter and became intent. "He did not. Do you tell me now."

"Laura?" said Ted.

Laura knew that he would do the telling for her if she felt shy, but she decided to go through with it. Ted might tell too much. Once again she explained at what times she would see things, and what things she had seen. This time she did include her vision of Ted and Randolph on the battlefield, but left out the one of Claudia and Princess Laura in the cellar, since she had already told Fence it was a dream. She did not, of course, mention her glimpse of Andrew in the North Tower, staring at the remnants of the Crystal of Earth. If Fence, by some miracle, did not know that Patrick had broken it, she was not going to tell him. She must remember to tell the others, or they would yell at her, however little it might matter now.

Fence looked at her consideringly when she had done. "This is a gift of thy mother's house," he said, "though she had it not and in her sister it turned to favor and to prettiness."

Laura thought that that did not sound like a bad thing to happen, but Fence did not seem to approve of it.

"Hath any of these come to pass?" Fence asked her.

"The one with Ted all bloody and Randolph looking unhappy did," said Laura. "I saw it myself, when Ted got killed in the battle. And the people and beasts all running around on the flat place, I think that was the battle, too."

"Was it for that thou took'st the magic sword to battle?" said Fence.

"Well . . . partly."

Fence was silent for a moment. "So many visions of Claudia," he said. "Claudia's face in a sword, with magical swords and a unicorn. Claudia regarding a mirror which regardeth not back. Claudia's face above misty shapes, as it were the sun."

"And I think the house by the Well that the dragon destroyed is Claudia's house," said Laura, suddenly enlightened.

Fence looked at her as he had when she said that Andrew was a traitor. "Why?" he said.

Laura gaped at him. Face and voice and vision had fallen together in her mind, and she knew that the woman with the broom in the Secret House was Claudia. But this, too, was not something she could tell Fence. She lied quickly. "I saw her in the house, when she was looking in the mirror," she said. "So I thought it was her house."

"It is not," said Fence, "but 'tis of one kind with her other deeds that she should put it to her uses. Well," he said, and fell silent.

"Please," said Laura, who was feeling extremely uncomfortable now that she had listed so many peculiar visions and seen Fence take them seriously, "what does it all mean?"

Fence smiled at her. " 'Tis a talent of thy house," he said, "a seeing of things far off, whether in time or space or thought. It is hard for thee now to know which of these thou seest, but I can put thee in the way of knowledge will help thee, when we return to High Castle. Meanwhile, tell all you see to me and I will help thee sift it."

"Can you sift what I told you just now?"

"I can sift nothing touching Claudia," said Fence, a little shortly. Laura had been afraid he would say that; she glanced at Ted, and as she had expected he was frowning.

Fence considered the frown for a moment, while Ted turned red, and then spoke to Laura again. "But what thou hast seen concerning the dragon and the House and the man reading on a book are visions of times past. Belaparthalion smote the House with fire in his wrath against the treachery of Melanie. King Conrad built it anew in its old fashion. The sight thou hadst of the five shadowy figures that thou knewest—of that I am less certain. It might be a vision of the land of the dead, in times past or to come. Fear not. Those visions that are of great moment come again until they are clear."

Oh, great, thought Laura. "Who was the man reading the book?"

"The book is King John's," said Fence. "From thy story I cannot tell who the man may be; but there are few who read on King John's Book. If thou seest him again, mark him well."

"All right," said Laura, feeling relieved. It was not until later that she wondered how she could have inherited a talent of the Princess Laura's house, and whether this was another instance of the peculiar remembrance that let Ted fence, and let her play the flute, without instruction.

"Thank you, Fence," said Ted, "that's all we wanted."

"A strange gathering for such a purpose," said Fence, looking around at them, still expectantly.

Laura wondered what he meant. Ted did not answer him, and they all got up and wandered through the trees back to the camp, talking of the weather, if they would have to march in the rain tomorrow. Laura lagged behind; Ruth and Ellen and Patrick went on ahead; Ted and Fence walked together in the middle. When Ruth and Ellen and Patrick were out of sight, Laura heard Ted say to Fence, "Randolph told me that you were drawing near the end of your conclusions about the King's death. Can you tell me what you've discovered? He said you'd found an antidote in the wine I spilled?"

Laura slowed her steps so they should not hear her, and then had to go faster so that she could hear them.

"I know no more than that," said Fence; he sounded distinctly annoyed. "If Randolph knoweth more, he hath not spoke his knowledge in my ear."

"Well, he didn't speak it in mine either," said Ted, in relieved tones, "but he did seem to think you had it, too."

"I am confounded by the matter," said Fence, definitely, " 'tis a riddle beyond my powers, unless we discover new events."

Laura slowed again, thinking. If things went according to

the game, Randolph would have to force Fence to his conclusions about the King's death; and he would do it in High Castle, in the Mirror Room where Agatha did her sewing. What Randolph had told Ted must have made Ted afraid that Fence might discover the truth sooner; which would give them that much less time to get the swords and make their escape. But things seemed to be all right. Laura thought of the unicorns; and despite the discomfort their sense of humor had caused her, she sighed. Then she hurried forward again, to pick up her flute and find out what other music the back of her mind could remember.

On their fourth and last day in the round valley, in a shivering desert dawn, they buried the soldiers who had no families. The bodies were put in a common grave, and there were no carved and painted coffins. Otherwise this funeral was much like the King's. Fence and Randolph conducted the service in the beautiful but infuriating, almost-intelligible language. This time Ted, listening painfully, not distracted by a recent failure, a downpour of cold rain, or having helped to carry a coffin two or three miles, thought he caught a phrase here or there. It sounded very odd, almost like Shakespeare spoken with a French accent. "What is this world? What asketh men to have? Now with his love, now in his colde grave, allone, withouten any compaignye."

He leaned over to Patrick, who, required to choose a language to study in the seventh grade, had selected French because Pasteur had spoken it. "Pat! Is that French?"

"*French!*" said Patrick, under his breath but with amazing vigor. "No!"

"Well, what is it?"

"I have no idea."

"Be quiet," said Ruth over Patrick's head.

Ted obeyed her, and listened, but heard nothing more that he could understand.

They had wild roses and goldenrod and daisies and a kind of tall purple flower that no one knew the name of, to throw upon the bodies before the grave was filled in.

Ted, watching his golden armful drift down and trying not to sneeze, was visited with an all-too-vivid memory of the land of the dead: the light too dim to show any color, the shifting shapes, the mood that made the ghosts draw back from those who laughed, the bodiless voices asking after blood. He felt horribly relieved and acutely guilty. The awfulness of that place struck him more forcibly now than it had when he was in it. Why should people who knew how to fight and who belonged here be doomed to something almost too listless to be called Hell, while he came back and walked under the sun? He had yelled at the others, over and over, that this was real, that they should take it seriously: but surely so long as he could come back like that, with no effort and through no merit of his own, he was only playing.

Such thoughts troubled him all the march back. Most of the marchers were merry. Now came all the singing Laura had missed on the way out. Other people than Randolph brought out pipes and flutes; there was not only singing and storytelling, but dancing in the evenings. Ted was glum; his sister and his cousins were glum; Randolph put his pipe away after the first night and was not so much glum as simply silent; but Fence was deliberately and doggedly cheerful, as Ted's mother would be when she was worried about something it was no use talking over.

Three days into the march back Ruth caught Ted during a noon break and hauled him off into the grass.

"What in the world," she demanded of him, "have you told Randolph about me?"

"I told him I didn't want to marry you."

"Did you tell him I wanted to marry him?"

"I told him he'd have to take it up with you," said Ted, thankful that this was the case.

"Well, he has!" said Ruth, pushing both hands through her hair and demolishing her crown of flowers. The night before they marched had been marked by music and merriment and feasting, and Agatha had found wild roses, growing quite out of season, and bestowed crowns upon as many people as would consent to wear them.

"Or I think he has," said Ruth. "He keeps talking to me—and giving me things—and looking at me—but then he seems to take it for granted that I won't marry him. Which I won't, but I don't know if I should say so."

"Could he be trying to get you to break the engagement, by pushing things until you have to tell him you won't marry him?" What in the world was Randolph up to? After what he had said to Ted the night Cedric gave Laura the flute, you would have thought turning around and courting Ruth the last thing he was likely to do.

"I hope so. I can't get married; I have to go to college. I haven't even gone to high school yet."

"You could ask him to wait," said Ted, knowing she could not marry Randolph and that Randolph would not marry her in any case, but drawn into argument in spite of himself.

"For *ten years?*"

"It wouldn't have to be ten years for him. You could use Shan's Ring."

"Let's sit down," said Ruth, a little wildly. "I can't think."

Ted found them a flat rock. Ruth pulled the remains of her crown from her head and hurled them into the grass.

"Now," she said, "it's still ten years for *me*. What if I meet somebody who can quote Shakespeare?"

"Randolph can quote Shakespeare."

"He thinks he's just talking. Come to that, I guess he *is* just talking. It's not the same thing."

"Well," said Ted, "if you don't want to marry him, just say so. It would have to be a relief to him, Ruthie. He can't marry you." He remembered Randolph's contempt for the king who could suggest such a thing, and went on hastily. "He's a murderer and he thinks he won't live long enough to marry you. I'm sure he'd feel better if you broke the engagement so you won't have the dishonor of being betrothed to a regicide."

"But he doesn't know I know he's a regicide," said Ruth, "and I don't want him to know I know; I mean, it doesn't matter if *I* know, but he wouldn't want Lady Ruth to know. And it will hurt his feelings if I break the engagement: especially," she added, glaring at Ted, "now that I don't have the excuse of wanting to marry you."

"You could talk to Fence," said Ted, "or Agatha. I bet they know the proper forms for rejecting a suitor without hurting his feelings."

"And tell them I want to go to Harvard?" said Ruth, bitterly.

"Maybe you could commute," said Ted. The conversation was ridiculous. They were going home. But he derived some small comfort from talking as if they were not, and would somehow have to live with what they had done. Ruth was looking at him as she more often looked at Patrick. Ted became irate. He added stubbornly, "Use magic somehow."

Ruth, to his surprise, appeared to consider the suggestion. Perhaps this mummery comforted her, too. "It would be an awful waste of magic," she said briskly.

"Well, it's not as if it were electricity," said Ted.

"How do you know?"

"We could ask Fence," said Ted. "As a matter of fact, we really should give some thought to telling Fence the whole thing."

"We'd end up in an insane asylum."

"There aren't any," said Ted.

"Or a dungeon. I'm not an initiate; I haven't taken any vows. And I've been faking my way around Green Caves ceremonies for months now, until I don't have to fake it any more, and I can tell you from what I've read that they wouldn't like that at all. And *you've* been letting them treat you as if you were King."

"I said, tell *Fence*," said Ted. "After hearing his oath, I don't think he'd give us up as spies."

"Fence!" said Ruth. "We've been acting like his friends, when we hardly know him. He's been treating us as friends, and we're strangers. We think we know him well, but he doesn't know us. And he'd hate the idea that we know him well because we think we made him up, even if we couldn't have. And—"

"All right, all right."

"And what would they *do* with *us* if they got the other ones back? Now if *we* got the other ones back, we might have some bargaining power. You're spoiled, Ted—we all are, because we're the royal children. This is not a very comfortable place for strangers. Do you know what the people of the Outer Isles say about us? 'Travel not in the Hidden Land: It will take all you have and laugh you to scorn for having nothing.' "

"All *right*."

Ruth pulled a red leaf from a bush and began to shred it. There had been no frost yet, but some of the trees were beginning to turn already. Ted thought briefly that back in Illinois it would still be summer; and then remembered with a shock that it would still be June.

"Besides all that," he said, "I think we should be getting home. We still have the rest of the summer to get through back there. Not that it won't keep, I guess, but—"

"Rest of the summer!" said Ruth, abandoning the leaf and pulling at her hair again. "It's winter in Australia, but never mind. We have to get through the rest of our *lives!*"

"We don't want to go home, do we?" said Ted.

"Not in the least. Do you suppose they have any good universities here?"

"Well, *you* can stay. I won't kill Randolph, and the only way not to kill him is to go home."

"If you're gone Patrick will have to kill him," said Ruth, with a despairing giggle.

Ted thought of Patrick's dream, and profound unease settled on him.

"Besides," said Ruth, "that would be cheating."

"This isn't a game," said Ted, automatically.

"But we can't help acting as if it were."

If he thought about that at all, he would think too much, and possibly become as dangerous as Patrick. He stood up and held out his hand to Ruth. "Well, let's ask Fence about the magic, anyway. It can't hurt."

"Your manners are improving," said Ruth, accepting the hand but sounding rather blank.

That did not bear thinking about, either.

They got Fence almost to themselves at dinner; Randolph and Matthew also shared their fire. Fence seemed as usual.

Matthew was unwontedly subdued, and Randolph did not so much as smile at them when they sat down. There was a great deal of hilarious laughter from the other fires.

"Fence," said Ted, "I wanted to ask you a question about magic."

Fence looked accommodating.

"Is it infinite, or does it run out?"

"Magic runneth not out," said Fence, slowly, turning the phrase over as if he liked it. "The limitation of magic is in the strength of those it must run through. In itself it hath no limits."

"Do a great many very small magics wear people out?" asked Ruth.

"Of a certainty," said Fence. "Those are more perilous than a single great deed of sorcery. They creep upon their doers like the sunset; little by little the light goeth, but in the end it is dark, and they without their torches."

"Suddenly one day you fall over?"

Fence nodded; he seemed, again, to enjoy Ruth's phrasing. He looked thoughtfully at Ruth. Ted, afraid he would ask why someone who had studied in the Green Caves for years would need to ask such questions, asked one himself.

"Fence, what do you know about other worlds?"

Ruth choked briefly. Fence turned his thoughtful look upon Ted. "Speakst thou of the stars?"

"Well . . ."

"Is the world round?" Ruth asked abruptly.

Fence was taken aback. "Of course."

"Ruth!" said Ted.

"Just checking."

"No doubt one day thy knowledge will check mine," Fence said to her, "but not in such questions as that."

"Fence," said Ted, bypassing the pun, which had made

Matthew grin and Ruth scowl, "how would you get to those other worlds?"

"Is there any magic for it?" added Ruth.

"No," said Fence; he seemed wary, but willing to answer. "There is no magic quicker than a dragon or a unicorn."

"What would you say," Ted asked him, "if you crawled under a hedge in High Castle garden and came out in the Border Lands?"

Fence sat bolt upright, joggling Matthew's elbow. Matthew, his wine soaking into his cloak, leaned forward, paying it no heed.

"Hast done this thing?" demanded Fence.

"No," said Ted, truthfully enough.

"My saying would serve me ill," said Fence. "The curses I know are many and deep."

"Curses?"

"Dost know what danger such things hold? Dost know what power to make such a place in the hedge would need? To that, I am a kitchen-wizard and Randolph is a spit-boy and Lady Ruth is a gardener."

"Oh," said Ted. He wondered if they should add to their note the information that Shan's and Melanie's swords held this power. Or was it the places under the hedge and the bush that held it? Or was it Claudia?

"Whence came such ideas?" Fence asked both of them.

"Well," said Ted, feebly, "well, we were wondering if we could shorten the march home."

Randolph laughed; Matthew sat back and began mopping at his cloak; but Fence looked Ted and Ruth over as if they were a book full of difficult writing, and said no more.

They received a tremendous welcome when they returned to High Castle. People cheered and sang and blew on horns and piped and threw flowers. Ted went cold when the first bouquets came down, scattering their petals on the wind: he felt like a body in some funeral of the spirit. He looked at Patrick's fair head strewn with petals white and red, and for the moment was entirely willing to go home and never return.

CHAPTER 18

A FTER two days of fruitless discussion, several unsuccessful attempts to catch Fence's door open, and a Council which confirmed Ted's guess that the weapons with which Fence meant to bribe Chryse and Belaparthalion were indeed Shan's and Melanie's swords, they decided to try stealing Fence's keys again.

Their only other hope seemed to be to wait for the last moment and somehow waylay the expedition to take the swords to Chryse. They thought that that seemed even less likely to succeed than using the keys again. Besides, since the entire business with the swords and Chryse and Belaparthalion was not in the game, they did not know whether it would take place before or after the revelation to Fence of Randolph's crime. Ted was sure that this unhappy event ought to happen in October. But he was no longer willing to put much faith in what ought to happen; and when he discovered that Ellen thought it happened in September and the others seemed not to have any idea of its date, he wanted to hurry.

He and Ruth and Patrick came to this conclusion in Ruth's room, and they had just begun to discuss when Patrick should make his attempt when Laura and Ellen burst in on them.

"Ruth!" said Ellen. "Fence and Randolph are in the Mirror Room; we went looking for Agatha and they were polite but they hurried us out and Randolph looks awful. I think this is it."

Ted and Patrick leaped for the door and pounded down the hall.

"Should we go back, too?" said Ellen.

"We're not there in the real scene."

"Neither is Patrick," said Ellen.

"I don't want to see it," said Laura.

"But if there's one more chance to stop it—"

"I don't think," said Ruth, "that anything can stop Randolph once he makes up his mind."

The door to the Mirror Room was closed. Ted and Patrick looked at one another, put their shoulders to it, and burst into the room. Fence and Randolph faced one another over a carved chest against the outer wall. The draperies were drawn over all the mirrors and windows; the room seemed dark and close.

"Fence!" said Ted, although both of them were already looking at him.

"What's the matter?" said Fence, coming forward.

"Not the matter, exactly," said Ted, and went on with the first thing that came into his head. "I just remembered that I never asked Randolph to tell me about the Council I missed, before we marched back, and—" He had no idea what to say next, but Randolph came forward, too, with a wry look.

"You come most carefully upon your hour," he said. "Fence and I were speaking of that Council even now."

He gestured at the only chair in the room, and Ted found himself sitting down in it. Patrick came and sat on the floor next to him. Fence and Randolph faced one another in the middle of the room, and seemed to forget about the two boys.

"Well?" said Fence to Randolph; in his face was a challenge, but in his voice a plea. Ted sat forward: he thought he knew what that Council had been about, and that he had delivered them all into Randolph's hands.

"Do you truly say to me," said Randolph, "that all the Council could make nothing of this matter? That none among them hath a thought upon it save that they know not what befell? Not one hath the glimmer of a thought?"

"Some have," said Fence, reluctantly.

"What is this glimmer, then?"

Fence scowled, and then ruined the effect by sitting on Agatha's sewing table and swinging his legs. "Their thought considers the matter too loosely," he said. "Where did the plot begin, and how long was it in the making? They have left unexamined the vintner, the merchant, the wine cellar, the butler, the kitchen, the page."

"Forget not the cupbearer," said Randolph.

Fence glanced at him and smiled, but Ted thought the smile looked more hopeful than confident. "Thou hast heard the whispers, then," he said. " 'Twill be easy enough to stifle such talk; trouble not thyself. I will see to 't."

Ted stood up quietly and backed for the door. He felt trapped and frozen, and could think only of getting out. Patrick looked at him in surprise.

"Consider first, my lord," said Randolph, "whether such talk ought indeed to be stifled."

Patrick stood up, too, not quietly enough.

"What ails the two of you?" demanded Fence.

They looked at him.

"There's no need," Randolph said to them. "If you know, what will it avail you not to hear me say it? If you know not," he added, as Ted tried to say something, "what do you fear?"

"Randolph," said Fence, who had stopped swinging his legs and was looking a little pale.

"Could vintners and merchants distill such poison?" said Randolph. "Could butlers, pages, cooks know its secret? You taught me the use of my wits: now where are yours?"

Patrick walked over and stood beside Ted, bumping shoulders with him. He was shaking. So was Ted.

"Tarry but a moment longer," said Randolph, not looking at them.

Fence slid down from the table, and as the folds of his starry robe fell into place again he seemed suddenly to dwarf the room. "If my wits are addled," he said, "I needs must make do with thine. Make them to work for me, Randolph."

"I know the truth," said Randolph. "I need not my wits to discover it. And knowing it already, how can I tell you in what way you should work your wits to discover it yourself?"

"Tell me this truth, then," said Fence.

"No, indeed I will not," said Randolph. "I would not betray your teachings thus. How many times, knowing the truth, have you made me dig it out for myself? Can I do less for you?"

"Knowest thou," said Fence to Randolph, "why I did thus?"

"I do," said Randolph. "It was that I might believe the truth when I saw it. For truth hath strange and terrible shapes."

"And this truth," said Fence, "a most terrible one."

"I will not hear these things," said Ted, as the game dictated he should; but he was far too late. They did not heed him. They saw only one another.

"Say it," said Randolph.

"Randolph," said Fence. In his round face the bones showed clearly. "You have betrayed all I ever taught you;

you have betrayed your liege lord and your solemn word; all this besides with the lowest and cruellest of all weapons, a weapon of cowards. You poisoned King William."

"Well done," said Randolph. "The master is yet master, and not pupil."

"Had the master been truly master," said Fence, "the pupil had not done what is done."

"He didn't!" cried Ted, hardly knowing what he said. "How could he have? I knocked the bottle out of his hand; I took the cup from him and brought him another; how could he have done it?"

Randolph looked over at Patrick. "Thy royal brother," he said to Ted, "following the philosophy of Andrew and scorning magic as tricks only, hath set himself to learn such tricks as, he thinketh, account for the doings of sorcery. And in an idle moment of the dull winter, he did teach some few of those tricks to me; and so I had them to hand when thou, Edward, took from me the cup I had prepared."

"But why did you have two doses of poison, that doesn't make sense!" said Ted.

"The second was for mine own use," said Randolph; he turned back to Fence in time to catch the look on his face. "I regret it most heartily," he said to him.

He looked at Ted again. "I thought thou knewest, and didst keep me here for thine own ends, fearing thy lack of skill."

Ted could not answer him.

Fence was so still that all his previous stillnesses would have seemed fidgety by comparison; he spoke very quietly and with no expression. "You must return what you have forfeited," he said.

Randolph took the circlet from his head and the ring from his finger as he walked across the room, and laid them upon the carved chest. Fence, following, took up the circlet. He turned it in his hands and said three words under his breath. It broke in pieces, and the pieces crumbled to dust, and the dust, floating down, was gone before it could touch the floor. Fence took up the ring. "And what of this," he said, without inflection.

"That too is forfeit," said Randolph; but now he, too, looked pale.

Fence closed the ring in his fist, and opened his hand again. Something glittered in his palm like a jewel, but he slid it into his robe too quickly for Ted to see what it was. They could have left now, without being noticed, but there seemed no point now in escape, or in anything else.

"Randolph," said Fence, "I am sorry I have so failed you."

"So even that is denied me," said Randolph.

"It is you who have denied it," said Fence. "Lay not that flattering unction to your soul, that not your trespass but my ruling speaks."

Randolph, suddenly and incredibly, smiled at him. "Thou seest, then," he said, "thou hast not failed me. To deny me all I have denied, in the courage of that is not failure. Hadst thou been kinder, Fence, that had been failure indeed."

"Carrion comfort," said Fence, as if he were reading a road sign, and he turned and went straight between Ted and Patrick and out of the room. Ted's throat swelled and closed.

Randolph leaned on Agatha's table, as if his legs had failed him suddenly. Now he was very pale.

"My lord," he said to Ted, "you had best set the trial soon."

"No," said Ted.

"My lord, I had thought to spare you."

"I didn't mean—"

"Choose your weapon, then," said Randolph, "and your time; but I beg you, my lord, that it be soon. And disgrace not your teacher."

He, too, went out.

"I told you!" said Ted, almost crying. "I told you!"

"Ted!" said Patrick. "He said, choose your weapon."

"So—oh!" said Ted. He knew Patrick's mind as if it were his own, and the relief was almost more than he could stand.

"Come on quick, and catch Fence!" said Patrick.

They caught up with Fence at the door to his tower.

"Fence!" shouted Ted. "Fence, wait!"

Fence turned to them a face like an accurate but uninspired statue of himself, and Ted's words clogged in his throat.

"He's come to choose his weapon for the duel," said Patrick.

Fence's aimless green gaze sharpened briefly. "Edward, is this wise?"

"I think so," said Ted. "It's quicker. Fence—just for this one thing, may Randolph and I use the swords of Shan and Melanie?"

Fence was silent, staring at the floor. "Shan's mercy indeed," he said at last, "but how dearly that would please Chryse."

"Well, that's all to the good, then, isn't it?" said Ted, hating himself.

"And it would comfort Randolph, maybe," said Fence. This made no sense to Ted at all, but since it seemed to be on his side, he said nothing.

"Wilt thou undertake that the bout is quickly over?" Fence asked him.

Ted saw no way that he, or the real Edward either, could

undertake any such thing unless Randolph helped him, but it did not matter. "I will," he said.

"And return the swords without demur, when thou hast done?"

"What would I want them for, after that?" burst out Ted.

"Very well, then," said Fence. "When wilt thou—"

"This evening," said Ted. "May I have them now? Randolph should have a little time to accustom himself to the blade, shouldn't he?"

"Bide thee here," said Fence, "and I will bring them."

He went slowly up the stairs.

Ted sat down on the floor, as Randolph had leaned upon the table. "Oh, dear heaven," he said. "I think we've done it."

"I'll get the girls," said Patrick. "And we should dress in our old clothes."

"No, someone might see us. We'll just take them with us. Can you and Ruth write the note to Fence? And, look, tell her to find a page and ask him to give it to Fence at five."

"No fear," said Patrick, and ran down the passage.

Ted leaned his head against the purple-stained stone wall and closed his eyes. He felt like someone who truly has to be home at five, but has had the misfortune to be given this instruction on the day his team is losing badly whatever game it might be playing. He was leaving behind a broken friendship, a shattered trust, an empty throne, a kingdom without an heir, and a snarl of riddles. And he still felt that all of it was somehow his fault.

"Here are thy weapons," said Fence's voice over his head.

"That was quick," said Ted, blinking and getting up. His foot was asleep.

"Thy thoughts have sped the time," said Fence. He still spoke without expression, but he was beginning to look less stony and more crumpled. Ted wanted to do something for him; but if someone's excellent good friend and first apprentice was a traitor both to his King and to his friend's own teaching, what could you say to him? Especially when you had once thought that his pain made a wonderful story.

"I prithee heed this warning," said Fence. "The sword of Melanie, that which gloweth green, doth enhance the skill of him that wields it; but the sword of Shan, that gloweth blue, doth increase the skill of him that it fights; for she was a warrior, but he was a teacher."

"So if I use Melanie's sword and he uses Shan's," said Ted, longing to get away but feeling it better to play his part to the hilt, in the little time remaining him, "I'll have my own skill enhanced and also get some of his?"

Fence nodded. "It will be quicker so."

"My skill is his anyway," said Ted.

"Oft do our gifts come back in strange guise," said Fence, with bitter meaning.

"Fence," said Ted, "it isn't fair!"

"What is foul today may be fair tomorrow," said Fence. He held out the swords, still in their sheaths and tangled in their belts. Ted took the awkward bundle, and the power of the swords shivered up his arms and prickled the hair on his neck.

"If thou wilt tell me the place of thy choosing," said Fence, "and what men thou wilt have for witnesses, I will arrange these matters for thee."

"The rose garden, I think," said Ted, whose composure was dwindling rapidly, "and—and choose what witnesses you will."

"And the hour?"

"Five o'clock," said Ted.

"It shall be done, my lord."

They looked at one another in the sickly light.

"Would a trial have been better?" Ted heard himself asking, as if he were indeed Edward, as if it mattered.

"No," said Fence. "He hath injured thee; let thy hand give him his reward."

"He's injured you more!"

"For that," said Fence, "he hath his reward already." He turned in a flurry of galaxies and went back up the staircase. When Ted could see again, he ran for the stables.

Patrick intercepted him in the courtyard. "The girls have four horses down by the moat," he said. "Come on."

"That was fast work," said Ted.

"Well, the grooms did all the saddling. Ellie spun them some story about how she and Laura and Ruth were going to pick so many wildflowers that they'd need an extra horse to carry them back on. I don't think they thought she'd manage it, but they gave her the horse. That child is becoming dangerous."

Ruth, Ellen, and Laura stood without speaking in the shadow of the four horses. They looked depressed. Ruth had the pack she had carried on the march; it bulged with their old clothes. She handed it to Ted and gave Ellen a boost onto her horse. Ted and Patrick scrambled onto their horses; Ruth helped Laura up behind Ted and mounted the remaining animal. They rode away from High Castle.

It was a clear, bright day, cooler than it had been for some time. Ted thought he could smell autumn coming. He wondered whether, in the woods where they had hunted the unicorn, it would smell like the soul of autumn, as when he had come there it had like the soul of summer. He sighed; and as if in answer Laura clutched at him and cried, "My flute!"

"We can't go back," said Ted.

"But I need it!"

"It's not yours, Laurie."

"But it will save us at the end!"

"Not us: them. We won't need saving where we're going."

"He gave it to me, not her! She's *dead!*"

"We can't go back."

Laura was silent, but a hot wet patch spreading through the back of Ted's tunic told him that she was not resigned.

They left the horses at the Well. Ellen wanted to water them, but Ruth refused to have anything more to do with the Well, and the horses showed a definite disinclination to go into the woods where the stream was. Ruth whispered sorcerous words in their ears again.

"Did you remember that with the back of your mind, too?" asked Patrick, and received no answer.

The horses went loping back toward High Castle, looking as if they were enjoying themselves.

"I always meant to get to know mine better," said Ellen, "and develop a wonderful bond with it."

They trudged through the woods, where the bushes and saplings were reddening and goldenrod thronged the clearings, and tramped hollowly across the wooden bridge. The stream was low, and the cracked mud revealed by its sinking reminded Ted unhappily of the desert where they had fought.

They came to the hedge before the Secret House, and stood silently in a circle. Laura was going to cry; it was just a question of when. Ellen looked solemnly furious, as if somebody had played a practical joke on her and she meant to get even. Ruth wore an air of vague irritation, as she would when she tried to make cookies and Patrick and Laura stole bits of the dough. Patrick seemed pleased, but was managing not to smile; probably, Ted thought, because he knew somebody would slug him if he did.

Ruth pulled a wad of crumpled clothing out of her pack and handed it around. The skirt that had reached her ankle when she came to this country now came to the middle of her calf. Ted's jeans were too short. He had grown, after all. He looked at his sister, whose shirt was too tight in the shoulders. He hoped Aunt Kathy and Uncle Jim were not observant, or, if they were, they lacked the imagination and the knowledge to figure out what their observations must mean. Ruth, quite uselessly, packed their tunics and dresses and velvet caps and the odd linen underwear into her pack, and laid it on the bank.

"Don't forget to throw your sword back through," said Patrick to Ted.

"Ruth," said Ted, "what'd you do with Shan's Ring?"

"I sealed it up with the note."

"All right, then."

"Let's all leave at the same time," said Ellen. "We'll go along to our bottle-tree, and I'll yell, 'On your mark, get set, go!'"

"We'll write to you," said Ted.

"See you next summer," said Ruth, and walked away. Her brother and sister followed her. Ted and Laura watched them slither along the bank of the stream until they went around a bend.

"Better get ready," said Ted. They crouched before the gap in the hedge, holding their sword. It sent up Ted's arm the strongest prickling he had yet felt, almost a pain. He saw by the flinching in Laura's face that she had felt it too.

"On your mark!" came Ellen's voice, a little wavery. "Get set! Go!"

Ted and Laura ducked under the hedge and stood up in the weedy yard of the Secret House. It was a clear, cool day there, too; but the sky was duller, the air heavier. Ted could smell cars, and dust, and rubber, and a whole collection of things he had almost forgotten about.

He held the sword up into a shaft of sunlight, and for the first time since they had found it, the runes they could not quite make out ran down the blade. This time, the back of Ted's mind knew them, and he read aloud:

"All may yet be very well."

"What a weird thing to put on a sword," said Laura; her voice wavered even more than Ellen's had.

"Help me throw it back," said Ted.

Laura put her hand on the hilt, and, awkwardly but with considerable strength, they swung their arms backward and forward, and hurled the sword through the gap in the hedge. Ted half expected to hear it clatter on the sidewalk. But there was only a brief rustle as it went through the leaves; a flash as a bit of sun hit it; and shadows; and nothing but hedge.

CHAPTER 19

"WHAT do we do now?" said Laura.

"We're in trouble at home," said Ted, absently. He felt that something was wrong, but could not place it. He tried to remember how they had left their cousins' house for the last time, to stay in the Secret Country and play their game through.

"Can't we get used to being here first, before we get yelled at?"

"I'll tell you what," said Ted, abandoning his effort with some relief. They would be reminded soon enough of everything they had done, when Aunt Kathy laid eyes on them. "Let's buy something we couldn't have there. How about some ice cream?"

He did not want any himself, and Laura did not look pleased with the idea either, but she nodded.

"Do you have any money?" she asked him.

Ted went through his pockets, coming up with a wad of rubber bands, a book of matches, a tangle of string, two dusty pieces of hard candy without their wrappers, and a grimy paper with instructions for translating things from the Secret Country's alphabet into English.

"I had that with me all along and never knew it!" he said. "But no money." He scowled. "I thought I had five dollars—I gave it to you, Laura, when we had that bet about the flashlight."

Laura fished in her own pocket. "I still say it turned into a lantern." She jabbed her hand viciously into the bottom of the pocket. "Ouch!" she said, and pulled it out. "Oh, Ted!"

The little ivory unicorn hurt their eyes in that shady light.

"Fence said there was a spell of finding and returning on it," said Laura.

"And it seems upon thee as well," said a husky voice behind them.

They turned around. Claudia stood on the porch of the house. She had a broom in her hand and a black cat at her feet. Like the ivory unicorn, she seemed too bright for her setting. She wore a red-and-white checked gingham dress that suited the house and yard well enough, but did not suit her at all.

Laura pulled on Ted's arm. "Run," she whispered. "Or she'll do it now, what I saw in my vision."

Ted had barely been able to hear her, but Claudia laughed. "That hath been done already," she said. "That was but thy shadow I buried. Thou art more use to me above the earth, for all that thy flight from thy dream frets me sorely."

"You mean it wasn't real after all?" said Laura.

"Oh, aye, 'twas real, fear not," said Claudia, with a most unpleasant glee in her voice; it made Ted like the glee of the unicorns better. "Soon thy horses will come back riderless to High Castle, and the page with thy missive to Fence will reach the top of the two hundred and eight steps. All things continue in their paths. Except my plans," she said, "which the two of you have very handily thwarted. Now I have a fancy to know how and why two mere younglings from a world without sorcery, whom I thought to bend easily to my purposes, have so easily bent me to theirs. Will you not come in?"

She smiled beautifully as she asked this question. Ted, wanting more than anything else to run, came slowly forward and climbed the steps of the porch; and Laura came with him. If this is magic, thought Ted, I don't blame Patrick for not believing in it.

The house was cool and smelled of cloves and cinnamon. Ted thought of the West Tower in High Castle. They followed the swish and rustle of Claudia down a long hall hung with odd dark pictures. In the middle of it glimmered a purple waterbeast, making a noise like a distant faucet dripping. It looked far stranger in this modern hallway than it ever had on the cold stones of High Castle. Laura stopped dead. Ted began to edge by the creature, but Claudia laughed and said something to it, and it ran in runnels through the polished floorboards and was gone.

They went on down the hall, to a doorway where another black cat sat. Claudia pushed the door open, and the cat graciously preceded them into the next room.

It was a sun porch running the whole width of the house at the back, and its three outside walls were all windows. From those of the right-hand wall they could see Claudia's weedy side yard and the neighbors' rosebushes and two toddlers covering themselves with mud. But the windows of the left-hand wall looked out upon the view Laura and Ellen had had from their bedroom window at High Castle: the glassy lake, the slopes of forest where they had hunted the unicorn, the insubstantial mountains and the high western sky. And each small diamond pane of each window of the back wall held a different picture.

Ted stared, and blinked, and stared again. Some of the

scenes were those they had seen on the tapestries in the East Tower, when they solved the Riddle of Shan's Ring. But these were not woven; these were real. He bent forward to look more closely.

Claudia laughed, more pleasantly this time. "You see," she said.

"They're moving," said Laura.

Ted walked right up to one of the windows and put his hand on the glass and pressed his nose to it. It gave off a faint warmth that was not altogether pleasant. He stared down from a great height onto a vast flat field whereon the small figures of men struggled with one another and with strange shadowy shapes shot with fire. He squinted, trying to see more clearly, and the height seemed to diminish. One piece of the battle grew in his vision.

He watched his sister, her sword flaming blue, kill the creature that had killed him. He moved over a pane and saw a thin young man with black hair and decided eyebrows sitting in a vast field of goldenrod, pulling his boots on. His face was dazed and his hands shook. He must be Shan. He looked too much like Randolph. Ted moved over another six inches, and watched himself and Patrick, on the lawn beside the Pennsylvania farmhouse, mime the last fight between Prince Edward and Lord Randolph. He regarded the figures with a practiced eye and was appalled.

"They don't know what they're doing," he said; and blanched. Indeed they had not known what they were doing.

"But I know," said Claudia.

"Do you make things happen?" whispered Laura.

Claudia laid a long hand upon the pane where Ted had seen the battle. "Here in the Hidden Land I can but watch," she said. The hand moved to the pane with Ted and Patrick. "Here, in your place, I can move matters. In the same way, here in your place you can but watch, but in the Hidden Land you can move. And," she said, "if I move aught from here to here," turning her hand from Pennsylvania to the Desert before the Mountains, where the battle with the Dragon King's army played itself out again, "then in a little measure may I move the matters and minds of my own country as well. Wherefore," she said, "having moved the five of you to my country, I gained a measure of power over that you walked on, and those you spoke to, and that you handled."

Ted, struggling with a sense of outrage so violent that it threatened to prevent speech, said at last, "How did you move us?"

Claudia took from a table a round mirror like the one Fence had used the night she stood on his stairs with a knife. "With this," she said, "one may look abroad, in time or distance. Having seen what would befall in my country, I bent your thoughts to enact it, that it might be familiar to you when you came upon it."

"You mean we didn't even make it up?"

"Too much you made up," said Claudia, with a flash of anger. "That talent of mind that in my country turns to sorcery, in yours turns to this making up; and hard put to it was I to turn your thoughts to my desires. The sorrows you have had you brought on your own heads. Now, the strong-minded are a trouble; but the weak-minded avail me not. Wherefore I ask you to join freely with me, and be my companions not my playing-pieces."

Ted and Laura stared at her; Ted was speechless with rage. Laura looked stunned.

"I have spoken freely with you," said Claudia. "Will you not therefore favor me with the tale of your power and your plans, that you could so neatly check one to whom all the wizards of the Hidden Land are but green apprentices?"

Ted found himself wishing he could answer her. There might be worse things than to be her companions. He considered her glowing face, her smooth black hair, her eyebrows arched like the ears of a cat, her clever eyes. He remembered his dream, of having tea with Claudia and of being offered by her all the castles of the Secret Country, and the glory of them.

"I don't believe you," he said.

Claudia, misunderstanding him, turned to the window again. "Come, then," she said. "Look and listen." Ted and Laura, still pulled by whatever spell she had used to bring them into her house, came and stood beside her, and peered into the diamond she pointed to.

"Time now flows for us as for them," she said, "since you have removed your spells. Here is what befalls in the Hidden Land."

Fence sat in his living room before the cold fireplace, his elbows on his knees and his head in his hands. A breeze from the narrow windows stirred his untidy hair. Someone knocked on his door. (Ted and Laura both jumped.) Fence lifted a hand, and the door swung open. One of the yellow-haired boys whom they had seen playing in the sun the day Fence came back, and later enacting the part of the eagle in the coronation play, Matthew's son John, walked into the room. He was red, and breathing hard.

"My lord, a message from the Lady Ruth," he said between gasps, and held a folded paper out to Fence.

Fence took it, turned it over, and quirked his mouth. Ted wondered what seal Ruth had used.

"Sit you down and have somewhat to refresh you," Fence said absently, and opened the letter. His fingers tightened on it; he sat up straight; he leaped to his feet as he read.

"Randolph!" he shouted, and ran out the door. They could hear his footsteps receding in the echoing stair. The yellow-haired page gaped after him, shrugged, and reached for the wine bottle.

"So," said Claudia. "Now, the Lady Ruth, who is of your country, whereof I may move its members, hath spoken to this page. Wherefore—" she said three odd words under her breath, and moved her hand before the little diamond pane.

They saw John, standing in the Banquet Hall, looking after Ruth, who ran across it and plunged out the door.

"To Fence's Tower," said the page, unhappily. He stood frowning, and began to shrug. In a moment he would resign himself and make the climb.

Claudia said three more words under her breath. The page's face brightened, and he went up stairs and through passages until he came to the Mirror Room. Randolph sat there, just as Fence had, his elbows on his knees and his head buried in his hands. He looked up when the page burst in, but so calmly that Ted shivered. Randolph looked as if nothing would ever make him jump again.

"My lord, I have a letter for the Lord Fence," said John, "but I sought him first in other places than his high rooms."

"He was but lately here," said Randolph.

Claudia muttered again, and Randolph's face changed, just a little. Ted, in a burst of illumination like and unlike his remembrance of fencing and flowers, understood. Claudia had made the page think of seeking Fence elsewhere than in his high tower. She had made Randolph's face change: what he said next, she would have made him say. Ted, in the outbursting of an intolerable outrage, put his fist through the diamond pane.

It gave before his hand like cloth, not glass; but the sound it made was like smashing crystal. It broke outward, with a flash and a brilliance like that of the shattered Crystal of Earth. Behind it was a diamond of darkness.

"How dare you!" shouted Ted.

How dared she, how dared he, how dared Laura. All of them had done this. Sitting in a summer meadow, sequestered in the dusty attic during a thunderstorm, fishing in the scummy pond, year by year, they had hammered out the fates of others. Fence is so young, he surprises everybody with his wisdom; Fence is Randolph's best friend; the King is very stubborn; Randolph poisons his wine; Edward is a milksop, but when his father dies he knows what he has to do; should he kill Randolph in the Council Chamber—no, let's make it the rose garden, and we can use ours. And Claudia, you had to believe, had sat here in this house, turning their thoughts just a little, this way or that. Once she had seen what was to be in the Hidden Land, she must have worked on all of them, his sister and his cousins and himself, as she had just now worked on John and Randolph. And they in their turn, by means even Claudia did not know, had also worked on Fence, and Randolph, and William, and Edward, making them what they were, sealing their doom. But Claudia had known what she was doing, and they had not.

Ted put cold hands to his hot face, and felt suddenly that the air was the right weight again and his blood flowing as it ought. His limbs were his own again; the spell was gone. He could run from here, or smash more glass, or—

Claudia, who had been regarding the ruin of her wall with no sign of dismay, opened her mouth, and Ted hit her as hard as he could in the stomach. Claudia doubled up, gasping. Then he kicked wildly at the wall of windows. The air was full of light; the room rang with violent sound; and from the blackness where the windows had been tongues of red and green flame began to lick upward. Claudia straightened up and shouted, in no tongue they knew.

"Run!" yelled Laura, pulling at Ted's arm.

Ted picked up Claudia's mirror and hurled it through the view of the lake and the Enchanted Forest; and there came a noise and a shaking as if the house were coming down around their ears.

Ted and Laura ran, past a hissing cat and a wailing one, out the open door, down the porch steps, across the untended lawn. They dove through the gap in the hedge, staggered to their feet, and ran as hard as they could go. They were not many blocks away when they heard the wail of sirens.

Ted stopped and looked back.

"Don't!" said Laura, and they ran on.

When Laura had fallen down for the third time, she agreed to stop, and they sat down on a bench at a bus stop, wheezing.

"I guess we fixed her," said Laura.

"I hope so," said Ted.

Laura took the ivory unicorn out of her pocket, and they looked at it. Its green eyes stared through them, enigmatic and unnatural. But something in its posture suggested the inhuman glee of the unicorns they had known.

"If we ever start forgetting, and thinking we imagined it," said Laura, "or if Patrick tries to tell us any more about hallucinations when we see him next summer, we can look at this."

"These fragments have we shored against our ruins," said Ted; and as he spoke, felt the back of his mind, whence he had learned fencing moves and the names of flowers and quotations such as that, close up suddenly. Edward was gone.

"What?"

"It was a stupid thing to say. What about that ice cream?"

Laura shrugged. They sat on for a little in the hot air. A bus roared past, sweeping them with a cloud of evil-smelling grit and rattling the squashed paper cups and abandoned candy wrappers at their feet. Two young women went by; Laura recognized their makeup as a type her father had called "anguish moist and fever dew."

"Ted," she said, "I don't suppose you'd rather you'd killed Randolph and stayed?"

"Laura!" Ted, perilously close to wishing that very thing, stood up. "Let's go get the ice cream, to strengthen us against the ordeal that lies ahead." They might as well remember how to play. They would need all the fragments they could muster.

Up in the soggy air a cardinal whistled, clear and piercing. Laura jumped up.

"Laurie, no."

The cardinal swooped down and perched on the chipped wrought-iron armrest of the bench. It fixed them with a round black eye that seemed far too intelligent for the size of its braincase, for its kind as they knew it here. Then it flew up, darted down the street, circled, landed on a telephone booth, and whistled so shrilly it hurt their ears.

"Oh, come on, come on!" said Laura.

The cardinal flew off, far too high and fast for them to follow. Ted laughed through a tight throat. It seemed that even imagination was no friend to them now. They could stumble from day to day, thinking they saw summons after summons back to the Hidden Land. But they had lost the Secret Country.

"There's ice cream in that direction," he said to his sister, firmly. "Lee's Drug. Our last omen."

They looked at one another. Tears trembled in Laura's eyes; but the familiar deep breath she took was not to release them in wailing, but to give her the steadiness to speak. Oh, wonderful, thought Ted. Next summer, I can tell Patrick that this was good for Laura's soul.

"Chocolate," said Laura.

"Pistachio," said Ted, at random.

And King Edward and Sir Laura, of the Hidden Land, went on their way in deliberate and meticulous squabbling.